DUST WALKERS

VIGILES URBANI CHRONICLES BOOK 2

KEN LANGE

Dust Walkers
Ken Lange

Published by Ken Lange
Copyright © 2018, Ken Lange
Edited by Danielle Fine
Cover Art by Natania Barron

This is a work of fiction. Names, characters, places, and incidents are products of the author's imagination or are used fictitiously and are not to be construed as real. Any resemblance to actual events, locales, organizations, or persons, living or dead, is entirely coincidental.

All rights reserved. No part of this book may be used or reproduced electronically or in print without written permission, except in the case of brief quotations embodied in reviews.

For my better half, thank you for always being there for me.

1

January 17th

My living room—along with the rest of my house—was a complete and total wreck. This was in no small part due to the NOPD, who'd been traipsing through my house for the last six hours. Because of that, it had been one of the longest, and most frustrating, days I'd been forced to endure since returning stateside. But if the slow trickle of officers filing out of the door was any indication, fate was turning in my favor.

I leaned back in my recliner and waited for their so-called boss, Captain Hotard, to make his way over with some shitty comment about…well, anything. This was his third such visit since I'd bought the place, and it was becoming a bit too routine for my tastes. I glanced down at my watch. 4:15 p.m. With a little luck, I might be able to make my dinner date with Heather, her best friend Justine and Justine's other half, Viktor Warden. Which was a good thing, because Heather would probably murder me if I screwed it up.

An officer I didn't recognize handed a report to Captain Hotard, who frowned and nodded. He waddled over and pointed at my wrist. "Got someplace to be, Randall?"

I shrugged. "Nothing that can't wait while I entertain New Orleans's finest. Can I offer you a beverage?"

He jerked his head back in revulsion. "I wouldn't contaminate myself by having a drink with *your kind.*"

I grinned. "Aw shucks. And here I was thinking you made these frequent visits to my home because you enjoy my company."

His cheeks turned crimson. "Being this close to one of *you* is about as much fun as being circumcised without anesthesia." He waved a pudgy hand around the room. "This place is disgusting. It's no wonder your neighbors think you're a criminal."

I frowned. "It was clean until you guys came in and ransacked it."

He shrugged. "That's not how I remember it."

Rolling my eyes, I ran my hand over the top of my head. "Of course it isn't."

Captain Hotard stepped forward and stabbed a chubby finger into my chest. "Watch your tone, boy."

My gaze flicked down to the offending appendage. "Are you done here?"

Beads of sweat trickled down his face, and he jerked his hand back. "For now."

I pointed at the door. "Then go. I've got things to do."

He snorted. "Careful, boy, you're not your uncle."

I shook my head. "No, I'm not...that's something you should keep in mind. He's a lot more lenient than I am."

Laughing, he spun on his heel. "Uh-huh. Have a good evening, Mr. Randall. I'll be seeing you soon."

A moment later, he was out the door, and I strode over to lock it behind him. Goddamn, that guy was a pompous little prick. My phone beeped, letting me know I had a message. Heather.

Change in plans. We'll be meeting Justine and Viktor at his place...something came up, and he has to work late, so I'll pick you up at 6:30.

That gave me roughly two hours to put the apartment together, get cleaned up, and dressed. At 6:20, I made my way downstairs and

Dust Walkers | 3

waited on the corner. Five minutes later, Heather pulled up and waved me in. It appeared we'd opted for a similar look, a pair of jeans and a t-shirt, but she, of course, made it stylish. She gave me a disapproving once-over before turning into traffic, headed for Warden Global on St. Charles Ave. A little while later, we were through the security gate, and a guard pointed us to one of the visitor spaces on the side of the building.

Leaning over, Heather brushed her hand up and down my chest several times. "That's the cleanest shirt you could find?"

I shrugged. "I pulled it out of the dryer this morning."

She folded her arms. "Would it have killed you to wear a button up and maybe a pair of slacks?"

I grinned. "That would've required me finding an iron after Captain Hotard and his crew left, and I wasn't exactly in the mood. Anyway, do you really think Viktor or Justine will give two shits how I'm dressed?"

She frowned. "Hotard was at your place today?"

"Yeah, he left about the same time you texted me the change in plans."

Sighing, she shook her head. "Goddamn it. That man is such an asshole. You'd think he would've found a new hobby by now."

That made me chuckle. "If only that were the case."

She dusted off my shoulder again then popped her door. "Let's go...and be nice."

I stepped out and laughed. "Aren't I always?"

Heather arched an eyebrow. "Do you really want me to answer that?"

Squeezing my eyes closed, I sighed. "No."

Eight months ago, I'd burned her wannabe boyfriend to a crisp and executed her father in front of her...so she was keenly aware of my shortcomings.

Christ, I was a dumbass.

I followed her into the lobby and stopped short at the sight of the place. The expansive room felt ancient, yet modern at the same time. Someone had taken great care in the design, creating a sleek feel heavily influenced by some eastern temple. Everything centered around a beautiful fountain that seemed to act as the life's blood for the structure itself. Several plants and trees were strategically placed throughout the space to give the feeling that this had somehow occurred naturally...which clearly wasn't the case. After all the stories I'd heard about Viktor, and his company, a sense of peace emanating from their headquarters was the last thing I'd expected.

Before I could contain my awe, Heather walked over to the reception desk and showed her ID. A moment later, an attractive woman made her way out of a back office to hug Heather. The newcomer was considerably shorter, with dark hair and green eyes. They stood there talking for several seconds before meandering over.

Heather was practically bouncing on her heels as she waved a hand at me. "This is Gavin." She turned to me and gestured at her friend. "This is Justine."

Justine smiled. "Pleasure to finally meet you in person."

I bowed my head slightly. "Likewise."

Justine stepped back and held her hand out toward a nearby hall. "You okay with taking the elevators?"

I shrugged. "Sure, why do you ask?"

She frowned. "Viktor hates the things." She patted her butt. "On the plus side, fifteen flights of stairs means I get to skip part of my workout."

I chuckled. "I bet."

Heather huffed out a breath. "That's just great. You've known my friend for less than five minutes, and you're already talking about her ass."

My mouth dropped open. "Hey...she brought it up."

Justine nudged Heather. "God, he really is easy."

Heather nodded. "I know, right?"

Glancing between them, I couldn't help but chuckle. "Wow, okay, if this is the way you two act when you're together...Viktor and I are in trouble this evening. And to think, you wanted *me* to be on my best behavior."

Heather straightened her shoulders. "I still do."

Justine rolled her eyes. "I told Viktor the same thing...we'll see if either of them can actually pull it off." She looked up at Heather with disappointment on her face. "I'm betting the answer is no, but let's find out."

Heather frowned. "You're probably right...but it's too late to back out now. We're here."

Justine nodded. "That you are." She stepped toward the elevators and stopped short. "Sorry about the hallway in advance. It's a bit of a mess due to a remodel."

I shrugged. "If I had to guess, we won't be eating there...will we?"

Justine snickered and shook her head. "No, we won't."

Grinning, I said, "Then I'm not worried about it, or the state of the house, for that matter. The only thing that concerns me at the moment is food, since I had to skip lunch today due to visitors."

Justine glanced over at Heather, who shook her head. "Oh, not me...Captain Hotard paid him another visit."

Justine pulled a card out of her pocket and walked around the corner. "Seriously? How many times does that make in the last six months?"

"Three."

She pressed the card against the scanner and punched in a code. "That man needs to get a life."

"I couldn't agree more."

There was a ding when the elevator arrived, and the three of us stepped inside. Justine placed a key into the control panel, and turned it. Less than a minute later, we were on the fifteenth floor. It wasn't as bad as she'd made it out to be. While the corridor was a bit of a wreck, it was a managed chaos. The walls were partially painted. Half the light fixtures were a brushed nickel while the rest appeared to be gold. Drop cloths lined the floors, and a great deal of scaffolding sat at the far end of the hall to give us access to the only door about a dozen yards away.

We were halfway down the hall when the door opened, and a rather large man stepped out. He looked familiar, and when he'd passed, I glanced over at Heather and whispered, "Wasn't he the chef at that wedding?"

She glanced over her shoulder and nodded. "I think so."

Justine held the door open for us. "Oh, you've met William?"

I shook my head. "Maybe… I think he was the one who catered the wedding that Heather took me to when we first met."

Justine frowned. "Is that the same night someone tried to gut her?"

I nodded. "Yeah."

She stopped me, and wrapped me in a hug. "Thanks for protecting her that night."

I patted her back. "You're welcome."

The scent of Italian seasoning, red sauce, and pasta wafted out of the apartment, making me hungrier than I already was. When I finally made it inside, it struck me how normal the place was. Given Viktor's supposed age, wealth, and status, I'd expected the place to be a bit more opulent.

Whoever designed the lobby had had a hand up here as well, but they'd somehow managed to fit in a set of recliners, a comfortable-looking sofa, and barstools without any of it looking out of place. Hell, I wouldn't have minded having a place like this…if it were about a tenth of the size.

Justine pointed at the sofa. "If you guys have a seat, I'll go see if I can't hurry Viktor along."

My stomach chose that moment to growl loudly. "Sorry."

Justine snickered. "No worries. William should've left some snacks on the bar if you're starved."

Not wanting to be rude, I declined the offer. "I can wait. Thanks, though."

Justine winked. "Suit yourself."

She ducked down a hall a second later, and my gaze drifted over to the bar.

Heather kept her voice low. "Don't even think about it."

I held up my hands. "Hey, I'm just scoping the place out."

She grinned. "Don't feed me that line of shit. You were looking for food."

Dust Walkers | 7

"Again, she brought it up."

She snickered. "They'll be out soon, and we can have a sit-down dinner."

A few minutes later, Justine was escorted into the living room by a stocky man with short black and gray hair, matching neatly trimmed beard, and three scars across his right eye...which happened to be entirely blue. In fact, it appeared to be a piece of glass instead of actual flesh and blood. Overall, he was a fairly average looking middle-aged man, someone you'd pass on the street without a second thought. Where things got interesting was the way he carried himself and his easygoing, yet confident demeanor.

While I'd missed the power my uncle wielded—partially by design —Viktor couldn't have hidden his charisma under a mountain of baggy clothes.

He strolled over and gave me an easy smile as he held out his hand. "Pleasure to meet you."

I took it and nodded. "Likewise."

He glanced over his shoulder at Justine. "Dunno about you, but I've been told to be on my best behavior tonight."

I snickered. "If it makes you feel any better, so was I."

He thumbed over at the bar. "Good, then let's have a few drinks, and see if we can't get ourselves into some trouble."

Justine cleared her throat, and we both froze. "Dinner first then drinks."

Viktor frowned. "But..."

She raised a finger and shook her head.

He sighed and glanced up at me. "Food first then drinks...but there will be drinks."

I nodded. "As if there were any doubt about that."

Heather nudged me and whispered, "I thought you were hungry."

I shrugged. "I am...but."

She pinched the back of my arm. "I swear you're easily distracted."

Viktor chuckled. "In his defense, it was my idea."

Justine snickered. "That's right, dig yourself in deeper. See where that lands you tonight."

Viktor grinned. "It might be worth it. He's the first vigil Lazarus has had in nearly a thousand years, so I might be willing to risk a night or two in the doghouse."

Justine giggled. "I swear, it doesn't matter the age, boys will be boys." She gently laid a hand on his shoulder. "You two can drink and talk to your heart's content...once the table is set."

He smiled. "I'll remind you that you said that."

She stifled another bout of laughter. "I'm sure you will."

When we were seated, Justine poured us a glass of wine to go with a healthy portion of lasagna, breadsticks, and Italian sausage and peppers.

Viktor gestured at the table. "Sorry about having to cancel our plans to dine out, but work ran late, so I asked a buddy of mine to step in to make us dinner. Plus, this gives us the privacy a busy restaurant wouldn't."

Justine's voice was full of humor. "That was sort of the point of going out...I wanted you two to get to know each other before you start telling stories."

Viktor grinned. "I'm quite capable of having a conversation without turning it into some random anecdote."

Her eyes widened, and her mouth fell open. "Really? That's what you're going with?" She folded her arms and narrowed her eyes. "Tell you what, if you're able to get through the night without regaling us with some story, I'll never mention it again. If you don't...we're going on a two-week vacation of my choice."

He grinned. "Sounds like I win either way." Putting on a serious face, he glanced over at me. "I hear Bryan Hotard stopped by your place today."

I swallowed my food and nodded. "Yeah, I'm starting to think he has a crush on me."

He snickered. "The man's a prick. He had me cuffed and locked in the back of a squad car a few weeks ago."

Justine frowned. "He's an asshole, no doubt, but you did have a dozen-plus corpses at your feet that day."

He choked down a bite of lasagna. "Hey, some of them were dead when I got there." He turned to me. "They were using necromancers to control a bunch of undead."

I frowned. "Another one?"

He nodded. "Yeah, I heard about Walter. It seems they've been cropping up a lot over the last ten years or so." Shaking his head, he grumbled, "I haven't got a clue why."

"Well, that's not good news."

Viktor's expression hardened. "No, it's not."

I leaned back in my seat. "Hopefully, they'll fade into the background for a while...I've got other problems to deal with at the moment."

He nodded. "You're talking about the new laws concerning the weres, right?"

At the mention of the global initiative I'd implemented, my stomach did a little flip-flop as my nerves set in. "Yeah, but I'm having trouble maintaining the peace. The Archive doesn't have the manpower to keep order while we work through the transition."

Viktor laid his fork on the side of his plate. "I could offer you a hand in that department if you wanted." He shrugged. "It'd stretch me a bit thin for the foreseeable future, but this is important."

I could hardly believe my ears. He was throwing me a lifeline...and offering me an actual chance at making this happen. "Really?"

He nodded. "Absolutely."

I blinked. "Thank you." Sighing, I said, "To be honest, I'm not sure how things got this bad in the first place."

Viktor frowned. "I am... Have you ever heard of Red Riding Hood?"

I chuckled. "Of course, but what does a fairy tale have to do with weres becoming slaves?"

Justine checked her watch. "Christ, that's got to be some sort of record. By the way, we're going to Hawaii at the end of the month."

Viktor opened his mouth, closed it then let out a belly laugh. "Looks like it." His expression instantly soured. "But back to the Brothers Grimm and their propaganda machine."

It turned out Red Riding Hood was a real person named Chandra

Raghnailt, and she wasn't the helpless little girl the stories made her out to be. In fact, she was a full-grown woman who happened to be an excellent swordsman, not to mention a powerful necromancer. While she did wear a red cloak, it wasn't the bright piece of clothing in the stories—it was dark, almost black, stained with the blood of the fallen. According to the legends, she'd spent centuries hunting and killing weres of all types, for no other reason than that she felt like it.

Viktor found out about the woman's rampage after she killed one of his friends. That was when he decided to hunt her down to put an end to her genocidal crusade. He'd nearly disemboweled her, but before he could finish the job, two of her henchman showed up, forcing Viktor to retreat. He hadn't seen or heard of her since then—meaning she'd either died of her wounds or gone underground.

Even though Chandra hadn't resurfaced, the Brothers Grimm brought back the tale of Little Red Riding Hood a few centuries later. They made it their life's work to brand all weres as evil. But their hatred hadn't stopped there as they were quick to include all supernatural folk in their propaganda disguised as fiction in an effort to turn humans against us.

We continued with our dinner as the subject changed from weres to necromancers and finally came full circle to Captain Hotard...and by extension the UCD and my position as the head of it. Which was a bigger deal than it sounded, as it was a division of Interpol.

Being the center of attention never sat well with me, so I thumbed over at the bar. "How about that drink?"

Viktor grinned and got to his feet. "Absolutely." He gestured Justine and Heather over. "Come on, after I pour us a whiskey, I'll give you a tour of the place."

I smiled. "Sounds good."

Viktor grabbed a second bottle of scotch and handed it to me. "We'll be wanting that later."

I glanced over at Heather and shrugged. "Okay..."

Viktor raised his glass and waved for us to follow. Tucking the bottle of scotch under my arm, I casually strolled up behind him as he opened an unassuming metal door. A moment later lights flickered to life overhead, and I damn near dropped my glass.

What lay before us was the most amazing collection of art, books, and artifacts I'd ever seen in my life. They were items he'd acquired over his exceptionally long life, and it was nothing short of awe inspiring. We spent the next several hours perusing the shelves and being patiently guided to its heart, which was a sunken firepit in the center of the space. That was where we stayed till almost dawn, talking and listening to the most fantastical stories I'd ever heard.

2

February 20th

Late last month, I'd called for a conference to be held to work out the particulars of giving the weres full rights. With Viktor's assistance, I'd been able to maintain order, but that was about as far as the good news went. While the governors were on board, quite a few prefects were not, and they were the ones causing all the problems. They were doing their best to negotiate a rewrite of the law I'd already passed. Which was never going to happen.

While I hated to leave them on their own, my duty as a vigil—okay, the vigil—made it necessary. I'd received a call from Heather yesterday morning about a situation in New Mexico. A man named Cole Pahe had phoned the triumvirate and spoken at length with Heather. She'd done some cursory checks on him, and it turned out that Andrew, my uncle and the governor of North America, held the man in high regard. In his words, if Cole needed to speak with me, it was important enough for me to stop what I was doing and tend to the matter sooner rather than later. The frustrating part was that Cole

Dust Walkers | 13

had refused to share exactly what the problem happened to be, saying he'd only discuss it with me personally.

Given all the small-minded racist shit being thrown around, it was probably for the best that I'd left anyway.

There were far too many holdouts amongst the old guard for my liking. No matter what they thought, weres were now on equal footing with the rest of them. I was doing my best to get them onboard with the new agenda without knocking anyone's teeth out. Which was proving far more difficult than I'd ever imagined. I had to remind myself that beating people within an inch of their lives wouldn't help.

Another upside to this return trip to the city: it allowed me the opportunity to speak with Alicia Sanders, my real estate agent. Captain Hotard had made it clear, along with several of the residents of my building, that I wasn't welcome there. Which was fine by me—I'd discovered very quickly after moving in that apartment living wasn't for me.

But I'd stuck it out while I searched for something more suitable. Although that hadn't happened yet, Captain Hotard had landed himself on suspension for excessive force, which made this the perfect time for a change without him up my ass.

I parked the Tucker a half block from my apartment and made my way up to meet with Alicia. She was a pretty woman, but definitely high maintenance. Just being around her for more than half an hour at a time exhausted me, but she was the best at what she did.

When I got to the top of the stairs, she smiled and waved me into my empty apartment before setting a clipboard on the counter. Like every other time I'd met her, she was meticulously dressed. She was the type of woman who wore her beauty like armor and wielded it as a weapon against the unsuspecting.

Which I wasn't.

She'd tried to seduce me on several occasions, which went absolutely nowhere. Even if I'd been single, nothing would've happened. There was something iffy about the woman, but I couldn't put my finger on it.

Maybe it was her flirting that'd turned me off. She'd once described me as 'tall, dark, and interesting.' The tall was easy enough to understand as I stood six-foot-six, and the dark was due to my native heritage. But if I had to guess, it was my heavily scarred hands that were the interesting bit. The left one looked as if God had shoved it into hell's forge for shits and giggles. Not to be outdone, my right bore the markings of my office: a wreath with crossed swords on the back, and the word Pax was carved into the flesh of my palm.

Alicia cleared her throat, bringing me back to the reason I was standing here. "Did you hear what I said?"

I shook my head. "Not a word."

Puffing out her bottom lip, she flashed me those brilliant blue eyes. It was an act meant to melt men, and I was sure it worked on most of them. But, while the woman was beautiful, she was also trouble with a capital T. She had a deep-down gold-digger quality that was hard to miss when you weren't distracted by the window dressing.

Alicia smirked and handed me a pen. "Since you paid for the place outright, I may be able to work it out so that you break even."

I signed on the first page, flipped through the next dozen, signing and initialing as needed, before handing the pen back. "Do me a favor...turn up the charm, and if you sell it within the month, I'll give you a five-thousand-dollar cash bonus."

I'd said the magic word. Her eyes lit up, and I could practically hear the gears turning as she picked up the paperwork. "You know I couldn't take cash like that...it wouldn't be appropriate. But I'm certain you'll find a creative way to make things right."

"Consider it done."

She stowed the papers in a leather folder and flashed me a big smile. "I'll be in touch in a week, maybe two."

And with those words, I knew the place was sold. Some poor guy, or maybe girl, would be suckered into buying the place sooner rather than later. Did I feel bad about bribing her? Hell no. It wasn't as if the cash made that much of a difference in the scheme of things. She was getting ten percent of a three-hundred-and-fifty-thousand-dollar sale. The five grand was more of a trophy for her. She hadn't been able to bed me during my search, so as far as she was concerned this was compensation for her *time*.

I followed her down four flights of stairs to the ground floor. She made a performance of climbing into her Mercedes, showing as much leg as possible.

The woman was persistent; I had to give her that.

She smirked. "If you ever get tired of looking…"

Smiling, I shook my head. "You can stop right there. It isn't as if I'm not interested. I'm male, for God's sake, but you're out of my league." I winked. "Take it as a compliment, get the bonus, and be a happy woman."

"If you say so." She shrugged as if she didn't have a care in the world. "Your loss, honey."

And in her mind, I'm sure it was. I gave her a wave and waited for her to drive off.

3

It was a bright, clear day in the city of New Orleans, and the moderate temperature allowed me to open the windows before making my way down Magazine. For my first trip to the great southwest, I'd be using one of the transport gates to get to my destination, instead of a plane, train, or some other form of *mundane* transportation.

The local version of which was in the heart of Audubon Park at a place called Newman Bandstand. Heather was meeting me there to show me how to activate the thing since it would be my first time using it. I pulled off Magazine, found a suitable spot for the Tucker, and grabbed my bags.

When I'd first arrived in the city, I hadn't been able to fill even one duffle, and now I had two crammed with gear. Heather had insisted I pack a jacket, but I doubted it would get any use. I'd always loved the cold. The heat, on the other hand, well, I hated that with a passion—especially when there was humidity involved.

I made the short trek to the oversized cement pavilion. Standing at the top of the stairs, Heather offered me a warm smile and a wave. Flatfooted, she stood six-foot-one, with sea green eyes and shoulder-length strawberry blond hair. This month. Last, it was black. Every

Dust Walkers | 17

time she went to the stylist with Justine, she wound up with something new.

When I walked up the stairs, Heather wrapped her arms around me and pressed her lips to mine. It was her favorite way to say hello, and I wasn't exactly complaining.

After several seconds, she pulled back and beamed. "Are you ready for this?"

I shrugged. "I guess."

She walked to the nearest pillar, and with a wave of her hand, a low hum reverberated throughout the pavilion. A few seconds later, a couple of pathetic looking trees popped into view.

Gesturing at the scene, she grinned. "Enjoy your trip. Cole should be in the parking lot past Frenchy's Field. Since he's been keeping mum about what's going on, he'll be the one to chauffer you around while he explains things."

Glancing from pillar to pillar, I frowned. "What do I need to do? Are there special words or something?"

She laughed. "No, this isn't the movies. Just walk through, and poof, you're there. It's like strolling across the room... You can manage that, right?"

Rolling my shoulders, I sighed. "We'll see."

She leaned over and kissed me again. "Call me when you get settled."

I smiled. "Sure thing."

With that, I stepped into the scene, and...nothing. Well, not *exactly* nothing. My skin tingled for a second as I passed through the paper-thin image. Turning around, I tried again, and nearly walked into Heather.

I sighed. "Houston, I think we have a problem."

Raising an eyebrow, she frowned. "What's going on? You can't just walk back through without opening the gate from the other end."

Holding up my hands, I said, "I didn't actually make it to New Mexico."

She shook her head. "I don't get it."

I thumbed back at the gate. "When I walked into the image, I felt tingly and then nothing." Stepping to the side, I pointed at the lagoon. "All I managed to do was get a good look at the moss growing on the water there."

Frustrated, she blew out a long breath. "Stay put. I'll be back in a minute."

She moved into the shimmering scene then there was a low pop as it vanished. A few seconds later, it reappeared, and she stepped into view.

Placing a hand on her hip, she let out a laugh. "I hadn't expected this to be a thing." She pointed at my bags. "Give me those."

Furrowing my brow, I asked, "Why?"

She snickered. "Because, silly, they won't make it through airport security."

I blinked. "What?"

Heather fought off a case of the giggles. "It appears you can't use the gate. I'm guessing it's due to your...unique nature."

That was a polite way of saying that I didn't possess any actual magic.

Handing her the bags, I grumbled, "Damn. All right."

She kissed my cheek. "You might want to get online and book the next available flight." Pausing, she pulled out her phone. "Smile." There was a flash, and she lowered the device. "I'll send this to Cole so he'll know who to look for."

She was gone a good ten minutes, giving me plenty of time to pay way too much for a one-way ticket to Santa Fe.

What a mess.

It shouldn't have come as a shock that the gate wouldn't work for me. They were created long ago to be used by those with magic in their blood. Until this moment, I'd thought being a member of the Archive and a vigil would be more than enough to allow me passage. Apparently not.

The fastest route to Santa Fe came with a connecting flight through Dallas on a civilian aircraft. Due to my size, I'd be lucky if they didn't charge me for an extra seat. The only thing in my favor was that I didn't have any luggage for them to lose.

The gate hummed, and Heather reappeared with her hand out. "Keys."

I stuffed my hand into my pocket to retrieve them. "Be careful with her."

She rolled her eyes. "I'm not sure who you like more, me or that car."

I laughed. "You, of course. But you have to admit, the car *is* special."

Heather nodded. "That she is." Eyeing my phone, she asked, "All set?"

Frowning, I ran my hand around the back of my neck and nodded. "Yeah, I'm on the 5:15 flight out. I should get there around 11:30 tonight."

She squeezed her eyes closed and winced. "Ouch... Flying isn't my favorite thing, but there are worse ways to travel."

I shrugged. "I suppose you're right...I could be forced to make my way there by camel."

Pursing her lips, she asked, "Other than the time, what's so bad about that?"

"For starters, they smell, they're irritable, and generally bad tempered."

She snorted and waved a hand at me. "Ever stop to think that you're massive, and that's why they're pissed off?"

Glancing down at myself, I sighed. "Could be..." I checked my watch. "I've got a little over five hours before I have to board. Want to grab a bite before you drop me off?"

She gave me a half-hearted grin. "Wish I could, but I have a triumvirate meeting. We still haven't agreed on a replacement for Martha, and it isn't as if you can keep doing it forever."

I nodded. "I suppose that's true."

She thumbed over at the car. "Come on, let's get going."

The thirty-minute trip to the airport was far too short, or maybe it was the following hour in TSA hell that was too long. Since this was my first trip via civilian aircraft, it took me a few tries to make it through. The final attempt required me to remove my steel-toed boots, belt, and empty my pockets before the scanner stopped beeping. Thank God, because I wasn't in the mood to be taken aside for a cavity search.

With that hurdle behind me, I passed through the checkpoint and found a place to eat. For some reason, I was finding myself hungry more often than not lately. The great thing about being in New Orleans was that almost every establishment in the city sold booze, and the airport was no exception. I couldn't think of a better way to pass the next several hours than to eat fried chicken and have a couple cocktails. Probably not the healthiest of combos, but it did soothe my frayed nerves.

At around three, I finished my last drink and meandered over to the gate to check in. Not long after we boarded the plane, a nice lady changed places with me, allowing me to have an aisle seat.

Believe it or not, I arrived in Santa Fe on schedule. Which was a shock, considering the puddle jumper we were flying sounded like it was about to fall apart at any moment. The pilot taxied up near the terminal, where a set of stairs were pushed into place, and we were allowed to disembark. That was when it hit me. I was an incredibly stupid man... While Cole knew me, I didn't have a clue what he looked like. Hell, I didn't even have his phone number. My head started to ache, and I massaged my temples. You'd think I would've learned my lesson by now and started doing my homework beforehand instead of jumping into shit and hoping it would work out.

To make matters worse, my stomach was growling. The booze and fried chicken had long since run their course. Hopefully, there was a place close by where we could stop and get something to eat. That was, if I ever found the guy. Standing in the middle of the airport wasn't going to help anything, so I made my way outside to see if anyone was there to flag me down.

The place was tiny, and it took less than a minute to make my way through the front doors. My mouth fell open slightly at the size of the parking lot, which was barely big enough to hold twenty-four cars across and only three rows deep. What sort of backwater town had I landed in? I'd seen forward bases that took up more space. Considering how famous the city was, I'd been expecting a massive airport in a thriving metropolis. Instead, what I got was a sleepy little town that had to have the best PR firm ever.

The quiet purr of a well-tuned engine floated in off the highway. Scanning the darkness, I was focusing on the entrance to the airport when a gorgeous 1957 Chevy Task Force turned in. Behind the wheel sat a rather small man, with shoulder-length black hair, dark eyes, and deep brown skin. His high cheek bones and angular jaw were made more pronounced by the odd shadows from the overhead lighting.

He coasted to a stop next to me and flashed me an easy smile. "Evening."

Apprehensively, I asked, "Cole?"

"Yep, pleasure to meet you." He thumbed at the bed of the truck. "I stowed your gear back there in case you needed it right away."

My gaze flicked over my bags, and the tension in my shoulders eased. "Mind if we grab a bite to eat before we dig into whatever it is you want me to check out?"

Grinning, he motioned for me to get in. "I think we can manage that." He paused, and his voice was full of wonder. "It's great to finally have one of our people as a vigil."

I popped the door and slid into the seat. "Thanks…I think."

Cole appeared confused for a moment. "Your grandfather is Isapo-Muxika, isn't he?"

Wincing, I nodded. "Yeah, he is."

He gave me a sad smile. "I suppose being blood doesn't make him any easier to get along with then."

"Not in the slightest." My stomach chose that moment to growl loudly.

He raised an eyebrow. "You weren't kidding about being hungry. Didn't they have snacks?"

I shook my head. "Nope."

Cole harrumphed. "In that case, I've got the perfect place to grab a bite."

Patting my stomach, I chuckled. "Sounds great."

Twenty minutes later, we parked on West Alameda and walked the remaining half block to the Del Charro Saloon. On our way, I took stock of my companion. He was around five-foot-six, and maybe a buck thirty soaking wet. He was dressed in a pair of dark jeans, a red flannel shirt, and a black leather fur-lined jacket that came down to his thighs. He grabbed the door and pulled it open, waving me ahead.

We found ourselves a nice table in the far corner.

Taking a seat, I picked up a menu. "What's good here?"

He grinned. "Everything, but my favorite is the stuffed green chili burger, extra spicy."

The way he said the last bit made me nervous. "The first half of that sounds great, but I'll skip the extra spicy."

Laughing, he said, "Smart man." He let out a long breath. "Once we finish here, we'll collect the trailer."

I grinned. "Don't tell me you called me here to help you move."

He chuckled. "Hardly, but where we're going, there aren't a plethora of places I'd like to stay, so we'll be bringing my airstream with us."

I leaned my forearms against the table, and my smile faded. "Sounds like this is going to take a minute. Care to fill me in on what's going on?"

Cole quickly scanned the restaurant to make sure we couldn't be overheard and lowered his voice. "In the last few years, the number of missing people in the area has spiked. A lot of the locals have brushed it off as tourists getting lost on hikes, or people trying to disappear in the hopes of finding a new life."

Frowning, I cupped my jaw in my hand. "But you're not buying it."

He shook his head. "Never have. One of the tribal elders and his wife went missing a few months back. And after a lot of poking around, I thought it best to call in some help since no one around here wants to listen." His voice turned hard. "Isaiah, another elder, seems to think they've gone on vacation without telling anyone. In his words, I worry too much."

I opened my mouth, but he held up his hand to stop me from speaking when an exceptionally beautiful woman with deeply tanned skin and long dark hair made her way out of the back. She wore a pair of faded denim low rise jeans with a light blue top that showed lots of cleavage and stopped at the bottom of her ribcage. Her nametag read Danielle P.

She dipped low and kissed Cole gently on the lips. When she spoke, her soft voice lilted across the table. "About time you showed up." She straightened and winked. "Your usual?"

Cole's cheeks darkened. "Yeah." He waved a hand at me. "This is Gavin, the man I was telling you about." He turned to me. "This is my wife, Danielle."

She stuck the pen behind her ear and held her hand out in my direction. "Pleasure to meet you." Her eyes narrowed, but her tone was light. "He's been awfully coy about why you're here, but don't go getting him in any trouble or you'll answer to me."

I held up my hands and grinned. "I'll do my best."

She clucked her tongue and smiled. "See that you do."

Cole sighed. "You've got it backward. I called him...so it's me who's getting him into trouble."

Irritation flickered in her eyes. "It would be in your best interest not to remind me." Keeping her eyes on him, she gestured at me. "Why are you involving the Archive at all? Everyone who's gone missing is human." Her tone softened. "Maybe if you told me what was going on, I'd be able to help."

He shook his head. "Not a chance in hell. I don't need, nor want, you to get on the elders' bad sides... One of us there is enough."

She gritted her teeth. "Like I give a shit about them."

Cole folded his arms. "I'm not going to involve you in this if it's at all possible."

Flipping him the bird, she said, "Fine."

He pointed at the pad in her hand. "Gavin is having the same... minus the habaneros." Turning to me, he asked, "How would you like yours cooked?"

Wanting nothing more than to stay out of their disagreement, I shrugged. "Medium rare, if it isn't too much trouble."

She smirked, and mumbled, "At least one of you knows how to eat a burger." Danielle spun on the heel of her boot and marched off to the kitchen.

Once she was out of earshot, I leaned in. "She did bring up a good point. If everyone who's missing is human, why am I here?"

He frowned. "That's something best shown. You'll have to trust me for a few more hours, but believe me, you're here for a damn good reason."

I shrugged. "That's fine with me."

He started to say something else, but Danielle returned with our drinks, pausing long enough to stare daggers at Cole before leaving without a word.

Once she departed, I shook my head. "I'm guessing whatever you called me in for is bad enough to suffer her wrath."

His expression hardened. "It is."

If his tone was any indication, whatever he was going to show me would most likely mess up my entire week. Armed with my greatest weapon, sarcasm, I said, "Fantastic."

A tiny smile broke through his dour expression. "It's good to see you have a sense of humor. You're going to need it."

I frowned. "I'm guessing you're not a motivational speaker."

He snorted. "Nope. Danielle and I own this place. Bought it about a year ago. She runs things here, though." Pausing, he sighed. "Mainly because my darling wife thinks I'm not a people person."

I raised my tea glass in his direction. "If it helps, people say the same about me."

Cole grinned. "Then we should get along wonderfully."

"Ha."

A couple of minutes later, Danielle arrived with our food and sat next to her husband. "I hope you two enjoy it."

Cole raised an eyebrow. "Why's that?"

She folded her arms. "Because that's the last meal I'm making either of you until you tell me what's going on."

Doing my best to change the subject, I asked, "How long have you two been together?"

Dust Walkers | 25

He picked up his burger and shrugged. "One hundred and eight years July. How about you and Heather?"

Wow. That was…impressive. I'd be lucky if she kept me around for the first year, let alone a hundred plus. Christ.

"We've been together about eight months…barely."

He smiled. "Still in the honeymoon phase. That'll pass, and you'll discover if you're meant to be together. If so, count yourself fortunate. A good partner is hard to find."

Danielle cut her eyes at Cole. "Tell me about it." Her expression softened, and she sighed. "This is the first time you've ever kept a secret from me."

Cole mumbled, "I'm sorry. If it helps, I don't want to be involved in this at all, but it's not in my nature to turn a blind eye."

She grimaced. "I know, but you don't have to protect me. You know damn good and well I can take care of myself."

He held out his hands, attempting to calm her. "I'm not trying to protect you. Goddamn, is that why you're so pissed off?"

Confused, she stammered, "Then…what?"

Cole chuckled. "I'm more worried you'll go wrecking stuff, and then Gavin here would have to come and arrest you instead of the actual bad guys." He shrugged. "So you see, I'm actually protecting the general populace from your wrath."

Danielle rolled her eyes. "Please, you're making me out to be some sort of hothead."

His voice was heavily laden with sarcasm. "You? Never. You're cool as a cucumber in deep winter."

She punched him in the arm. "Smart ass." Turning to me, she said, "I may occasionally be…overzealous, but only when someone deserves it."

I nodded and smiled. "I'm sure."

Cole laughed. "The last time you lost your temper, you burned down half the house."

Shaking her head, she said, "That was an accident."

He winked at her. "I know, but it's always good for a laugh."

Her voice turned catty. "For you, maybe. The rest of us aren't laughing."

The last part was true. I'd taken the liberty of keeping my mouth full in order to participate in this conversation as little as possible. When their gazes fell on me, I shrugged and took another bite of my burger, which, I might add, was awesome.

Danielle grinned. "He's a smart one."

Cole sniggered. "What makes you say that?"

She pointed at me. "He knows when to keep his mouth shut." Leaning over, she kissed him on the cheek. "At least I don't have to worry about you as long as he's around."

I swallowed my food. "Maybe you've got me confused with someone else. You do realize I'm new to the Archive...right?"

Danielle gave me a dismissive wave. "Please, if even half the stories about you are true, my husband will be fine."

And there went my appetite. "Care to be more specific?"

Arching her eyebrow, she said, "There are a few circulating, but my favorite is when you supposedly showed up at the triumvirate and burned a man to the ground... Is it true Andrew's kept his remains on display?"

I frowned. "Sort of. Brad was burned to a crisp, and the process fused his charred skeleton to the floor. With all the enchantments in my uncle's place, they're having a hell of a time removing it."

Cole winced. "Ouch."

The memory of that day washed over me, and my voice came out in a growl. "Traitors irritate me."

Danielle shivered and gestured at my hand. "I can see that."

I glanced down. My right hand had turned onyx and my left was covered in blue flames. Thank God we were the last ones in the place. It took a moment, but I suppressed my anger, and my flesh returned to normal. "Sorry about that."

Cole cleared his throat. "No worries. It took me years to get my powers under control. You've been at this, what, nine months?"

I nodded.

He grinned. "Give it time, and it'll become second nature." Sighing, he pushed back from the table. "But for now, we should probably get on the road."

Danielle leaned over and kissed him on the cheek. "Be safe, my love." She placed her hand over her heart then held it out toward me. "May the gods watch over you." Bowing, she said, "It was a pleasure to meet you, and I'm so happy one of our own has finally become a vigil. It'll be nice to have someone who understands our ways." Her voice dropped. "Martha was nice enough, but she was an outsider."

That was code for Martha relying on information she got from the townsfolk. Which wasn't entirely her fault, if I had to guess. The way it tended to work—where I was from, anyway—was this: Everyone on the reservation kept to themselves, even refusing to cooperate with outside law enforcement, who didn't typically try very hard. In the end, all it did was create misunderstandings on both sides. There was a good chance I'd meet with the same resistance, since I was only half native.

"Let's hope others share your viewpoint."

Her forlorn expression told me everything I needed to know. "With luck, the others will see you as a bridge between our people and...everyone else." Lifting her steely gaze to mine, she squared her shoulders. "You are the future, and if we hope to survive, everyone will have to adjust their perceptions."

Cole beamed. "Well said."

"Thank you." She curtsied. "Be safe, and call if you need anything."

She took our plates and left us. I pulled some cash out of my wallet, and Cole held out a hand. "It's on the house."

"Thanks, but I need to leave a tip...I wouldn't feel right otherwise."

He frowned. "Fine."

I folded two twenties and placed them under my glass. "Where's the trailer?"

"Around back." Cole walked toward the door then stopped at the bar and yelled, "We're leaving. Need anything before we go?"

Danielle popped out of the back and smiled. "No thanks." She shooed us out. "Now hurry up and get this over with so we can get back to our lives."

Cole snickered. "Yes, ma'am."

He pushed open the door, led me out into the darkness, and pointed down the block. "The trailer's around the corner, in one of the storage units. We'll need to hook everything up before we get on the road." Gesturing at the door, he said, "You're welcome to catch some shut-eye while I drive."

Shaking my head, I took a deep breath. "That won't be necessary. I got a few hours' sleep on the plane, and I'd like to do a little sight-seeing since this is my first time out this way."

That was the funny thing about my life; I'd traveled the world a couple times, but I'd only seen a few of the states in the country I was born in.

It took a half hour to get the airstream in order, another three to make it to the tiny city of Grants, and our destination, the Ice Caves, was still thirty minutes away. While Cole didn't seem impressed with them, I thought it was pretty damn neat to have a year-round frozen grotto in the middle of the desert.

4

February 21ˢᵗ

Stars shone brightly in the night sky, and the silver moon lit the vast emptiness of the desert, giving it an otherworldly quality. About ten minutes outside of Grants, the old-growth evergreen forest came into view. The primeval landscape jutting out of the rich volcanic earth was made up of junipers, firs, and pines. It was a scene that had changed very little over the last few million years, and with luck would remain as pristine for many lifetimes to come.

What remained of the extinct Bandera Volcano dominated the horizon, and while it wasn't a giant mountain oozing lava, it was still quite impressive. Cole turned off the highway onto a well-kept dirt road. After about a half mile, we found a paved lot where we parked. At the far end of the asphalt, there was a pale green wooden shack with a flat roof that looked as if it had seen better days. A big sign across the front read *Trading Post*.

Cole waved a hand at the hovel. "This is our first stop."

I furrowed my brow. "Seriously?" Gesturing at the shop, I said, "You brought me here to go to some tourist trap that isn't even open?"

His voice dropped. "Not quite. We'll be taking the path down to the caves themselves. The owners know I'm stopping by, so they won't mind us doing this before business hours."

Hmmm. "Okay then. Will all our stops be so touristy?"

A small groan escaped his lips. "God, I wish."

I pulled air through my front teeth. "I take it that things get worse after this."

His tone soured. "You could say that... The nightmare I'm about to show you will be an absolute joy, compared to what's next."

Grimacing, I shook my head. "Damn, dude. I never thought I'd be the one saying this to someone else, but you seriously need to work on your interpersonal skills."

He grinned as he got out of the truck. "Nah, I think it's best to temper people's expectations, especially when it involves the Grants."

Curious, I asked, "Are they related to the folks the town's named after?"

Cole snorted. "Nope, they *are* the ones who founded the place." His expression turned hard. "You should be aware that they're going to be pissed you're in town without their permission."

"Huh?" I shrugged. "Last I checked this was a free country, and people could go wherever they wanted, whenever they wanted."

His voice had a hard edge to it. "Maybe most people can, but you're part of the Archive, and more importantly...you're a vigil." He huffed out a laugh. "Technically speaking, you're the man in charge, which will only serve to complicate things even more." He pointed at my bags. "Might want to grab your things."

I'd changed into tactical gear before leaving Santa Fe, so all that was left was my backpack, where I'd stored the gladius and a few other items. After strapping on the sword and a pistol, I said, "That still doesn't explain why they'll be angry."

He shrugged and started walking toward the trail marked with a weather-beaten sign that read *Ice Caves* with a big red arrow. "In their mind, they own this land, and the people in it. Plus, they really don't like outsiders—and that's especially true when it comes to a member of the Archive telling them what they can and can't do."

I rubbed my face, trying to wake up. "You keep saying they... How many of them are there?"

Cole grunted. "There's the head of the family Lewis, and his two brothers Angus and John. Out of the three of them, there isn't a nice one in the bunch." He turned toward town and gave it a middle-finger salute. "Which is why I didn't bother telling them I was going to contact you."

I glanced out toward the lights in the northwest. "Fuck those guys. If you ever need to speak to me about anything, call, and we'll work it out. If that's a problem for them, they can kiss my ass."

A half-smile crept onto his face. "Good to know." He pointed past the shanty. "We should get going."

It was a quarter mile before we came to a rickety wooden staircase that led down into a collapsed lava tube. A couple of twists and turns later, we stood on a flimsy wooden patio that overlooked a sheet of green ice.

It probably made me an asshole, but I totally lost interest fifteen or twenty seconds after seeing the place. Suffice it to say, a bunch of blue-green ice in the bottom of a cave sounds a lot more interesting than it actually is.

Turning to him, I shook my head. "Okay, am I missing something?"

He grinned. "Took it all in, did ya?"

With a dismissive roll of my shoulders, I frowned. "What can I say? I've seen it. Now what?"

Cole pointed his flashlight at the far side of the chamber. "What we're looking for is over there."

Leaning over the railing, I did my best to find something worthy of attention. "Could've fooled me."

He waved for me to follow. "Come, you'll need to get closer to see what I'm talking about."

I looked around for a ladder. "How do we get down?"

Laughing, he said, "Don't tell me this is your first time jumping a fence."

Bewildered, I shook my head. "No, but..."

32 | KEN LANGE

"But what?" Pointing at the far end of the cavern, he said, "Once we're there, it'll be just around the corner."

Throwing my hands up in surrender, I sighed. "All right, let's go."

It didn't take long to make our way down to the slick frozen surface of the cavern. Cole stuck close to the side, using the rockface to stay upright. I, on the other hand, simply walked behind him, easily matching his pace. Cole ducked around an outcropping of rock before disappearing into a smaller tube. When I rounded the ledge, the scent of death and decay nearly took me off my feet. Unconsciously wiping my upper lip, I grimaced before following him in. Due to the tight quarters, I was forced to stoop and do a little shuffle in order to catch up.

About fifty feet in, Cole dropped his voice and held his finger to his mouth for quiet. "Over there."

He lifted his light to illuminate the far corner. My mouth went dry, my stomach started doing flip flops, and my mind did its best to make sense of the scene before me. Two bodies had been flayed and left here in the cold. Gore pooled at their feet, and their muscle tissue was a weird pinkish color as they'd long since dripped dry. Given the amount of blood on the ground, it was obvious this was where they'd been murdered. This was the part of the situation that made sense.

Where things went off the rails was them squatting under their own power and trembling here in the darkness. Every now and again, they twitched oddly as their desiccated sinews contracted. The sudden movement made weird clicks that echoed throughout the chamber as bones ground against one another. Anytime they shifted their footing, it made a vomit-inducing sucking noise due to the goo on the floor. There was no way they were alive, yet...they were still functional somehow. For the first time in my life, I viscerally understood the word abomination.

Shivering, he grimaced. "This is why I called you here."

I was numb for a moment then fury crept through my system, making my hands quiver. Keeping my gaze locked onto these...things, I asked, "Is there any reason I shouldn't end them right now?"

He shook his head.

Dust Walkers | 33

I strode past him, tugged the gladius off my hip, and quickly removed their heads. While I hadn't a clue what they were, the Grim was incensed by their presence. I hoped Kur would have some insight, but he was trying to rouse himself out of stasis, which left me on my own for now.

Anger coursed through me. "What the hell were those things?"

Cole prodded one of the heads with his boot. "They were the chindi of the tribal elders I told you about." He gestured at the way back. "Let's get out of here and find some fresh air. This place reeks."

We were a bit quicker making our way up to the surface than we'd been getting down. It was as if the stench was following us... Hell, for all I knew, I'd stepped in some tribal elder and was tracking it up the stairs as I went. About halfway across the parking lot, the putrid odor seemed to dissipate. Thank God for the great outdoors and a good steady breeze.

I pointed back at the stairs. "Mind filling me in on what chindi are, and why they're skinless?"

He chewed on his bottom lip and was quiet for a moment. "I'm guessing you've never heard of them."

I blew out a long breath. "Can't say that I have."

Nodding, he leaned against the railing. "Well, that's sort of a blessing and a curse for you."

"How's that?"

He let out a rueful laugh. "It's good you've gone this far in life without ever having to deal with one. Today, however, I'm sorry to say that's changed." Sighing, he shook his head. "The chindi have many forms. Normally, they're what you would call ghosts, spirits, specters. In the form you just saw, the spirit's left the body, leaving only the flesh behind to continue without direction or purpose. Popular culture calls them zombies, or the undead."

A shiver ran up my spine. "How does something like that happen?"

He kicked a rock off the pavement. "At a guess, there's a necromancer in town, which is why I called you. From what I hear, you've dealt with them before."

I facepalmed myself and sighed. "Just one, and that didn't exactly turn out well for either of us. But as far as I know, he never created anything like those things down there. Specters, yeah, but nothing like that." Squeezing my eyes closed, I leaned heavily against the truck. "No other possibilities?"

His face screwed up in disgust. "If I believed the old myths, sure, there's a chance they were created spontaneously, but I don't." He thumbed over his shoulder, and anger colored his tone. "And when we add in the fact that they were skinned, we're likely looking at not only a necromancer, but a flesh-walker as well."

My stomach tied itself in knots, and Kur finally pulled himself out of his slumber, whispering, *"Necromancer, body snatcher, thief."*

Images of a flayed body were quickly followed by someone chanting a spell over the flesh before they wrapped it around themselves to be transformed into their victim.

I covered my mouth to keep from losing what was left of my dinner. "Christ. They're real?"

Cole nodded. "I've never seen one before, but it's the only thing that makes sense."

I really wanted to argue, but he was right.

God help us.

5

It was well after sunup by the time we made our way to the far side of town. We'd just turned off Iron Avenue onto 101 Grants Loop when the Grim stirred, and suddenly it was as if someone were standing on my last nerve.

The closer we got, the more irritated I became. I was already concerned about meeting these guys, and this sudden foul mood wasn't helping matters. Not that I was too worried about making a good impression, but I didn't want this to go any worse than it had to. Although, based on what Cole had told me, I'd probably end up pissed off no matter what.

It was nearly a full mile before we arrived at a small fortress for overly privileged dickheads.

A massive eight-foot adobe wall surrounded the sprawling estate, giving it a prison vibe, and the heavily reinforced steel gate did little to detract from that impression. If you asked me, this was all a bit overkill, and whoever'd had it built was compensating.

Two armed guards made their way out of a portcullis, took one look at us, and scowled.

The taller of the two gave us the finger. "What the fuck are you doing here, Injun?"

36 | KEN LANGE

Cole slowly got out of the vehicle. "We've come to speak with Lewis."

He growled. "That's Mr. Grant to you, boy."

Cole grimaced, and his voice came out with an edge to it. "Fine." He thumbed over at me. "We've come to speak to Mr. Grant."

The guard huffed and shook his head. "Should've made an appointment. He's busy this morning."

Cole smirked. "He might want to make an exception for a vigil."

The tall man laughed. "Unless Martha grew a beard, I'll pass on interrupting his breakfast."

I stepped out and held up my right hand. "Martha's dead, and I'm filling in until someone suitable is found to take her place."

His gaze swept over my hand, and he staggered back a step. "You're the new guy...the one who took over for Naevius."

It appeared certain bits of information traveled faster than others. "That's right."

He glared at Cole, and his voice became tense. "What's he doing here?"

I moved in front of Cole and gestured at myself. "You'd be better off addressing such questions to me."

Puffing out his chest, he sneered. "Okay then, what the hell are you doing here?"

I was conflicted. On one hand, I wanted to take the man down a peg or two for his arrogance. On the other, his utter lack of human decency made me pity the jerk. "That's something best discussed between me and your employers."

He gestured at his partner, who made a hasty exit. "Why?"

Wow, this guy's snotty attitude was making me want to punch him in the face, and this was only the hired help.

It took a great deal of effort to keep my growing annoyance in check, but I managed it. Barely. "That's really none of your concern. At this point, you have two options. Either let me in, or don't. Frankly, I don't care one way or the other, but I'm guessing your bosses will."

His expression soured. "Fine." He turned and yelled, "Open the gate..."

Dust Walkers | 37

Cole waved me back to the truck. "That was a risky move."

I shrugged. "Maybe, but it got us in the door."

He bobbed his head up and down. "That it did, but I'm saying you could've been a bit politer about it."

I rubbed my temple. "Probably true, but according to what you told me earlier, they're going to be pissed off that I'm here anyway. Besides, something about this place irritates the shit out of me."

Cole choked back a laugh. "Really? I couldn't tell." He gave me a dismissive wave. "At least now I know you're a good judge of character."

It was a real fight to keep my annoyance at a manageable level. "Even a deaf, dumb, and blind man couldn't miss this much concentrated assholery."

The gates swung back, allowing Cole to coast around the circular drive... Guess we'd found that loop they were talking about.

As I got out of the vehicle, an attractive, dark-haired woman wearing battered leather armor was being ushered toward the front doors by two rather unpleasant looking men. They wore matching disdainful expressions when their gazes fell on Cole. The sunlight glinted off the purple streaks in the woman's hair as she stepped into the open, but one of her companions caught her arm and pulled her back toward the house.

Her remaining companion stormed over, glaring at Cole. "You should've called."

Cole shrugged. "Sorry about that, Steve, but you know as well as I do that cell reception outside town is shit. So, I did the only sensible thing and brought him here as soon as we crossed the city limits."

The big man frowned as his gaze landed on me. "When did you get here?"

Last thing I wanted was to get Cole and his wife into more hot water, so I lied. "Not that it's any of your business, but I came through the gate early this morning, commandeered the first Archive member I could find, and now I'm here." Taking a deep breath, I said, "And that's the last question I'll be answering until I meet Lewis or one of his brothers. If that's unsatisfactory, I'm gone."

His haughty expression faltered, and beads of sweat popped up around his graying hairline. "No...the Grants are waiting to meet you."

I waved him ahead of us. "Then by all means, show us the way."

Steve's annoyed expression said he wasn't thrilled with my presence, but that was all right by me, since I wasn't happy about being here either. He pivoted on the spot, and lumbered through the entrance with us in tow. Several twists and turns later, we arrived at a set of intricately carved doors. He knocked but didn't bother waiting for a response before pushing them open.

In the center of the room was a large solid wood desk. The man seated in the leather chair behind it wore a tailor-made black suit with silver cufflinks. He appeared to be in his fifties, but since he'd founded this city, he was much older. His dark hair had only the slightest hint of gray in it, and his brilliant blue eyes stood out against his tanned skin.

Judging by his position at the desk, this had to be Lewis, and the two men standing to either side of him were his brothers.

He got to his feet and gestured at me. "So, you're the infamous Gavin Randall."

His condescending tone grated on my last nerve, but I was in his house so I probably needed to at least try to be polite. "That's right, and the three of you are?"

He waved a hand at the small sickly blond man to his left. "This is my brother John, I'm Lewis, and this is Angus." The latter was a slightly less attractive version of himself. "Have a seat, and tell me what I can do for you, *vigil*."

I meandered over to the nearest chair and plopped into the seat. "I'm sure you're aware that Martha O'Neil was murdered last year."

Annoyance crossed his face. "I'd heard rumors, but nothing definitive until this moment."

Clearly, he was all broken up about it. "Well, since the area is currently without a vigil, I've taken it upon myself to tour the territory and make sure everything is as it should be... With that being said, is there anything around here I should be aware of?"

Lewis frowned as he shook his head. "I don't think so."

John leaned over and whispered something in his ear.

The man's eyes lit up, and he grinned. "My brother has reminded me that there've been some strange reports coming out of Highland Meadow." He turned to Cole. "The abandoned bridge by the old Route 66…you're familiar with the place, aren't you?"

Cole nodded. "Yeah."

Lewis continued. "Great, then you can do what your people are best at and guide your betters, or in this case, somewhat better to where he needs to go." His gaze landed on me. "That way you can get the hell out of my town as soon as possible."

The arrogance was strong with this one. Biting back a nasty retort, I managed to keep my tone civil. "Care to be more specific about what's happening?"

Shrugging, he said, "If I could, I would. Perhaps you'll find out when you get there." He put his elbows on the desk, and his expression hardened. "After that, I'd appreciate it if you kept moving. Maybe the res could use your help, but the rest of us are fine."

Craning my neck from side to side, I sighed. "I suppose this is your polite way of telling me to get out of town before sunset. That's a bit of an old west cliché, isn't it?"

He wagged a finger at me. "Boy, if I wanted you gone, I'd throw you out. What I've offered you is a bit of friendly advice."

When I clenched my hand into a fist, several of my knuckles popped. "I'm not big on being told what to do…especially by the likes of you." The moment his brothers started to move, I was on my feet. It was all I could do to contain the Grim as he begged to be let loose. "You two really don't want to try my patience today."

Lewis held up a hand, and they both stopped. "Easy now. This is a friendly conversation, and I'm sure Gavin here will see reason." He pointed at the door. "Look into the situation at the bridge, and then go. If you don't…" He waved a hand at his brothers. "I'll let them have their way with you."

I laughed. "That'll be a lot less fun for them than you might think."

He snorted. "You really should get going. You're not the only one running low on patience." Lewis held up a finger. "And one more thing."

Resisting the urge to roll my eyes, I blew out a long breath. "Yes?"

Lewis got to his feet, and while he was tall, he was still a few inches shorter than me. "Don't come back unless you're invited."

The doors opened, and six armed men stepped into the room.

I glanced at them then Lewis. "I'm beginning to get the feeling you don't like me very much." He started to answer, and I held up my hand. "That's okay. The feeling is mutual. But you should know something."

He chuckled. "And what's that?"

My tone hardened. "If I come back to this place, invitation or not, you won't like the way it turns out."

The guards fell in beside us and escorted us to the drive.

Steve stood next to Cole's truck with a smug look on his face. "You'd do well to remember that your kind isn't welcome here." His gaze drifted over to me, and he spat on the ground. "That goes double for you, half-breed. I don't care who you are. If you show up here again, I'll bleed you out slowly and leave you in the desert for the coyotes."

I smiled. "Pleasure to meet you as well...Steve."

He flipped me the bird. "Go on, get, before I change my mind about letting you leave."

Cole slipped into the cab of the truck, and I made my way around to the other side to do the same. The gate swung open, and we idled out onto the road. My anger dissipated as we got further away from the Grants. What a bunch of assholes.

Cole cleared his throat. "You all right?"

I nodded. "Better with every mile we put between us and those arrogant, racist pricks."

He laughed. "That sums them up nicely."

Turning to him, I put my shoulder against the door. "Who was the woman they were taking into the house when we got there?"

Cole frowned. "That was Jessica... She's supposedly Lewis's daughter."

Dust Walkers | 41

I cocked an eyebrow. "What's that mean?"

He shrugged. "Well...Lewis sort of showed up with her as an infant in late November of 1970."

Cocking my head to the side, I blinked. "That's an awfully specific thing to remember...month and year."

He chuckled. "I guess it is, but for me it marked the end of several months of peace. Lewis and his brothers had been out of town, and it was the first time for as far back as I could remember that any of us could breathe easy. That all ended when they showed up with Jessica. Everyone around here has speculated that she's some sort of love child, but the mother's never shown up, and as you can tell, they aren't exactly the talkative type."

Weird, but not unheard of. "Not to mention protective as hell. I thought the guy was going to have a stroke when she stepped toward us."

He took his hand off the wheel and patted me on the shoulder. "We should be so lucky. That guy is a massive prick. Same with his buddy Steve."

I nodded. "Yeah, I got that feeling." Gesturing out toward the road, I asked, "Where are we headed?"

He sighed. "Highland Meadows. It was the next stop on our list anyway." Glancing over at me, he said, "I've heard of a few people from town going missing in the area and wanted to check it out."

I yawned. "Sounds like we're in for a long day."

Cole bobbed his head in agreement. "Probably, but we'll try to rest after we make camp." He gestured at me. "You're welcome to catch a few winks while I drive."

Highland Meadows was a speck of a town fifty miles outside Grants. I leaned against the truck to take him up on his offer and fell asleep almost instantly.

6

The sound of the truck door clicking closed woke me. I wiped my eyes and squinted in the bright light of the mid-morning sun. The landscape reminded me how different the world could be. All deserts were barren wastelands, but this one had more greenery than most, giving the area a unique beauty and a sense of agelessness.

I stepped out of the cab and stretched before making my way around back to find Cole. He was busy cranking the hitch for the trailer, so we could set up our basecamp.

Gesturing at the ravine behind us, I yawned. "Is this the spot everyone is so hyped about?"

He nodded. "Yeah, this used to be part of Route 66, but they cut this section thirty or forty years ago."

The rickety bridge spanning the crevasse was barely holding itself together. There were numerous planks missing, dry rot had long since set in, and the entire thing was in danger of collapsing at any moment.

I wiped the sleep from my eyes. "So, we're making camp here?"

Cole shrugged. "I can't think of a better place. Being here will give us an opportunity to scout the area, and with the townsfolk too spooked to come out this way, we'll have the place to ourselves...

hopefully. But for now, I thought we'd get a few hours' rest and see what pops up after the sun sets."

I frowned. "That's the extent of your plan?"

He grinned. "Yep."

Honestly, I couldn't come up with anything better, but sitting out in the open waiting for something to show itself wasn't my idea of fun.

Resigning myself to the situation, I rolled my shoulders. "All right. How can I help?"

He pointed at the end of the trailer. "Make your way down there and drop the stabilizers."

It took another thirty minutes to set up the solar array atop the Airstream, and with it active, the lights flickered to life.

Inside, Cole pointed at a door at the opposite end. "You'll be in the guest room, which is back there." Thumbing at the door behind him, he said, "I'll be up here. The kitchen is fairly well stocked with the basics, but we'll probably need to find a local grocery later to pick up a few items." He glanced over his shoulder. "I'm going to get some sleep, and I'd suggest you do the same."

Stifling a yawn, I nodded. "A little more sleep sounds really good right about now."

He turned on the spot and disappeared into his sanctuary. I was obviously more tired than I'd thought since it took me several seconds of standing there alone to realize that the conversation was over.

I made my way down the length of the trailer, pushed the door open, and locked it behind me to make sure I wasn't disturbed. What I found was nearly enough to shock me awake. Nearly, but not quite. There was a queen bed in a surprisingly spacious room, along with the rest of my gear. After taking off my boots, I moved the comforter onto the floor and placed my rucksack at the far end before curling between the wall and the box springs. I needed to get some decent rest, and, even now, this was the best way for me to do that.

It wasn't long after that I drifted off to sleep. The gentle swaying of the trailer and the sound of sand beating against the metal skin of the Airstream woke me. My watch read 4:35. I rolled over and got to my feet, my body doing its version of the snap, crackle, and pop song. I grabbed a clean set of clothes and stepped into the hall to find the head. Thirty minutes later, I was clean, dressed, and in the kitchen, quietly searching the cabinets for a glass. Which was more of a chore than you'd think because most of the *dried goods* were actually bags and bags of habaneros.

I was starting to think Cole was a little obsessed with the things.

There was a brilliant flash of lightning in the distance, quickly followed by a low rumble of thunder that caused the trailer to vibrate. I shivered at the thought of being caught in a major sandstorm in this thing. Maybe they weren't terrible here, but in some spots of the world there were serious consequences when one of them rolled in... such as having your skin sandblasted off your body.

Over the following two hours, the storm moved in, and the sand pelting the trailer was replaced by a steady rain. Cole stumbled out of his room a half hour later and silently made his way to the bathroom.

I pulled some eggs and bacon out of the fridge to whip up a late breakfast. It was his good fortune that Cole meandered out of the bath just as I was finishing.

He pointed at the table. "That for me?"

I inclined my head. "It is."

A big smile crossed his face. "You, sir, are a godsend."

Snickering, I shook my head. "You might want to wait to taste it before you pass judgment."

Ignoring me, he opened a cabinet, grabbed a bottle of tabasco, and doused everything on his plate. "I'm sure it'll be fine, and even if it's not, there's always more hot sauce."

Horrified, I stammered, "Ah...wow...Christ, I already put a few ghost peppers in there to spice things up. What are you, half dragon?"

He crumbled a few more of the dried peppers over the dish and chuckled. "Nah, nothing as fanciful as that. Not in my opinion, anyway."

I raised an eyebrow. "Hey, don't stop there. Now you've got to explain yourself."

Wiping his mouth, he snorted. "I don't fall into the standard categories within the Archive... My father is Haashch'eezhini, and my mother is Na'ashjéii Asdzáá, or at least that's what I'm told by the tribal elders."

Even with my limited knowledge of the Navajo, I'd heard those names. They were powerful deities in their pantheon...and here I was, possibly talking to their son. "I'm sorry? Did they just drop you off at the elders' doorstep or what?"

He wobbled his hand back and forth. "Not exactly. An ancient advisor to the tribal elders, Łééchąą'í, carried me out of the desert and presented me to them. According to him, I was birthed by the earth and given form by the universe." His voice turned hard. "Which is way nicer than saying that my parents abandoned me at birth..."

I jumped when a heavy thud of something striking metal sounded outside, and a shiver ran up my spine as the wind howled. I glanced over at Cole, who still had his mouth open.

He closed it and got to his feet. "Guess it's time to get to work."

I leaned over, grabbed the gladius off the counter, and clipped it onto my belt. "Let's go then."

When I stepped out of the trailer, it was already dark, and the rain had changed to snow. I scanned the darkness. The only thing out of place was the raised hood on the truck. Between the snow, haze, and general lack of light, it was impossible to tell if anyone was standing there. That put a little extra oomph in my step as I made my way over to the vehicle. After checking the immediate area to ensure I was alone, I inspected the engine. While I wasn't a mechanic, I knew enough to see that someone had removed the distributor cap and done a number on the spark plug wires.

This wasn't exactly the work of the supernatural, but it was sure as hell inconvenient.

Dozens of footprints in the damp earth were starting to freeze, and a faint trace of decay hung in the air. Cole strolled up next to me, wearing a thick brown leather duster and matching gambler cowboy hat. He frowned, and his eyes turned scarlet as he scanned the horizon. The sound of shuffling feet came from the nearby ravine, and the Grim tugged at my consciousness.

Cole pointed toward the bridge. "There's a lot of movement out that way." He gave me a once-over then thumbed back at the trailer. "Want to grab a jacket before we find out who's come calling?"

I shook my head. "Nah, I'll be fine."

He gestured at a nearby crevasse. "Give me a minute to get on the other side of the bridge then push whoever's there toward me."

I gave him plenty of time to get into position before making my way down into the gully. Unfortunately, I was less than stealthy about it as the thin layer of ice cracked beneath my feet with every step. By the time I reached the bottom of the ravine, the lingering scent from earlier had become an overwhelming wall of death.

A half second later, the ground crunched behind me. I spun on the spot, and recoiled as three bloated corpses sped my way. The very sight of these things made my skin crawl, and I did my best to put distance between us. But all I managed to do was clumsily stumble backward as I pulled the gladius from its sheath. My eyes adjusted to the evening gloom, painting everything in shades of crimson. Well, not everything. The undead appeared as black silhouettes highlighted with gray mist.

Finding my footing, I lifted the sword and brought it down quickly, nearly cleaving the first one in two. The moment the blade pierced the creature's flesh, a putrid odor made me gag. I kicked it in the chest, causing the motionless thing to fall back and hit the ground with a dull thud. Swinging the blade to my right, I caught the next one in the head, slicing through its skull at eye level. A cold, viscous fluid ran down the hilt onto my hand, and bile caught in my throat. The third hit me hard in the gut with its shoulder, lifted, and drove me into the rocky wall. As I was already about to lose the contents of my stomach, it was all I could do to keep from vomiting on the thing's back.

Wisps of shadow wrapped around me as I allowed the Grim to manifest. When the tendrils of my robe passed through the dead thing, it didn't as much as flinch. Frustrated, I slammed my flaming fist into its face, and was met with less than dismal results. All that I'd managed to do was burn through its cheek to the bone, but the creature didn't seem to feel pain. It appeared that the Grim was more or less useless against anything that didn't have a soul...which meant that I was left without my best, and perhaps only, weapon against these things—a massive flaw in what little superpower I had.

I brought the pommel down on its forehead, and it staggered back a half step. The vile thing recovered quickly and swiped at my abdomen with its bony fingers in an attempt to gut me. I deflected the blow with the gladius before kicking out and snapping its knee. It collapsed, and I drove the black blade through its brainpan. Thankfully, the thing stopped moving. The gladius, however, was vibrating, and a weird violet mist surrounded it.

I glanced over at the first corpse, and it was just as dead as the others, so maybe headshots weren't the only way to kill these things. Or maybe the gladius was doing the heavy lifting for me.

Near the bridge, a bright orange glow lit up the night and highlighted the horde moving toward Cole. The Grim shimmered out of existence to reveal a thick layer of clear ice crawling up my legs and torso until it enveloped me. The blue flames normally confined to my left arm spread under the ice and danced across my new form. When I stepped forward, I'd expected to be met with some sort of resistance, but there was none. This new armor was practically weightless and moved with a fluidity I hadn't expected.

I didn't know what was happening to me, but a low rumble from Cole's direction meant there was no time to figure it out. Testing my grip on the gladius, I gritted my teeth and leaped into the fray. I drove the sword into the back of the first body, and it dropped like a rock, taking the blade and me to the ground with it. Dozens of the corpses fell on top of me.

The combined weight of their bodies forced me face-first against their fallen comrade. I lost my grip on the hilt, my hand slid down the blade, and it sliced through my palm. More of the things piled on, and the pressure built until I couldn't breathe. It took all my strength, but I balled my fist and tried to force it up toward the sword once more. But a sudden impact from above forced my hand down. The moment my knuckles connected with the frozen earth, a massive shockwave rolled out in every direction, obliterating all it touched.

The fire under the ice armor seeped through the cut, lapped at the blood I'd spilled before igniting an inferno that engulfed the area an instant later. The canyon walls funneled the flames in both directions. When it cleared, there was nothing left but ash, and an odd, silver man-sized sphere coated in ice.

I swayed as the world around me spun faster and faster. It was difficult to breathe, my body ached, every bone felt bruised, and my head pounded in time with my racing pulse. My vision narrowed. Unable to catch my breath, I collapsed on the spot, and darkness overtook me.

7

February 23rd

The darkness ebbed away as light shone through my eyelids, which were crusted shut. My pulse was drumming out a rhythm against the back of my skull, making it difficult for me to recall my own name. To be honest, the last time I'd felt this awful was when I was a guest of the Iraqi government twenty years ago.

It took some prodding to kick my brain back into gear, but when it finally came online, the recollection of being trapped in a canyon filled with shambling corpses flooded my mind's eye.

When I tried to open my mouth, my dry, cracked lips burned, and a low groan escaped me. Lifting my hand to my eyes to wipe away the grit took a monumental effort. Eventually, I opened them. Massive mistake. The curtains weren't fully drawn, and the sun was doing its damndest to burn out my retinas.

My body objected when I attempted to sit up. Agony coursed through me, but my scream was cut short when my chest seized, shutting off the flow of air to my vocal cords. I'd only managed a couple of inches, but when I fell back onto the mattress, it jolted every bone in my body.

A second later, the door popped open. Cole stopped in his tracks, and relief spread across his face. "Thank God." His body slumped as he took a deep breath. "You had me worried...I wasn't sure if you were going to wake up."

I tried to speak, but all I could manage was to choke on my own tongue and make some incoherent noises.

Cole held out his hands. "Hold on, let me grab some water."

The first sip was cold, refreshing, life affirming. Honestly, it was difficult to think of a time when something so simple had tasted so good. But my hands were still shaky, and I spilled the rest before I could get a proper drink. With Cole's help, I managed the second glass a little easier, even if it did take ten minutes to get it down.

Again, it took the two of us to prop me against the wall of the trailer, but I was feeling somewhat better. Taking a deep breath, I gave Cole a once-over. "Not that I'm not grateful, but how in the hell did you manage to carry me back here?"

Cole blew out a long breath. "It took a little doing with you being unconscious and all, but I'm stronger than I look. The most difficult part was trying to balance you as I made my way up the wall of the gorge out there."

My cheeks burned. "Sorry about that...and thank you for taking care of me." My hands shook as I lifted a third cup of water to my lips. "How long was I out?"

He winced as he rubbed his forehead. "A day and a half."

I blinked. "Shit. Any idea what happened?"

His hands shook, and he sat on the edge of the bed. "Not exactly. In truth, I was hoping you had some answers. There were a crap ton of the chindi then there was a rumble a few seconds before the gorge turned into a raging blue inferno. Once that cleared, you were covered in the same weird flames. You staggered, fell to your knees, and promptly went to sleep on the job."

His summation made me laugh, but the pain made it come out more as a series of coughs. "Is that what I did?"

He shrugged. "After being forced to carry you back, that's how I'm seeing it."

I grinned. "When you put it like that, I sound like a lazy bastard."

He nodded. "Yeah, you do…but it gave me some time to work on the truck while you slept."

A pain shot through my hand, and it made me wince. "How's that coming?"

Getting to his feet, he growled. "Whoever it was didn't fuck things up too badly, but they did steal the distributor cap. Without that, we're dead in the water."

I leaned my head against the wall. "Goddamn it." Shaking my head, I sighed. "What happened to the zombies?"

Cole threw up his hands in defeat. "They're ash…not that I understand how you managed it. And while that's impressive, and a wee bit terrifying by itself, that isn't the weirdest part."

I popped my head off the wall to give him a curious look. "What do you mean?"

Rolling his shoulders, he sat on the edge of the bed again. "Those flames, they didn't feel hot. I mean, they turned a bunch of corpses to dust, but when they surrounded me, I thought I was going to freeze to death on the spot. That's fucking strange, man."

Thinking back to the incident with Brad, it made sense. For a fire to burn hot enough to turn a body into a charcoal briquette, the room should've heated up like a blast furnace, but none of the triumvirate members had as much as broken a sweat.

I took a moment to mull that over, before turning my attention back to him. "Okay…that is a bit weird."

He snorted. "Just a little, but, believe it or not…there's more." His gaze hit the floor, but after a few seconds, he glanced up at me. "The sword you were using is stuck in the bedrock…I can't even wrap my hand around the hilt without getting thrown back on my ass. It's almost as if the thing is alive and knows I'm not its master."

That wasn't really a surprise. While I couldn't tell you how, or why, the gladius was sentient, possessing a keen intellect…and perhaps even a soul. I know that talking about an inorganic object like it has a life of its own is a bit peculiar, but there you have it.

Nodding, I said, "I'll tend to it shortly."

Cole patted my leg. "I'd suggest some food and a shower first. After that, let's see how you're feeling."

I ran my hand over the top of my head. "Probably a good idea."

He insisted on feeding me before I got clean, which wasn't an awful deal, but the real turning point in my day came with my shower. Nearly all the cobwebs in my head cleared up, and the aches and pains became manageable. While I was still pretty messed up, I could walk and talk without too much effort, so I counted that as a win.

An hour later, I stepped out of the trailer to find a massive black scar marring the land around the mouth of the ravine, and the ragged evergreens caught in the blast radius were now dead.

Kur shivered. *"Such is the power of a Reaper's blood...it is able to give or take life, depending on the intent."*

I glanced down at my hand. It was completely healed, and as per usual these days, there wasn't a scar to show for it—not that I needed another one. Cole guided me down a fissure that gradually led into the canyon, so I didn't have to climb down, which was an absolute bonus given how unsteady I was on my feet.

He stopped short and stepped out of the way. "Here it is."

The gladius was wedged into a crack in the charred sandstone. I slowly wrapped my fingers around the hilt, took a deep breath, and jerked up. That was a mistake, because the blade came free the moment I tugged on it. Which meant the rest of the momentum I'd built up landed me on my ass.

Cole chuckled. "I guess you didn't need to pull so hard."

I sheathed the sword and pushed myself onto my feet. "Ya think?" Before he could respond, a moan drifted out of the distance. Frowning, I turned to Cole. "Tell me you heard that."

He nodded, and his voice dropped to a whisper. "Yeah."

Pushing the pain aside, I quietly jogged over to the far side of the gorge and made my way up, with Cole right beside me. The whimpering was becoming more frequent, which made it easier to follow.

There was a large boulder in front of us, and I motioned for Cole to go left while I went right.

I picked up the pace, and a few seconds later, I found a wounded man propped against the sandstone rock. The side of his face, both arms and legs were charred. He must've gotten caught by the blast when I destroyed the zombies.

His head listed my way, and his eyes bulged. When he finally spoke, it was with a heavy Russian accent. "St...stay back. I'm dead already, thanks to you. Just let me die in peace."

My gaze swept over the man's exposed chest. There was a thick black circle with nine blades running to a center ring, giving it the look of a deadly wagon wheel. At the base of each blade was an inscription I couldn't read. Kur's consciousness squirmed at the sight of them, and the Grim stirred with an inexplicable anger.

Kur whispered, *"Necromancer."*

Even though I tried to fight it, the Grim wrapped itself around me, and long black tendrils shot out to heft the dying man off the ground. Without much thought, I lifted my onyx-covered hand. A thick pillar of darkness poured out, tearing through his tattoo and chest before slamming into the sandstone hard enough to crack it. It stopped, and I removed his soul, mixing his power with my own. Shadows of red and orange swirled into my cloak and backlit the darker strands before it returned to its natural state.

Just as quickly as he'd arrived, my alter ego vanished, leaving me to tend to the now-lifeless man, who fell back to the earth with a squishy thud. *Shit.* On the upside, my wounds were healed, and I felt normal again, but it would've been nice to question the man before executing him. Mind you, it was a little late to beat myself up about it. All I could do was hope to do better in the future.

When I glanced up, Cole was standing there, white-faced, and shaking. Eventually, he found his voice and stammered, "What...what the hell was that?"

I held up my hands and stepped back from the body. "It's okay, I promise... That was the Grim."

He shivered. "And that is what, exactly?"

I shrugged. "No idea. As I've said, I'm still new to this world." My gaze fell on the corpse, and I sighed. "And my inexperience has just killed our one and only lead... Any chance you know the guy?"

Shaking his head, he frowned. "I haven't the faintest idea who he is..." He squared his shoulders, and his tone hardened. "Just how new are you to your abilities?"

My cheeks burned, and I suddenly found the pebbles near my feet very interesting. "They manifested the day I became vigil, and a day or two after I found out I was a Stone Born."

His jaw dropped. "Seriously?"

I nodded. "Why would I make something like that up?"

Cole ran his hand over his mouth. "That's the craziest shit I've ever heard, but the denarius is never wrong about power. Those things are drawn to it like moths to a flame."

The comment caught me off guard. "Huh? What's that supposed to mean? What—"

He held up a finger to stop my questions. "Let's take care of one thing at a time." Pointing at the corpse, he said, "This guy isn't ash, so we'll need to bury him."

I stepped toward the corpse and gestured at it. "Whoa, slow down there. Don't you think we need to call the authorities or something?"

A sly smile slowly broke across his face. "You *are* the authorities."

That was something I'd have to get used to. In the end, there was no higher authority to contact about such situations. I blinked dumbly. "Oh...yeah. Sorry, I keep forgetting that."

He gestured at the corpse. "Do me a favor? Pat the guy down, and see if you can find anything useful before we stick him in the ground."

I shook my head. "You search, and I'll walk back to the trailer to find a shovel. No need for you to suffer because of my mistake."

He grimaced. "I don't carry gardening tools with me when I go camping." Cole kept a healthy distance. "On top of that, I need a few minutes to get comfortable with the idea of...what did you call it...the Grim?" I nodded, and he continued. "Well, I'd like to...you know... keep you where I can see you, until I get used to you having multiple...forms." He held out his hand to stop me from saying anything.

"Think about it, in the last few days, I've seen you as...whatever that was in the canyon, this Grim thing. and your *normal* self. It's a lot to take in. You understand...right?"

Nodding, I sighed. "I suppose I do."

He gave me a nervous smile. "Good."

I grabbed my phone and started taking pictures. "Are you sure you don't want any help digging that hole?"

Cole frowned. "I'll be fine, and in case you missed it, I'd like to keep some distance between us for the moment. I'm not saying I'm scared, but watching you punch a hole through someone's chest without meaning to makes me a bit gun-shy."

Wish I could say he was being overly dramatic, but I'd gotten a good look at myself in Reaper form, and it was nothing nice.

After snapping several photos of the area around the hole in his chest where a few of the markings remained, I flipped him over and repeated the process. Checking his back pocket, I found a wallet with thirty dollars American, twenty-five hundred rubles, and a battered ID that read Mikhail Ivanov. I knew enough Cyrillic that I didn't need Kur to translate it for me. Holding the photo up, I compared the faded black and white image to that of my newly dead friend; they were a match. According to the birthdate, he was supposed to be sixty-one years old, but he didn't appear to be out of his twenties.

If I had to guess, this was his first state-issued identification card. Heather told me that a lot of the supernatural community held onto the mementoes of their youth. Witness protection offered by the U.S. government didn't have a thing on the Archive. They'd perfected the art of building entire new identities for their members, thanks to centuries of practice.

This was due to one of the less popular Archive laws that required every member to move to a different city, or preferably country, and take on a new persona every so many decades. In fact, it was my good fortune that I'd returned home when I did, because Andrew wouldn't have been there in a few more years. I wasn't looking forward to the day it would be my turn, but it was unavoidable.

56 | KEN LANGE

Holding up the tattered piece of paper, I asked, "Does the name Mikhail Ivanov mean anything to you?"

Cole shook his head. "Nope, but as small as the towns around here are, someone is bound to know who he is."

A long strand of silver emerged from each of his hands and merged into a thick tendril of gleaming light about two feet in front of him. It stretched out another several feet, and he moved it toward the ground. It cut into the soil, disappeared for a few seconds, and when he lifted his hands, a large mound of dirt came up with them. He deposited it at the side of the six-foot-long by three-feet-wide oval pit.

I understood now why he'd wanted to dig, because that meant he didn't have to fondle a dead guy.

He stepped back and eyed Mikhail's remains. "Done with him?"

"Not yet. Give me a second." I'd lied—it took nearly another minute, maybe two, to ensure I'd searched him thoroughly and emptied his pockets. "Okay, all done."

Cole took a few steps back and pointed at the hole. "You killed him. You drop him in. After that, we can move on with our day."

I glanced between Cole and the wide berth he'd given me and sighed. "Honestly, there's nothing to worry about. I've got the Grim under control. Promise."

He shrugged. "I believe you, but if it's okay, I'll believe you from over here... Don't worry, I'm kind of getting used to the idea, which is why I'm not halfway back to camp by now."

"Fair point."

I scooped the corpse up, walked over to the makeshift grave, and unceremoniously dropped the asshole in.

After filling in the hole, Cole cautiously made his way over and knelt next to the things I'd laid out on the ground. "Anything useful in here...other than his name, that is?"

I frowned. "Doubtful. The biggest clue in there is a receipt from Gems Home Center for some propane canisters."

He arched an eyebrow. "Can I see that?" I leaned over, picked it up, and handed it to him. After several seconds, he grinned. "I know the place. It's in Grants."

I cleaned up the last of his things and pocketed them. "Guess we've got somewhere to start looking, once we get out of here."

His expression soured. "True. We need to fix the truck, and to do that, we need the distributor cap."

I nodded. "Yeah, that's what I was thinking. Guess that means searching the desert till we find it...or till we give up and walk into town."

He crinkled his nose. "Trust me, you'll want us to find it. Highland Meadows is nearly as friendly as Lewis and his brothers."

It took us about half an hour to find Mikhail's basecamp. He'd holed up in a nearby cave outfitted with the bare minimum. An old green Coleman stove with several propane canisters, both used and new. A water collector to take moisture out of the air, attached to a plastic fifty-five-gallon drum, and a host of other things to turn any cave into a home away from home. While I couldn't tell you how long he'd been out here, it looked like a while.

I wasn't sure how necromancy worked—no one was, except necromancers, of course—but it was my guess he'd stayed out here to watch over his horde. It wasn't as if he could leave them unattended for long. There was a chance they'd wander off, or someone might stumble on them and alert the authorities.

The state of the undead last night told me they'd been decomposing for quite some time, which led to several questions: Why had he built up such a large force so far outside of town and kept them around for so long? What had he meant to use them for? If he'd intended to overrun the nearby towns, he could've done that without too much resistance. Until he showed up in Grants. At that point, I was sure Lewis would send his attack dogs, John and Angus, out to deal with the problem.

Lewis didn't seem like a man who would take kindly to anyone trying to infringe on *his territory*.

Then again, maybe he'd known about this guy all along, and had used me to take care of the issue. And by issue, I meant me or the now-deceased necromancer, because this was sort of a win-win for him. One of us was going to die here, and he didn't have to get his hands dirty to make that happen.

What an asshole.

My dislike for the Grants family continued to grow by the second. I wasn't happy that the jerk thought he was running his own fiefdom out here, and I got the distinct impression he believed he wasn't beholden to the Archive. That was a misconception I'd have to rectify sooner rather than later.

Cole made a racket when he pulled the distributor cap out from under the cot and held it up for me to see. "Found it."

That was one bit of welcome news. I smiled. "Great. Does that mean we can get the truck started?"

He frowned. "No idea, but we're one step closer."

It took us twenty minutes to make it back to the trailer. I went inside to get a drink, and Cole popped the hood to see what he could manage. A half hour later, we were still stuck. Two of the spark plug wires were mangled beyond repair. With no cell service, we had about an hour's walk to get to Highland Meadows.

8

I'd spent a lot of years out in the deserts of the mid-east, and while they had a particular beauty, it paled in comparison to the terrain here. There were a lot of reasons for this—the unique vegetation, the fact that it was winter, which meant I wasn't sweating my ass off, and that this wasn't a warzone, which meant no one was shooting at me. So you can see how I might find one much more appealing than the other.

The only bad thing so far was that it'd taken longer than anticipated to reach the town. Personally, I didn't think a few dirt roads, several shacks, and some power lines warranted the title, but then again, it wasn't up to me. There was a shanty on the edge of the city limits that doubled as a general store, but that was it. Long and short of it was, there wasn't a parts store nor a mechanic for fifty miles. Our only hope was to find a landline, call Danielle, and pray she could get the parts to us before dark. The last thing either of us wanted was to go for round two with the zombies...especially since I wasn't sure there was a repeat performance in me.

Glancing over at Cole, I asked, "Any chance they have a public restroom around here?"

Cole bumped his hand against my chest and pointed. "The bathroom is around back. I'll go in and see if they'll let me use their phone."

I nodded. "I'll be back shortly."

When I pushed open a battered wooden door, the rancid scent of a toilet gone wrong took my breath away. Bile caught in my throat, and I was suddenly struck with a dilemma...did I really need to pee that badly? Unfortunately, the answer was yes. A few minutes later, I was desperately praying someone would turn a firehose on me to knock the stench off.

When I made my way back around, four of the locals were spread out in front of Cole. For his part, he was casually leaning against the building, taking their insults in stride. This was a scenario I'd seen often in my youth. Someone from the reservation would come to town, and inevitably they'd find themselves the target of wannabe thugs. I'd long since moved past anger at this type of thing; now all it did was disappoint me.

The leader, a heavily muscled blond man, wagged a finger at Cole. "What are you doing here, boy?" He spat on the ground. "You stupid or something? I'm certain you know your kind ain't welcome in this town."

Cole sighed. "All I need to do is find a phone that works, and I'll happily leave. You wouldn't happen to have one I could use, would you?"

The big man laughed. "My line doesn't do smoke signals. Isn't that what your people use to talk to one another? Or is it drums these days?"

His cohorts laughed at the lame joke.

Cole rolled his eyes. "Gee, I've never heard that one before."

A tall man with dark hair who seemed a little slow glared at Cole. "Don't roll your eyes at Charles."

Charles grimaced as he glanced up at his buddy. "Good job, numb-nuts. He knows my name now."

His slow friend bowed his head. "Sorry."

Charles shook his head. "It's okay." Fixing his gaze on Cole, he said, "You'd best learn your place...especially when you're in the presence of your betters."

At that statement, I laughed, and everyone's gazes turned to me.

Charles gritted his teeth. "Who are you, and what are you laughing at, punk?"

I put my hand on my chest and grinned. "My name is Gavin, and as for what I'm laughing at...that would be you."

He shook his head. "Are you one of them city folks who thinks people like him are human?"

I snorted. "If being human means being like you, I'll pass on that *honor.*" Pausing, I let the insult sink in for a second. Trust me, they needed it. "If I had to guess, the lot of you don't have enough brain cells put together to make a functional adult. That's why you stoop to bullying folks who are different, not to mention smarter, than you."

The doofus who'd gotten upset about Cole rolling his eyes dropped his shoulder and lumbered my way. "I'll crush you."

That was a bad move on his part, because this fight would've gone poorly for these assholes even if I hadn't recently absorbed the soul of a necromancer.

Sidestepping the shambling oaf, I slammed a fist into his ear. He staggered to the side and fell to the ground, clutching his head. Two of his buddies sprinted my way with Charles taking up the extreme rear for this little shindig. I brought my knee up to catch the shortest in the gut, before hammering my fist into his jaw with a loud thwack. Pivoting on my back heel, I rammed my boot into the pudgy man's throat then turned and backhanded Charles, knocking him into the side of the building. Normally, getting physical with these guys would've been the last thing on my mind, but I wasn't about to let these assholes beat on me to keep the peace.

A siren blared, and someone laid on their horn. I stepped back with my hands in the air... Seemed a jail cell was in my near future.

A few seconds later, the godawful sound stopped. Turning, I found a firetruck sitting there. I dropped my hands and gave Cole a questioning look.

A small man with long black and gray hair stepped out of the cab.

He quickly surveyed the situation and frowned as he looked at Cole. "Was this necessary?"

Cole held out his hands. "Hey, this wasn't our doing. Charles started running his mouth then his buddy got pissed and got stupid with Gavin. After that, things went south before I could stop it. Not that I tried to, mind you, but that's beside the point."

The small man glared up at me. "I suppose you're Gavin?"

I nodded. "I am."

He held out a hand in my direction. "I'm Atsidi Sani."

The name sounded familiar, but it took me a second to place it. "The silversmith?"

A smile broke across his stern features. "Among other things." Atsidi glanced over at Cole. "Why are you traveling with an outsider?"

Cole pushed off the wall and walked over to us. "I'm not. This is Isapo-Muxika's grandson."

Atsidi stepped back and blinked a few times. "You're bigger than I was told." He pointed at the downed men. "We can't afford this type of shit, and you should've known better."

If he wanted me to feel guilty about downing these assholes, he was in for a surprise. "All I did was defend myself. It's not my fault that Goofy and his buddies are a bunch of racist pricks. Who knows, maybe this will teach them some manners."

Atsidi jerked Charles up by the collar. "Get up, boy. You and your friends need to make yourselves scarce before something bad happens." Once Charles was on his feet, Atsidi guided him toward the parking lot, gesturing at me as he passed. "Charles, when you were a boy, you asked me what I was afraid of...do you remember my answer?"

Charles spat blood on the ground. "That was a long time ago, old man."

Atsidi grabbed his arm and spun Charles around to face him. "Do you remember my answer?"

Charles's voice cracked as he spoke. "You said there wasn't anything in this world you feared."

Dust Walkers | 63

He let go of the young man. "That's changed recently, and if the stories are true, I fear only one thing in this life."

Charles moved out of reach. "And what's that, old man?"

Atsidi pointed at me. "Him." His voice softened. "Do not test this man, Charles. You won't live to regret it. Consider yourself fortunate that you've met death and walked away."

Charles sneered as his gaze tracked over me. "Please, he's a man, just like you." He puffed out his chest. "And men have a habit of getting dead."

Atsidi's melancholy laugh made the boy flinch. "You're young and stupid. I hope you live long enough to realize the folly of your ways." He stepped aside and pointed at a beat-up sedan. "Now go, before you miss the opportunity."

The four bruised young men took the long way around us before getting into their dilapidated, multicolored Cadillac and slowly driving away. Not that Charles didn't try to gun it, but when he did, the car nearly died on the spot. Which meant he had to settle for puttering away at a snail's pace while the engine clanked loudly.

Watching them drive off, I sighed. "You were laying it on a bit thick back there, don't ya think? I mean, that was a little overdramatic."

He took in a deep breath and shook his head. "If anything, I wasn't explicit enough." Turning his gaze to me, he said, "When the elders learned about you, we sought to discover your destiny by asking those beyond the veil about you." He shivered. "But we've been met with mostly silence."

Cole cocked his head. "Mostly?"

Atsidi nodded. "The one vision we've been granted was one of pain, death, and suffering." His gaze locked onto mine. "And what little of your future we can see says you'll find your home in the stars and walk with the gods as an equal."

I didn't mean to laugh, but I couldn't help it. "No disrespect to you, but maybe you've foreseen someone else's future. I'll be lucky to make it through the next year without getting myself killed."

His expression turned neutral. "We are many things, Gavin, but

64 | KEN LANGE

wrong isn't one of them." Before I could respond, he turned to Cole. "Why are you traveling with a vigil?"

Cole sighed. "It's a long story, and one best told indoors."

Atsidi thumbed over at the truck. "Get in. We'll talk on the way to the firehouse."

There were out-of-date tanks that rode better—and quieter, for that matter—but beggars couldn't be choosers. Over the fifteen-minute ride to the firehouse, Cole gave Atsidi the short version of the last few days' events. There was a chance, slim but still a chance, that Atsidi might have the parts we needed. If not, he had a landline we could use.

Atsidi pulled up in front of a fairly new metal building and turned off the engine. Before I could open the door, he held up a hand. "Wait."

I leaned back in the seat. "What's up?"

He puffed out his chest. "Before you go traipsing around out back, I do have a condition for my help."

Cole turned to him, and his voice had an edge to it. "Oh...what might that be?"

He grinned. "The two of you have to break bread with me this evening."

Cole snickered and patted him on the shoulder. "Of course...I'd be happy to sit down with you for dinner anytime."

"Agreed." I checked my watch. 5:30 p.m. "Mind you, it's a bit early, but I can always eat."

He gestured at Atsidi. "The old man is on Golden Corral time."

I furrowed my brow and gave him a questioning look. "Huh?"

Cole frowned. "Have you been living under a rock for the last thirty years or something? That was a solid old people joke."

I shrugged. "Might as well have been, because I didn't get it." Thumbing out the window, I asked, "Think we could get out now? This seat is exceptionally uncomfortable... I think one of the springs is trying to give me a prostate exam."

Cole frowned. "That's less funny and more gross...just in case you were wondering."

I grimaced. "Wasn't going for funny as much as factual."

Atsidi snickered. "Bah… This would normally be where I'd chastise you about being overly sensitive." He clapped Cole on the shoulder as he popped his door open. "But any excuse to keep from being subjected to his terrible jokes in a confined space is good enough for me."

Cole glanced between us and sighed. "Figures."

I hopped out of the cab and looked back at Cole. "What's that?"

His expression soured. "I finally make a terrific joke, and the one person who should laugh doesn't get it."

Atsidi chuckled and climbed out his side. "Face it, you're just not that funny. Or at least not funny in the ha, ha way."

Cole flipped him the bird and followed him out. "Please, I'm fucking hilarious."

Atsidi smirked and gestured at the firehouse. "If you're done, I'll show you two around."

The white steel walls of the volunteer firehouse gleamed brightly in the evening sun. The faded red metal door was a stark contrast to the rest of the building as it appeared to have seen its better days two or three decades ago. It didn't take long for him to show us all the important bits, such as the bathroom and dinner table. While Atsidi cooked, Cole and I went out back to see what we could salvage from the three retired firetrucks sitting there. While not a perfect match, the wires we were able to recover would likely work long enough for us to make it to Grants and purchase replacements.

By the time we got cleaned up, dinner was ready.

Atsidi handed us each a plate and pointed at the counter. "Help yourselves. If you want anything else, let me know, and I'll see what I can do to round it up."

I loaded my plate with shredded…pork, or possibly chicken, fry bread, and some beans. Seated at the table, I inclined my head at the old man and slid a small piece of silver across the table. "Thank you for your kindness."

Ever since I left home, I'd always carried a tiny portion of the precious metal with me as a gift to anyone who might take me in for whatever reason. It was customary among my people to present the host with a token to show gratitude for their generosity.

Atsidi picked it up and smiled. "You are most kind."

His eyes turned white, and the silver stretched out to wrap around his finger. It continued to morph until it turned into a beautiful band with symbols carved into it that I didn't recognize.

He raised an eyebrow. "Interesting."

I couldn't tear my gaze away from the ring. "What is?"

Atsidi handed it to me. "This obviously belongs to you." He beamed. "I've never seen anything like it before. I hope you enjoy it."

"I couldn't possibly take it back." I shook my head. "It was a gift."

He grinned. "And one I freely accepted. Now, it would be rude of you to reject mine."

Reluctantly, I gave in and took it. "Thank you. How were you able to create something like this, anyway?"

Laughing, he said, "That part is easy. I'm an elemental, and metal is my specialty, so to speak. Normally, pieces like that are created through force of will. But, there are times that the energy stored inside chooses its own form. Such was the case with this one."

The symbols appeared to be laser cut into the metal, and the softness was gone, replaced by something stronger.

Hesitantly, I slipped it onto my right ring finger. "Thank you."

He grinned and patted my arm. "You are most welcome." Atsidi glanced over at Cole. "I'm really glad we ran into one another."

Cole sat up straight. "Why is that?"

Atsidi frowned. "I was out at the old Sohio Mine in search of new material when a few thugs claiming to work for the museum confronted me. By the look of the place, they'd been out there for quite some time, but that's beside the point."

I leaned my elbows on the table. "Why would a museum be interested in a mine?"

Cole tittered. "It's not what you think. The places you're thinking about have paintings. The one he's referring to is dedicated to uranium mining."

"Oh."

Atsidi nodded. "The weird part was they all had thick Russian accents."

I handed him Mikhail's ID. "Was he one of them?"

He nodded. "Yeah, there were a few other men and a woman with him, but he's the one who told me he'd shoot me if I came back."

Cole grumbled. "You don't have to worry about him. He's no longer amongst the living."

Atsidi looked between us. "Is that so?"

I frowned. "It is. He was the necromancer we were telling you about."

Hanging his head, he sighed. "Necromancers are an abomination upon this world. If he was with the others, you can bet they're of a similar ilk. They tend to stick to their own."

Kur quickly agreed.

Finishing the last of my fry bread, I nodded. "That'll be one of the things we check into next."

He gave me a sad smile. "I'm sorry to burden you with such a task. I'd only wanted you to find out if they were smugglers or some other sort of thief."

I shook my head. "Think nothing of it. I was going to look into the man anyway, and thanks to you, we now know he has friends. That means we have more people to find, and tend to."

Cole grimaced. "We'll go to the museum after we get the parts for the truck. After that, we'll stop at the mines to see if the others are there."

Once we finished our meal, Atsidi guided us around to the far side of the building and uncovered a perfectly preserved 1943 Willys MB...the iconic Jeep used during World War II. I'd expected it to ride rough, but much like my Tucker, it glided over the terrain with ease.

It was well after sunset by the time we made it back to the trailer. It took us about fifteen minutes to put everything right with the truck. Satisfied we were safe, Atsidi headed home. It was too late to make it to Grants before the parts stores closed, so we chose to stay put for the night.

9

February 24th

In the interest of safety in numbers, we moved the Airstream to Atsi-di's an hour before sunrise. After we finished setting up camp behind his house, I relaxed in a folding chair next to the RV to watch the reds and oranges push back the night.

Due to the spectacular display of Mother Nature's handiwork, it took Cole a little prodding to convince me to get back in the truck. In that moment, I would've been content to sit there and watch the sky paint itself, but he was insistent that we needed to get to Grants as soon as possible.

An hour later, we were parked outside the Auto-Zone across the street from an abandoned hotel called Lava-Land. Considering the volcano hadn't been active in a million years or so, this was a bit of a stretch, marketing wise. Maybe that was why it was out of business. More likely, this tiny town didn't have a need for multiple hotels.

The parts store opened a half hour later, and it didn't take us long to get what we needed to make the necessary repairs. On the way into town, we'd decided we would stop in at the museum first and see where that led us. There was always time to visit the hardware store where Mikhail had bought the propane canisters later if that didn't pan out. But, if they treated us anything like the residents of Highland Meadows had, the owners wouldn't be much help anyway.

Grants was home to the New Mexico Mining Museum, and if you wanted to know what it was like to mine uranium, they had a hands-on simulation for you to try. Seriously, that was their biggest draw... Come in and learn what it would be like to be trapped underground with massive power tools while you try not to irradiate yourself. As you could probably guess, I'd be skipping that part of the tour.

We were parked for about twenty minutes before a white Mercedes SLK convertible pulled into the side lot. The woman inside made a show of applying her lipstick and checking her makeup. Eventually, she stepped out of the car, and the morning sun glinted off her copper hair. The dark navy-blue pantsuit she was wearing was a stark contrast to her alabaster skin. She glanced over at us before making her way to the front door to unlock it.

Cole and I got out of the truck and hustled across the sidewalk to where she stood holding the door open for us. When I got close enough, I read her name tag: *Ruth Miller, Curator*.

Ruth offered us a warm smile as she stepped back to make room. "Good morning, gentlemen." Once we were inside, she made her way over the threshold. "Welcome, I hope the two of you enjoy your visit. If there's anything I can do to assist you, please don't hesitate to ask."

I inclined my head. "Thanks... Actually, there is something you might be able to help us with."

Annoyance flashed in her eyes, but the smile remained. "Oh, and what's that?"

I suppose the offer to help was just one of those things she said, since it was clear she wasn't happy about following through. If that wasn't enough to make me dislike her already, her ingratiating tone was exceptionally irritating.

Even so, I fished Mikhail's ID out of my pocket and showed it to her. "Do you know this man?"

Her expression soured as she shook her head. "No. Why do you ask?"

Tucking the photo away, I shrugged. "It appears he's been telling folks around here that he works for you...or the museum, more accurately."

Ruth's lips twitched downward. "I see." She folded her arms and blew out an irritated breath. "May I ask who you are, and why you're interested in him?"

I grabbed my wallet and showed her my Archive ID. "My name is Gavin Randall, and I'm with the Uncommon Crimes Division of Interpol. The man I showed you earlier is a person of interest." Pausing, I let the implication set in for a second. "Are you sure he doesn't work here?"

Her gaze fixed on the back of my hand, she pointed at it. "You must take your job very seriously to get it etched into your flesh like that."

I closed my eyes and put away my wallet. "It's part of the initiation process. Or so I've been told, anyway."

Disapproval wrote itself across her delicate features. "Boys and their fraternities...I'll never understand the thrill." She flicked a manicured nail at my pocket. "As for the man in the photo, I can assure you he isn't an employee." Her laugh was short and bitter. "Our budget here barely pays my salary. The other two full-timers are in their sixties." She waved a hand out at the empty room. "Everyone else who comes here to help out is a volunteer...and there are fewer and fewer of them these days."

Frustration crept into my voice. "I see..."

Cole cut in. "Do you have any *volunteers* at the old Sohio Mine?"

Ruth cut her eyes at him and furrowed her brow. "I don't think so. Why do you ask?"

I held out my hand to stop her questions. "I'd rather not get into specifics, but if you could somehow make sure no one from the museum is out there, we'd be grateful."

She rolled her eyes. "Fine." Spinning on her heel, she gestured for us to follow. "Come with me, and I'll double-check the books...if that's what it'll take to get you two off my case. I do have a museum to run, after all."

She made a show of sashaying her hips from side to side as we followed her up the stairs. While I was sure most men would've appreciated the view, I wasn't one of them. Even the Grim stirred, and that same irrational irritation cropped up in the back of my mind. There was something about this town, or maybe it was being so close to the Grants, that annoyed me on a fundamental level.

At the top of the stairs, Ruth pulled open a glass door that led into a spacious office. "If you two will have a seat, it'll only take a moment to grab the logs and see if we've got anything going on...anywhere." She let out an exasperated breath. "It's the least I can do for... Who did you say you were with again?"

She damn well knew who I was with, and why I was here. Pushing down my indignation, I answered. "The Uncommon Crimes Division of Interpol, better known as the UCD."

"Uh-huh." She flipped through several files as her tone became disinterested. "I'm not sure what you guys are doing out here. This is one of the dullest places on the planet." Glancing over her shoulder, she huffed out a laugh. "In fact, having an Interpol agent in my office is probably the most exciting thing to happen in this town in the last century."

I shrugged. "That may be, but I still need to know if you have any stray volunteers you may've forgotten about."

She let out an annoyed groan. "If you'll give me a minute, you'll see that I'm trying to help... Oh, here we go." Pulling out a thick leather-bound ledger, she turned around and kicked the cabinet closed. "Believe it or not, this place isn't as popular as it used to be, and it's rare to have an offsite dig going on. I mean, it isn't as if we get a lot of funding. What little we do get goes to keeping the doors open. So, even if we wanted to do something out that way, we don't have the resources."

Sloths were faster than this woman. "I understand. There seem to be a lot of governmental budget cuts going on lately."

Ruth strolled over to her desk and opened the ledger. "You're telling me." She slowly scanned several pages before shrugging noncommittally and handing it to Cole. "As I've stated, no one on the books is doing any sort of work for us...anywhere...just in case you have questions about other locations." Leaning against the desk, she gave me a haughty look. "Ever think that there's a chance the information you were given was wrong?"

Cole didn't even look at it before handing it to me. More out of aggravation than anything else, I leafed through it. The only thing of interest in the pages was the fact Lewis's name was scribbled into the margins over and over again. It appeared he never missed a chance to snap up a piece of property that'd been managed by the museum over the years. While it didn't appear criminal, it did strike me as odd. Why was he buying up so much property?

I got to my feet and returned the book to Ruth. "Thanks, for your...help. Sorry to have troubled you this morning."

She held up a finger to stop us from leaving, and her voice had an edge to it. "Wait."

Eyeing her curiously, I rolled my hand for her to continue. "Yes?"

Ruth squared her shoulders. "If you find anything of note when you visit, would you be kind enough to call the office and leave a message? We don't need to be caught up in some sort of PR nightmare. It could mean the end of this place."

Her request seemed legitimate, but much like Lewis's name in the ledger, it struck me as strange. "I might be persuaded to do that, if you answer a question for me."

Her eyes narrowed, and her tone became frosty. "What's that?"

Nodding at the book, I grimaced. "It appears Lewis Grant has bought a lot of land from the museum that was once owned by either the local or federal government. Any idea why?"

She balled up her fists, and blood rushed to her cheeks. "Not that it's any of your business, but Mr. Grant has been kind enough to purchase those parcels to help keep us afloat. It isn't like the feds are going to bail us out or anything. So, we have to do whatever it takes to ensure our survival. Sometimes that means a cash influx from a sale of useless property."

Dust Walkers | 73

Cole growled. "Of course, the fact that the Navajo were disputing the ownership of that land in court had nothing to do with it."

A dangerous smile crossed her lips. "You know, that never occurred to me until just now... Interesting."

He stepped forward, and I put a hand on his chest. "Easy now. I'm sure it'll all work out."

Ruth tittered. "I have a feeling you're right." She glanced up at me. "Other than Mr. Grant being a philanthropist, are there any more questions?"

I frowned. "Not exactly the word I'd use for the guy, but no...no other questions for now."

She held up her hand. "I did fulfill my end of the bargain, so you'll tell me if you find anything when you go out to the mine?"

I folded my arms. "I said I might be persuaded, and at the moment, I'm not."

She giggled. "Oh, did I hurt your feelings?"

Laughing, I shook my head. "Not in the slightest, but you aren't exactly on my Christmas list either." I pulled out my card and handed it to her. "Tell you what. If you can be civil and come up with anything helpful, we can renegotiate."

Ruth tossed it on her desk. "Hardly seems worth it." She pointed at the door. "If that's all, I really do need to get to work."

I nodded. "Have a good day, Ruth."

She folded her arms. "Ms. Miller will be fine."

Resisting the urge to punch her in the face, I clamped my mouth shut before following Cole down the stairs out to the truck.

He grimaced. "That woman knows something."

I shrugged. "She might, but we don't have anything on her other than that she's a bitch." My stomach growled, and I patted it. "I guess getting irritated makes me hungry."

Cole checked his watch and grinned. "We've got time to stop at Taco Village before we head out."

I rubbed my forehead. "Is it any good?"

He laughed. "You'll love it."

"Fine, let's do it."

He started the engine and pulled into traffic.

10

To me, the word mine had always evoked an image of a cave, but this place was more or less a deep squarish pit. So, needless to say, not what I was expecting. Weirdly, it was supposed to have been abandoned sometime back in the nineties, but the earth had recently been tilled. And I wasn't talking about a spot here and there. Someone had gone to a lot of trouble to dig up the entire thing...that being about a half mile wide and deep.

Why would anyone bother?

At the far side of the pit, near the murky green pools of water, the sunlight glinted off something small and shiny. When it happened a second time, I put a hand on Cole's shoulder, and pushed. Maybe I'd put a bit too much oomph into it, though, because he landed hard against the fender of his truck.

As for me, my subconscious must've thought I was moving a bit too slowly, because a thick layer of hardened darkness wrapped itself around my body. Something hit me in the chest with enough force to take me off my feet and knock the breath out of me. As my back slammed into the ground, the sound of a high caliber bullet being fired reached my ears.

I lay there for a second as I tried to catch my breath, which came back in a painful, ragged gasp. Grunting, I rolled onto all fours and crawled over to Cole, who hunkered nearer to the wheel as I approached.

His gaze continued to trek up and down my body as his expression fluctuated between horror and annoyance. "What the fuck, man?"

Shaking my head, I leaned against the tire. "Huh?"

He waved a hand at me. "What the hell is that? And is someone *shooting* at us?"

I shrugged. "No idea, and yeah, someone's taking potshots from across the way."

Closing his eyes, he nodded, and in an instant, a silver light enveloped him from head to toe. He dropped his hand onto the six-shooter on his hip and eased up to the bumper.

I grabbed his arm to stop him. "Hey, they're at least a half mile out. There's nothing you can do with that thing."

His eyes flickered down to my hand, and I removed it. Adjusting his grasp on the grip, he grinned. "About that…"

Cole leaned around the front of the vehicle and fired a shot, and the earth exploded in front of the pool across the way.

Stupidly, I got to my feet and sprinted down the hill. My only thought was to pour on the speed in the hope of getting there before they got their shit together and put a hole through me. While I was sure that this…armor was some stout stuff, I wasn't so sure it'd take a second round at close range, and I really didn't want to find out the hard way, if that were at all possible.

I reached the base of the mine, where it leveled out into little more than a killing field, and pondered my mistake, because this was one of my dumber ideas. There was no place to hide, no cover, and if some asshole were to fire again, they'd be hard-pressed to miss. It wasn't like it would be any smarter at this point to turn back, though, so I kept running. I was about a hundred yards out when the telltale flash of a sniper scope glinted in the sun once more. Well, shit.

In an instant, the world around me turned blue, and I was across the expanse. My forward momentum carried me into a thin yet muscular man with straggly blond hair and ice blue eyes. The impact

Dust Walkers | 77

knocked the gun barrel aside, and he stumbled back as he fired the weapon. The explosion made my ears ring, and the muzzle flash blinded me for a second. Before I could catch my balance, a fist slammed into my jaw.

My sight returned as I lurched back. He ducked low and drove his shoulder into my gut. Twisting, he forced us into the deceptively deep, murky water and pulled me several feet below the surface. It was a matter of seconds before the light dimmed. When he released me, the water turned thick, and it was difficult to move. Then he was gone. Holding my breath, I struggled upward, eventually breaking through the water and gulping in a breath of air. I clawed at the hard earth, and it took all my strength to tug myself free of the gelatinous muck.

Staggering to my feet, I looked around. Cole was about halfway across, and a minute or two later, he jogged up beside me, panting hard. "How the hell did you get here so fast?"

I shrugged. "Where did the guy go?"

Cole frowned. "You two disappeared for a second then he resurfaced, clasped a hand to his chest, and vanished."

Finding the nearest rock, I took a seat before I fell down. "How in the nine hells is that possible?"

He rolled his shoulders. "If I had to guess, an atman stone, but they're rare and very hard to come by." He scanned the horizon and sighed. "In all my years, I've never even seen one."

Furrowing my brow, I leaned over and rested my elbows on my knees. "What's that, and why are they so rare?"

A disgusted expression rolled over him. "Because they're pure evil. The necromantic ritual used to create them involves murdering someone in order to power the stone. From what I understand, only the most powerful of their kind can use one."

"So, to summarize, the guy is uber powerful, and his teleportation devise is run off the spirit of some poor soul unlucky enough to cross his path."

He nodded. "About right."

Shaking my head, I said, "Well, isn't that fantastic." The shadow armor faded as I reached over and picked up the sniper rifle. "By the way, that was one hell of a shot you made back there."

He patted his weapon and chuckled. "Thanks, but that wasn't anything compared to the vanishing act you pulled a few minutes ago." Running his hand over his head, he sighed. "You never did answer... How did you manage it?"

I sat up, still trying to catch my breath. "Not a clue. One second I was running, and the next, I was here."

He huffed out a laugh. "God, you really are new at this."

Cupping my face in my hands, I nodded. "Yeah, I am."

He waved a hand up and down me. "So, the whole futuristic black and blue body armor is a mystery as well?"

With a great deal of effort, I placed my hands on my knees and pushed myself upright. "Blue?"

He nodded. "Yeah, it was mostly solid black, but the helmet, chest, and back all had blue highlights."

"Huh...weird." I took a deep breath and shook my head. "If you're looking for a better answer than that, I'm sorry to say that I haven't got one. Normally when something like that envelops me, it's the Grim's doing...but I'm pretty sure it wasn't involved this time."

Cole flinched. "That's the thing I saw when you punched a hole through the guy's chest, right?"

Grimacing, I allowed my gaze to hit the ground. "Yeah."

He shivered. "And just what does he have to do with this?"

I rubbed my forehead and sighed. "Well, he's like my alter ego... and all my abilities seemed to stem from him. Until now."

Leaning over, he patted me on the shoulder. "I'm glad to see you're branching out." He paused and brought his gaze up to meet my own. "But, if you think for a second that this new form is any less...startling than the others, I'm sorry to tell you that it's not."

"Gee, thanks." Wanting to change the subject, I said, "Sorry about earlier."

He cocked an eyebrow at me. "For what? Saving my life? Being a general badass or being new?"

I chuckled and slung the rifle over my shoulder. "The new part…
The rest of that sentence was a bit of an overstatement."

He rolled his eyes. "Hardly." Glancing around, he frowned. "But
maybe that's a conversation best had when we're back at the truck and
safely on our way out of here. Last thing I want is for that asshole to
show up with his buddies." He gestured at me. "I'm not sure we'll get
lucky a second time."

I nodded in agreement. "Yeah, you're right. What in the hell did
you get me into?"

His expression hardened. "No idea, but you can see why I didn't
want to involve Danielle."

"That I can."

Almost drowning in the mutant water had drained me, and it took
me considerably longer to make my way down the steep slope than it
had earlier. It was all I could do to keep up with Cole as he picked
through the uneven terrain. Something soft and squishy caught the tip
of my boot, and I nearly fell on my face. When I turned around to see
what it was, a hand was sticking out.

With a low whistle, I got Cole's attention.

He turned. "What?"

I pointed back at the fleshy stump. "Maybe we should've taken the
long way around."

Raising an eyebrow, he gave me a weird look. "Huh?"

I stepped over, kicked away a little more of the dirt, and the thing
twitched. "Shit."

Cole put a finger to his mouth. "Keep your voice down."

Throwing my hands up in a 'what the fuck' gesture, I grimaced.
"This is a mine full of dead folks, not the goddamn library. Do you
really think they're going to give a shit about the volume of my voice?"

He glared at me. "Maybe not—then again, maybe the louder you
happen to be, the more likely they are to rise up and pull us limb from
limb."

With a low groan, I glanced around the massive grave. "Christ. So,
what, they're like a clapper?"

Cole shook his head in disgust. "You can make a clapper joke, but you don't get one about Golden Corral?"

I blushed. "Well, they show infomercials about the clapper."

He choked back a chuckle. "This is going to be a very long trip back. Now be quiet, and tread carefully."

The desire to be back at the truck grew, and there was a tugging sensation in my chest. I stepped forward and grabbed Cole's shoulder. Blue fire wrapped around us, blotting out everything for a second, and when it faded, we were next to the orange Chevy.

Cole's knees buckled, and he fell to the ground, shivering. I knelt beside him and rolled him onto his back. "Are you okay?"

His teeth clattered together loudly. "Wha...wha...what happened?" He turned his head, and his eyes locked onto the rims of his vehicle. "How'd we get here?"

I glanced back at the pit and shrugged. "At a guess, we teleported. As for how...that's a bit more complicated."

It took a little doing, but eventually I managed to get him into a sitting position, leaning against the tire.

Tapping my chest, I said, "There was this tugging sensation, and the desire to be up here grew, so I grabbed you. And here we are."

His head listed toward the pit. "I'm not sure which is worse, being down there surrounded by chindi, or having you *save* me with your blue ball of death."

I did my best not to laugh. "That somehow sounds way dirtier than intended."

He cocked his head to the side. "Oh, that you find funny... But I'm serious, that was one of the most awful things I've ever experienced." His tone curious, he asked, "What do you feel when it happens?"

I rocked back on my heels and found a comfortable place to sit. "Nothing really. Everything goes blue, and, *poof*, I'm where I wanted to be."

He waved at himself and took a deep breath. "Well, for me, it took my breath away, and I had the distinct feeling of being turned into a Cole-sicle." His hands shook as he held them out and inspected them. "Thank God...there doesn't appear to be any frostbite."

Dust Walkers | 81

I frowned. "It's that bad?"

He shrugged. "Maybe if I'd had a little warning, it wouldn't have been." Clenching his hand into a fist and releasing it, he smiled. "Apparently the effects wear off pretty quickly, so that's nice."

Embarrassed, I bit my lower lip. "That's great, and I'm sorry about the…discomfort?"

Cole chuckled. "At this point, I'm almost sure I'll get over it." He pointed to the mass grave. "What are we going to do about them?"

I got to my feet and shook my head. "No idea. The Grim can't do anything to them."

He forced himself upright and glanced over at me. "What's that mean?"

Frowning, I sighed. "The chindi don't have souls, and without a soul, it appears the big bad Grim is all bark and no bite." He still looked puzzled. "In short, I don't have the ability to hurt them."

Cole scowled. "But the other night you burned them all to ash."

Yeah, that had been bound to come back and bite me in the ass. "That's true, but I haven't a clue why, or even how, that happened." My shoulders slumped forward as I moved to the edge of the pit. "Believe me, if I did, I'd happily do it again."

He mumbled a few things I couldn't make out before sighing. "Well, that's going to make this very tough on us."

I stepped back and cocked my head to the side. "Care to be a bit more specific? Because I don't have a clue what you're talking about."

Cole closed his eyes as he let out a soft laugh. "We have to make sure they're incapacitated… Which means removing their heads. One at a time, from the sound of things." He gestured at the truck. "I hope that sword of yours is sharp."

I groaned. "Seriously? We can't just set fire to the place?"

He shook his head. "We'd have to uncover them all to make sure they were incinerated." Rubbing his chin, he grimaced. "Or…"

I pointed at him. "I'm liking this plan better."

He frowned. "You haven't heard it yet."

I gestured for him to continue. "Go on then."

His tone hardened. "We could go get Atsidi and have him ask the tribal elders for help. They might know how to deal with a mass grave better than I do."

I gave him a thumbs-up. "Yep, I still like that idea. Go see if someone will give us a hand, and I'll keep watch."

He rolled his eyes. "You really want to stand here alone—possibly all night—while I go look for help?"

I shrugged. "Well—"

Cole cut me off. "That's about the dumbest thing I've heard anyone say. We know there's at least one powerful necromancer around, and if Atsidi's right, he's got friends. The last guy you dealt with nearly drowned you by himself. Do you really think you could handle them all on your own?"

When people start arguing with logic, it gives me a headache. "Ah...well..."

He shook his head. "Let me spell it out for you since you seem to be a little slow on the uptake. If you stay, they'll kill you, and that wouldn't be good for any of us."

I gestured at the pit. "But there's a good chance the jerks will be back for their toys."

He nodded. "And if they are, they'll leave a trail a mile wide, and we'll be able to track them."

Shaking my head, I said, "I don't like the idea of leaving them here alone."

Cole shrugged. "Then it's cutting off heads one at a time."

It took forever for us to knock back enough dirt to pull one of them free and promptly remove its head. By the time the sun went down, we'd managed about fifteen executions. And given the pit's size, we wouldn't finish this in our lifetimes. We needed shovels, or perhaps a dozen backhoes, and several times that in manpower to do this properly.

I hung my head in defeat. "Fine, how about we fall back to your other plan?"

He snickered. "The one involving getting some help?"

I sighed. "Yeah, that one."

He stood up straight and grinned. "You ready to risk them coming back for these deadheads?"

"I am." Gesturing back at the wide expanse, I said, "It's clear we'll never be able to finish this, and who's to say they won't come back while we're in the middle of the job and too tired to fight back?"

Cole grimaced. "Agreed."

We climbed up the side of the pit to the truck and made the forty-five-minute drive to Atsidi's place. Given the hour, I doubted we'd make it back before morning. If I had to guess, there was a fifty-fifty shot the necromancers would move the horde before then. But digging them out by hand, cutting off their heads, and repeating wasn't making a dent in the problem.

11

February 25th

It was nearly midnight by the time we'd told Atsidi the full story. He was reluctant to face a single necromancer, let alone one with friends at the height of their power. And when the untold number of undead at their disposal came into the mix, he flat out refused to go anywhere until morning.

I couldn't blame the guy. I mean, he did have a point. Necromancers were more powerful at night, or so the stories said. Not only that, we were hampered by darkness and a lack of intel. Even I wasn't hardheaded enough to go into such a situation totally blind, outnumbered and probably outgunned. While I'd spent most of my life fighting the odds, I'd always had a chance of survival—tonight didn't afford me such an opportunity.

Between that, and my inability to control my powers—such as the blue-flamed teleporter—sleep evaded me. In my boredom, I tried to figure out how it worked. That turned out about as well as you might think...I got nowhere fast. It appeared the only things that triggered it were imminent death or the desire to kill someone.

I made about as much progress figuring out how the shadow armor worked. The ability to teleport or create armor on demand would prove useful…if I could ever figure out how to summon them. With every failure my frustration grew, as did my list of questions. Did the teleporter have a specific range? Where could I go, and how could I bring someone with me without damn near killing them in the process?

The only good thing about being up all night was that I was the first one in the shower, which meant it was piping hot. I'd only just gotten dressed and made my way into the kitchen when Cole stumbled through to the bath. By the time he was dressed, I had breakfast ready.

There was a knock at the door as I was finishing the dishes.

Cole turned and yelled, "Come in."

Atsidi pulled open the door, carrying several thick silver spikes about two and a half feet long.

Setting them on the counter, he said, "Morning."

I pointed at the metal stakes. "What are those?"

He frowned. "If theory holds, they'll sever the necromancers' hold on the corpses."

The silver was intricately carved with numerous conflicting inscriptions, and according to Kur, they shouldn't have been able to coexist on the same object. But since they were sitting right there in front of me, he was obviously wrong.

I picked up one. "How were you able to do this? From my understanding, more than a few of these engravings conflict on an energetic level with others."

Atsidi sighed. "The man who taught me how to use my elemental abilities was exceptionally knowledgeable about necromancy."

I gave him a questioning look. "Seriously? I've done a ton of research in the last nine months, and I haven't been able to find out anything that wasn't purely hypothetical." A small chuckle escaped my lips. "It probably isn't a surprise to anyone here that Lazarus is obsessed with them, and even he hasn't got a clue who they are, how they're created…or much of anything else, for that matter. The only thing he's certain about is that they're evil, and they need to be eradicated from the face of the planet."

His shoulders slumped as he fell into a nearby seat. "I don't think he's wrong, for the most part. But Nakai Tsosi was a good man. Or at least, he was when I met him."

Cole's expression faltered. "The old smith was the one who taught you?"

He rubbed his chin. "Yeah."

I glanced between them and frowned. "Please remember there's a newbie in the room. Would one of you mind filling me in?"

Cole leaned back in his seat and let out a long breath. "Nakai Tsosi is famous around here for how he died. Well, more accurately, how he was murdered. Someone tortured the man, and when they got tired, they lowered his body into a vat of molten copper."

Atsidi winced. "I was the one who found him." His voice cracked as emotion overtook him. "He took me in as an apprentice and taught me how to control my powers. He was kind to me when no one else could be bothered. It was through him that I learned about the Archive, and their laws." He wiped away a tear. "One day when I arrived, there was a dark-haired woman sitting in the corner of the forge. She never spoke, but the way she watched us made me afraid. There was something about her that completely unnerved me. Once the lesson was complete, Nakai informed me that it was my last one. He gave me several books and told me not to come back...ever. He walked me out then closed the door behind me, and I heard the bolt slide closed, locking them in."

While reading through the books he'd been given, Atsidi found a drawing of the woman with the name Inna below it. According to Nakai's notes, she belonged to something called the Black Circle. These journals detailed the history of necromancy and explained at length how the artform was passed from master to student—which involved some sort of bonding ritual where blood was exchanged.

In the historic portion, it went into what the Black Circle called the great war...and I couldn't get past how much it sounded like the dream I'd had shortly after becoming vigil. The tomes spoke of the battle between the Children of the First, Life, and Death. The representative of the latter, Ankou, created nine lich lords, and it was through their blood that necromancy was passed from one person to another—almost like an infection. As for their symbol, the solid black circle represented the infinity of death.

Their form of climbing the ranks was...interesting. Each initiate was made more powerful with subsequent blood rituals, until they were finally initiated into something called the Onyx Mind. These were the elite of their kind and, until a thousand years ago, had been led by Inna and Nakai. Their main goals were to keep order amongst the others and protect the lich lords at all costs. The abominable rituals involved corrupted certain schools of magic. It was these polluted practices that allowed the conflicting magical scripts to work, thus creating things like the silver stakes Atsidi had brought with him.

That was some of the most godawful information I'd ever heard. The necromancer problem wasn't just some random issue, with one cropping up every now and again. Nope, these assholes were organized, and had been around several millennia longer than the Archive.

They clearly had a goal, but I had no idea what that might be. They also had shock troops who were nothing short of badass. I was betting Lazarus hadn't had a clue how big this problem really was when he'd nominated them as public enemy number one.

When I combined this new information about how organized they were with Walter's warning about what was coming, I was certain the long-standing peace we'd enjoyed was about to end. That was something none of us were ready for. Not by a long shot.

Frustrated, I ran my hand over my face. "For fuck's sake." Taking a deep breath, I shook my head. "I'm surprised we haven't heard of the Black Circle before."

Atsidi blanched. "Hey, I did my part and told Samuel Estes, the last vigil I met, what I knew." He hung his head as he mumbled the next bit. "But I'm unsure he was able to do much with the information before he disappeared."

The name didn't ring a bell. "He was the guy in charge of the area at the time?"

Atsidi nodded. "Yep."

I frowned. If he was a vigil, the coins would've retained the information. Kur searched for his memories. Sure enough, Samuel had been the vigil for the southern district for nearly fifty years. The weird part was, his death had always been a mystery to the Archive. To both Kur's and my astonishment, all Samuel's memories were wiped clean for at least three months prior to his arrival in New Mexico.

Well, goddamn it.

Leaning against the counter, I chewed on my cheek. "It's safe to say he wasn't able to do much with the information you gave him." Atsidi's body slumped. "Don't be so hard on yourself. You followed the proper protocol, and that's more than most people would've done in your situation."

He sat up straight. "That might be true, but it feels like I should've done more—especially now."

I patted his shoulder. "Don't worry about it. What's done is done... I'm just grateful you clued me in on what's going on." Curiosity got the better of me, and I said, "I know this might be a bit personal, but when we wrap this up, is there any chance you'd let me borrow those books? That is, if you still have them."

His tone instantly lightened. "If you promise to take them with you, they're yours... I would like nothing more than to be rid of them, but they were too valuable to destroy."

It concerned me slightly that he was so anxious to rid himself of the things, but I nodded. "Agreed. When this is over, I'll take them off your hands."

Atsidi relaxed as he leaned back in his seat. "Thank you."

Cole harrumphed, and I arched an eyebrow at him. "Yes?"

He shook his head. "There was a weird coincidence after Samuel's disappearance."

"What's that?"

He chewed on his lip. "A few months after, a stranger came to town, asking questions about him."

Atsidi balled his hands into fists. "That was when Lewis made his move and nearly got burned to the ground."

Cole laughed. "Yeah, that was one hell of a week."

"What's that mean?"

Cole grinned. "Most of the accounts are sketchy... Some say the person in question was a redheaded man, others say it was a woman... Not that it really mattered in the end. What's important is that Lewis was using the absence of a vigil to bring in mercenaries to solidify his control over the area, even if he denies it. Anyway, this stranger burned the entire company of soldiers to the ground and pushed the Grants' plan back decades."

Furrowing my brow, I asked, "And what plan is that?"

Atsidi shrugged. "No one knows for sure, but for as far back as I can remember, he's done everything he could to buy, steal, or annex as much property as he can."

Cole sighed. "He's always wanted the tribal land, but we've been able to stonewall him so far. God only knows what the future will hold, though. Everyone is desperate for money these days...and Isaiah's been pressuring the other elders to sell."

The more I learned about Lewis and his brood, the less I liked them.

Nodding, I said, "The Grants are definitely a bunch of shits, and while the history lesson gives me an entirely new perspective on them, we've strayed off topic." I tapped my finger against the silver stake. "Are you sure these things will destroy the corpses."

Atsidi shook his head. "I think you misunderstood. All they'll do is sever the necromantic hold on them. If a necromancer were to perform the ritual again, they'd be up and running in no time."

I grimaced. "Well, that's better than nothing, I suppose."

Cole nodded. "And its way better than digging those things up one at a time to sever the connection."

Rubbing the blister on my palm, I nodded. "Agreed."

We piled into Cole's truck and hit the road. On our way out of town, we passed Charles on the side of the road, changing his tire. He was kind enough to flip us the bird and yell a few obscenities as we passed. It probably made me a bad person, but I was sort of hoping his spare was flat. Maybe the long walk back to town would give him time to reflect on his assholery... Not that I believed it would make a damn bit of difference in his case, but you never know.

It took us a little under an hour to make our way back to the pit, and when we arrived, my worst fears were realized. Judging by the tracks in the soil, they'd come back with three semis to collect their toys. All we were left with were a bunch of holes in the dirt where the chindi had been...except for the ones we'd decapitated, which had been left to rot in the sun.

I thought we should track them down, but Atsidi insisted we continue with the plan. He thought they may not have gotten them all, and that we should err on the side of caution rather than tempting fate.

He handed me three stakes. "You need to put one as close to the center as you can get, and the other two at either corner." He turned and handed the others to Cole. "Put these at either corner on this end."

I hefted the silver spikes in my hand. "You're sure this will help?"

He shook his head. "No idea, but if there's another layer of those things down there then yeah, I think it'll do us some good."

Forty minutes later, we'd connected all the stakes with a thin thread infused with silver filaments. Once we were clear, Atsidi walked around and placed a drop of blood on each spike. Seconds after he finished the last one, an X-shaped blast of gray light shot into the sky, followed quickly by a loud crack.

The earth all around us shook, and fissures formed in the dirt along the lines of the thread...then everything stopped. It was spookily quiet. When the dust settled, the freshly tilled earth was flat and hard. The silver spikes were gone, but it seemed they'd done what they were supposed to do.

Atsidi climbed up to us and frowned. "There must be a bunch more of those things down there. Otherwise, nothing would've happened."

I hung my head and sighed. "Well, that sucks."

Cole frowned. "Why's that?"

I pointed back at the pit. "Once you do the math, it gets scary as hell."

Atsidi glanced up at me questioningly. "I'm afraid I'm not following."

Facepalming myself, I squeezed my eyes closed for a second. "If I had to guess, you could stuff around two hundred and fifty people into a trailer if they were standing... If you stack them or go with some other configuration, you could probably get more. So, we're looking at about seven hundred and fifty of these things...if they only filled the trailers once." I gestured at him and groaned. "And from what you just said, there's a bunch more down there."

Atsidi shook his head and held out a hand in my direction. "I don't even want to know how you figured that out." Crinkling up his nose, he looked a little sick. "And just for the record, that's some weirdly specific knowledge of trailers that I never needed to know."

I let out a long breath and leaned against the Chevy. "If it helps, I'm not any happier about knowing it than you are."

Atsidi shrugged. "Wish it did... Good God, you really think they have nearly eight hundred of those things?"

I frowned. "Probably closer to seven, but yeah. They have a boat-load of them."

Cole sighed. "Christ, that's a depressing thought."

A morose chuckle escaped my lips. "Isn't it though?"

I couldn't see how things could get much worse, but knowing my luck, they would. So, with that thought firmly entrenched in my mind, I decided to start making calls as soon as possible in hopes of finding some sort of lifeline. There was no way in hell I was prepared to deal with an army of corpses on my own.

Not that there were a lot of options at the moment. Gabriel was in Rome, busy with training, and Isidore already had his hands full with Andrew. Alexander might be able to help, but that was kind of iffy since they were probably still neck deep in negotiations. All in all, my chances of finding help were slim to none, but I had to try.

12

February 26th

We dropped Atsidi off at his place, hoping he'd be able to convince the tribal elders to lend us a hand. He wasn't sure he'd make it past Isaiah, but it was worth a shot. That left me to work what little mojo I had to recruit some help. We were a few miles outside Grants when my phone finally picked up a signal, and I made the first of what would undoubtedly be a series of short, and disheartening, phone calls.

The phone rang twice before Alexander's deep voice came over the line. "Good to hear from you. How have things been since you left?"

I sighed. "Busy, and before I even get started, I feel a need to apologize up front."

He chuckled. "No worries. Tell me what's going on."

Leaning my head against the window, I grumbled, "I'm not sure if I told you, but I'm in New Mexico. Suffice it to say, shit's gone sideways here, and I need a hand."

I spent the next ten minutes filling him in. He was a trusted lieutenant, and as such, I didn't bother holding anything back. Which meant that other than Atsidi, Cole, and myself, he was one of the few

Dust Walkers | 93

people outside the ranks of the Black Circle who knew their name. I wasn't sure if that was a privilege or a death sentence.

When I finished, he sucked in air loudly. "Christ, man, you don't believe in half measures, do you?"

I rubbed my temples. "I guess not."

Alexander sighed. "You know I'm at the conclave, and there's no way I can get out of here for at least two days. Normally, I'd be able to call some of the local weres to help you out, but they're here, and will be for another week." He paused, and papers shuffled in the background. "There's a chance I can scrape up a team when I come, but there won't be a lot of us."

The fact he was considering coming at all brought a smile to my face, and I instantly relaxed. "Thanks, and believe me, I'll be grateful for whatever help you can muster."

His voice dropped. "Sorry we won't be able to be there sooner, but we're finally making headway with the Germans. Though the French and the Irish are still giving us fits… We'll get there, it's just going to take some time."

No one in their right mind could argue with progress, even if it meant that I'd be on my own a bit longer. "I'm glad things are moving forward, and while having you here would make things easier on me, that takes precedence."

There was a loud noise of something brushing against the mic, a few muffled words that I couldn't understand then it was gone.

He cleared his throat. "Sorry about this, but I've got to go. Be in touch soon."

Nodding reflexively, I sat up in my seat. "I really appreciate this."

Chuckling, he said, "It's the least we can do."

The line went dead. I stared at the phone for several seconds before scrolling through my contacts to find Viktor's number…only to get a fast busy. Ending the call, I shuffled through to find Justine's number.

It barely rang once before she picked up. "Hello, Gavin."

Forcing as much cheer into my voice as I could, I said, "Good morning, Justine. How are you today?"

She let out a tiny groan. "I've been better."

That surprised me because I'd never heard her complain about anything before. "Oh?"

Justine sighed. "Yeah, we've got a bit of a Lamia problem here in town."

Confused, I asked, "What's a lamia?"

She growled. "It's not a what. It's a *she*, and she's a psychotic snake lady who was involved in a prison break last month."

That jolted the memory of my dinner with them into the forefront of my mind. "Oh, yeah, okay... I think I remember Viktor mentioning that."

Well, shit, sounds like he's tied up too.

She paused for a moment. "What's going on with you?"

I put my elbow on the armrest on the door and cupped my face in my hand. "Well...I was going to ask Viktor if he could lend me a hand. But, given the circumstances, that sounds unlikely."

Justine grumbled. "Unfortunately, you're probably right. Still, tell me what's going on...maybe we have some people nearby."

I really hated to repeat myself, but since I hadn't been smart enough to conference her in on the first call, I did.

She was silent for a moment when I finished. Then she laughed and laughed. Finally, she calmed down enough to speak. "Sorry, I don't mean to laugh. It's just that I thought Viktor was the only one who had a penchant for falling into such shitty situations."

I wasn't sure if I should be amused or offended, so I opted for confused. "Ah...okay."

Justine giggled. "Truly, I'm not trying to make light of your circumstances...it's just been a really bad few days. Scratch that. It's been a rough four months. If I didn't know better, I'd think he went looking for trouble. Now, here you are in the deep end of the pool, and, well, it makes me realize that you two have more in common than either of you might think."

I chuckled. "Can't say that I see how, but I'll take your word for it, especially if that means you guys might be able to help me out."

Her amusement faded in an instant. "Sorry, I'm not sure we have anyone close enough to be of assistance right now, and Viktor's definitely tied up—but I know someone who might be available. If not, he'll have a rapid response team that'll be able to handle the crisis."

I would rather have worked with someone I knew, but reluctantly, I agreed. "All right...so do I call this guy, or do you?"

Her tone turned serious. "I'll tend to it. Give me an hour, and one of us will be in touch."

I let out a long breath. "Not a problem. I'll make sure we stay in town where our mobiles work."

She took a deep breath and did her best to sound reassuring. "Good, and don't sound so down. You did the right thing by calling. This is exactly why Viktor created Warden Global, and by extension, the Ulfr."

Confused, I asked, "The who?"

Her voice hardened. "The Ulfr. Ignatius is their leader. They're an independent arm of Warden Global, but our goal is the same: to stop the darkness from destroying this world. And you can't get much darker than a bunch of creepy necromancers. So, hold tight. One way or another, help is on the way."

Reassured, I nodded. "Don't they work with the Archive as well?"

Justine cleared her throat. "Sort of. They do their own thing, but if you're in a bad way, they're the people you want on your side."

I rested my chin on my balled-up fist. "I really hope you're right."

Her voice dropped a little. "Don't worry. They'll help." She paused for a second before continuing. "One question before I go...have you called Heather?"

I shook my head. "She's next on my list, but she's tending to Archive business in Rome this week."

Justine made a *doh* sound. "Damn it, I actually forgot about that with all the shit going on here."

I chuckled. "Totally understandable from what you've said about this Lamia person."

She let out a long breath. "No kidding. Now, hang tight and wait for one of us to call back."

"No problem."

Justine cleared her throat. "Take care."

Nodding, I said, "You too."

The line went dead.

Cole frowned. "Sounds like you're striking out."

I shrugged. "Mostly, but my friend Justine thinks someone named Ignatius can help."

His mouth fell open. "Wait, when you said Viktor earlier, did you mean Viktor Warden?"

"Yeah—Heather is best friends with his significant other, Justine Dupree. Is that a problem?"

He shook his head. "Not at all, but since he can't make it, she's calling Ignatius MacKay? As in the Ulfr commander?"

Frowning, I sighed. "I guess so...she did mention he was with the Ulfr—he's supposed to give me a call within the hour. Is that a big deal or something?"

Cole snorted. "Goddamn, this is one of those times when your newness to our world really shines through."

Pocketing my phone, I shook my head. "That might be true, but it didn't answer the question."

He chuckled. "Then allow me to be clear here...it's a *huge* deal." Taking his hand off the wheel, he patted me on the shoulder. "And one that works out in your favor."

I blinked. "How so?"

His voice dropped as he scanned the horizon. "I don't know if you know this or not, but vigils aren't known for their long lifespan." He glanced over at me and offered me a sad smile. "But with those heavyweights in your corner, there's a real possibility that you, and the people who serve you, might be able to change that."

I cocked my head to the side. "Really? As far as I can tell, Viktor's a pretty normal guy—once you get past the age thing, that is." I held out my hand to stop his retort. "I know he's supposed to be dangerous, but I doubt he's any deadlier than anyone else in the Archive."

His body instantly relaxed, and he let out a big belly laugh. "Wow, if even half the stories about him are true, you've severely misjudged the man."

Dust Walkers | 97

I shook my head. "You know as well as I do that people exaggerate."

He rolled his shoulders. "That might be, but the man has a proven track record…so much so that the odds of us surviving this shit storm have gone up significantly." He tapped his cell. "In fact, I'll be waiting to see if Ignatius is coming here himself before calling Danielle. If he is, she probably won't even yell at me…much."

Well, wasn't that special? My chances of living through this ordeal were looking better and better. Considering that a single necromancer had nearly overwhelmed me with his undead, and another had almost drowned me, things hadn't exactly been going my way.

Rubbing my forehead, I sighed. "Do you really think she'll be that impressed with a single man showing up?"

Cole nodded. "I do… Look, you don't get it because you've never heard of the guy before. But Ignatius is one of the most powerful people on the planet. That's it, end of story. So, if he shows up, the wife will be a little more accepting of the situation. Mind you, she's still going to be pissed off, but she'll be way more understanding with Ignatius in the picture."

It took a second for everything to sink in. "Oh…"

Cole backhanded my chest. "Don't look so distraught. Things really are looking up for us."

I forced a smile onto my face and nodded. "If you say so."

He laughed.

In another fifteen minutes, we stopped at a place called Lotaburger. Where my uncle had been endeavoring to murder my liver with scotch, Cole was trying to kill me with fast food. Don't get me wrong, it was awesome, and just what you'd expect from a place like this, but I was going to need to put in a few extra hours at the gym if he kept this up.

Cole went to dump our trash and head to the restroom when my phone rang.

I held the phone to my ear. "Hello, this is Gavin."

A man with a thick Scottish accent said, "Good day to you, Gavin. It's a pleasure to finally have an opportunity to speak with you. My name is Hayden Ignatius MacKay." He paused for a second before continuing. "Justine tells me you've landed yourself in a bit of a mess. Is that true?"

I got to my feet and walked out to the truck for some privacy. "Nice to meet you...sort of. Did she fill you in?"

He chuckled. "Not really, no. She was called away before finishing, but from what I was able to gather, there are a number of necromancers involved."

Not sure why, but when I opened my mouth, I couldn't stop myself from telling him everything, which took the better part of twenty minutes.

He sniggered. "Sounds like your arse is out the window... Mind if I ask a personal question?"

I leaned against the truck. "If it means you'll help, sure."

The good humor faded from his tone. "I was always going to help, lad."

Closing my eyes, I tilted my head back to the sky. "Ask away then."

He paused for a long moment before letting out a breath. "How did you arrive in New Mexico?"

Holding the phone away from my ear, I blinked at the absurdity of the question. "Commercial airline. Why?"

He took a sharp breath. "So, you didn't use the gate?"

My confusion left me as embarrassment took center stage. "No, not the gate. It doesn't seem to work for me...I think it falls into the same category as most things in the Archive."

Curiosity laced his tone. "How's that?"

I let out a nervous chuckle. "Well, if it requires magic to activate, I can't use it... Simply put, I'm magically challenged. Mostly, anyway."

"But you do have abilities."

Nodding, I said, "Yeah, but they aren't what you'd expect."

His tone suddenly turned serious. "They rarely are. I'll be there by nightfall. It appears we have much to talk about over the next few days."

Arching my eyebrow, I asked, "Oh?"

Ignatius's voice was hard. "Yeah. I'll call you when I get to town."

A mild case of panic started to set in. "Wait, don't hang up."

He paused. "You need something else?"

Shaking my head, I said, "No, I just needed to let you know it'll take us a few hours to get back to Santa Fe."

He laughed. "Oh, yeah, don't bother. Stay put, and I'll meet you in Grants. I was there once, a very long time ago... I'm pretty sure I recall the way. After I get there, I'll call, and you can come pick me up."

Shrugging, I chewed on my lip. "Okay, I can do that."

"Great. See you soon."

I ended the call and glanced over as Cole sat down. "It looks like Ignatius will be here by nightfall."

He grinned and patted me on the back. "That's awesome. When are we picking him up at the gate?"

I shook my head. "We're not... He said he'll meet us here in town."

His lips twitched up into a smile. "Fine, then I guess we're stuck here for a while."

Looking around the dusty parking lot, I asked, "What do you want to do till he shows up?"

Cole shrugged. "No idea, but I'd rather sit someplace where there aren't as many people." Thumbing over his shoulder, he got to his feet. "I say we camp out by the abandoned station until he calls. It's close enough to grab a bite, use the toilet, and still have cell service."

Glancing over at the spot, I said, "Sounds good to me."

We used the time to call our significant others. As expected, I got Heather's voicemail. Cole, on the other hand, had to deal with an irate Danielle, but just like he'd said, she calmed down when she found out Ignatius was coming in to give us a hand. While she didn't like the idea, he convinced her to stay put until we were able to get a better handle on the situation.

The day was dragging on, until a few minutes after three, when a bolt of energy shot through my body. I turned to Cole. "Did you feel that?"

He gave me a quizzical look. "Huh?"

I opened my mouth to explain when my phone rang.

Unable to shake the uneasy sensation in my gut, I answered. "Hello."

Ignatius took a deep breath and said, "Afternoon. Sorry to keep you waiting. I'm at an abandoned hotel called the Desert Sun."

"All right. One second." Covering the mic, I relayed the information.

Cole thought for a moment then nodded. "I know the place. It's just down the road from here. Tell him we'll be there in ten minutes."

Moving my hand, I opened my mouth to speak but Ignatius cut me off. "I heard the man. See you shortly."

Ending the call, I shrugged. "Guess the cab is about to get crowded."

Cole shook his head. "Not if you ride in the back."

I chuckled. "Already playing favorites?"

Cole smirked. "What can I say? The man scares me more than you."

After I climbed into the truck, Cole put it in gear, and we turned back toward Highland Meadows. Ten minutes later, we pulled into the abandoned parking lot to find a short, stocky, redheaded man standing there, holding a duffel with a small pack thrown over his shoulder.

I couldn't tell you what it was that set me on edge, but there was something familiar about him. A shiver ran up my spine as I got closer, and his emerald eyes locked onto mine. Holding out my hand, I said, "I'm Gavin Randall."

Ignatius froze for an instant before shaking my hand. The moment he touched me, a shockwave of power rocked us back onto our heels as it spread out in every direction. It hit Cole with enough force to knock him back several steps.

Ignatius's eyes instantly burned blue, and bright orange flames cut through his flesh. As his visage flaked away, his right hand turned a brilliant shade of orange, and black swirls enveloped his body, covering him in the familiar silhouette of the Grim—only his was much shorter.

It took me several seconds to comprehend what I was seeing.

Dust Walkers | 101

When Ignatius spoke again, he lacked an accent, and his voice was feminine. "Well, isn't this a sack of shit."

Stepping back, I said, "It's something, all right."

He—or she?—threw back her head and laughed. When she released my hand, our respective alter egos faded from sight. And where the stocky man had stood was a woman with long copper hair. She didn't fill out the clothes in quite the same way, but that did little to detract from her beauty.

Ignatius stepped back and sighed. "Fifteen thousand years of hiding, and you go and ruin it in ten seconds... Christ! Oh, and please call me Hayden. I prefer that in this form."

My mind was stuck in neutral for several seconds, but eventually I found my voice. "I don't...I don't understand. What's happening here?"

Hayden pointed at me. "You're a Reaper, and so am I." Turning to Cole, she flicked out her index finger, motioning for him to come closer. "And you are?"

His voice cracked when he spoke. "I'm Cole Pahe."

She sighed. "Well, Cole, I'm going to assume you know how to keep a secret."

His neck would've snapped if he'd nodded any harder. "Absolutely."

Hayden frowned. "See that you do. I can't have this getting out."

Cole leaned to one side and then the other. "Are you Ignatius? Or did something happen to him?"

She gave him a look that said he must be a special type of stupid. "What the hell do you think? Of course I'm Ignatius." Closing her eyes, she held up a hand to stop his reply. "Sorry, I didn't mean that." Waving a hand at me, she said, "Doofus here has inadvertently let my secret out... Goddamn it." She shook her head and bit her lip. "I apologize for being a bitch."

My brain finally kicked into gear, and I gave her a dismissive wave. "No worries...but would you mind telling me why you've been pretending to be a guy for, what did you say, fifteen thousand years?"

Hayden glanced around the empty lot and grumbled, "This is

hardly the place or the time... Besides that, I need a change of clothes. I'm not going to walk around looking like this the entire time I'm here."

Gesturing at the truck, I sighed. "Give me your things, and I'll put them in the back." We piled into the truck. "It'll take us an hour to reach a place with enough privacy to change. Mind answering a few questions on the way?"

Hayden shook her head. "That's not how this is going to work. Once I change, we'll talk. Not a moment before."

13

True to her word, she remained silent for the entirety of the trip back to the trailer. Once there, she stepped inside, looked around, and walked to the back. She pointed at my door. "Mind if I borrow the room for a bit?"

I shrugged. "Not at all, but how's that going to help?"

She pointed at her bag. "I'll need that."

Handing it to her, I shook my head. "Okay, so you packed a spare set of clothes?"

Hayden gave me a look that said that I must be the star pupil on the short bus. "Yeah, I planned for you to be the first person to shatter my disguise in fifteen millennia." She clenched her fists and let out a low growl before regaining her composure. "Just sit tight and wait for me to get back." She stepped through the narrow door and turned around to face us. "It's probably best you don't come in here. There isn't a lot of room to maneuver, and with this being a moveable structure, sticking the landing is a bit tougher than normal...which means the more space there is, the better."

Before I could say anything, a bright ball of orange flame appeared to engulf her, and then she was simply gone.

Cole's mouth dropped open, and he smacked me in the chest.

"Okay, that's weird as hell."

Glancing between him and the empty spot, I nodded. "You're telling me."

He shook his head. "You don't get it…that's the same thing you do, except yours is blue instead of orange." Plopping into the nearest chair, he cupped his face in his hands. "This is crazy as hell. There are two of you." He appeared to be mumbling more to himself than actually talking to me. "I can't fucking believe this shit… Two Reapers, one scary-ass vigil, and the goddamn legendary leader of the Ulfr."

Fifteen minutes passed, and she still wasn't back. A part of me was starting to think she wouldn't return at all, but I really wanted to be wrong—she was my best hope of surviving this mess. Twenty minutes later, my optimism had gone, and I was getting to my feet when the blinding ball of flame reappeared. When it vanished, Hayden stood there wearing advanced body armor that fit well without being revealing.

The bag in her hand hit the floor with a thud, and she folded her arms. "In all my years, you two are the only ones who've discovered my secret." Taking a deep breath, she sat across the table from Cole. "I know how crazy this has to look to you, but you have to believe that there's a very good reason to keep this between us."

He let out a nervous laugh. "Like you'll kill me if I don't?"

Shaking her head, she reached out and patted his arm. "If I was going that route, you'd be dead already."

A bead of sweat popped up along his hairline, and he shifted on the spot. "Okay…good to know."

Hayden forced a smile onto her face. "There's a lot more at stake here than my identity becoming public knowledge." Sitting back in her seat, she sighed. "For reasons I can't really get into, there are certain people in this world who aren't ready for me to make my appearance in my true form. If it were to get out, it would mess up eons of planning."

Cole wiped his forehead. "You have my word that no one will hear about this from me."

She nodded her thanks and turned to me. "And you?"

Dust Walkers | 105

"Like anyone would believe me." When she didn't seem reassured by my answer, I tried again. "I promise not to say anything." Before she could open her mouth to reply, I continued, "Forgive me here, but I've got a ton of questions, starting with...how in the hell have you managed to pull off being a guy for centuries? Is that some sort of spell, or a cloaking device...or something else entirely? And how—"

She held out her hands to slow me down. "Easy there, big fella. Let me answer that question first."

I gestured for her to continue. "Okay, go for it."

Leaning forward, she placed her elbows on the table. "What you saw was a construct, and as far as I know, it's unique to us. It allows me to create a near indestructible outer layer of armor in any form I wish." She eyed me for a long moment before continuing. "I'm sure that with enough time, you'll be able to create one as well. But, given your size, the only thing you'd be able to pass for is a giant or something of the sort."

Cole's eyes went wide. "I hate to interrupt, but could this manifest into some really...interesting-looking black and blue body armor?"

She cocked an eyebrow. "Huh?"

He sat up straight. "We were out at the Sohio Mine when someone took a shot at us." He waved a hand in my direction. "This weird black stuff covered him from head to toe to create some really advanced body armor with blue highlights."

Her gaze tracked up and down me a couple of times before she spoke. "Seriously?"

He nodded. "Yip."

Her tone became curious. "Interesting... I wouldn't have thought someone so young would be able to manifest a construct—especially one that's able to withstand a sniper."

I shrugged. "Well, if it makes you feel any better, it wasn't quite indestructible."

She cocked her eyebrow. "Why do you say that?"

Opening my shirt, I showed her the bruise on my chest. "Because the bullet hurt like hell."

She pursed her lips. "Odd...maybe because it was your first time using it."

"Maybe."

Hayden smiled. "Don't worry, it'll get stronger as you do."

I folded my arms and hung my head. "How does that work for us anyway? It isn't as if I can hit the gym a couple extra days a week to make that happen."

She tittered. "No. What you need is more experience and more souls at your disposal, along with a host of other things. All of which you'll acquire as the centuries pass. You've been at this what...less than a year?"

Absently nodding, I leaned my head against the wall of the trailer. "So...hurry up and wait is what you're telling me."

Hayden wobbled her hand back and forth. "More or less. Just give yourself time to develop your abilities." She gestured at me. "You should be proud of yourself for getting this far, this quickly."

The information wasn't exactly a surprise, but it was still a disappointment. "I guess."

Cole leaned his forearms against the table. "Sorry to cut in, but you said you've visited Grants before... Do you mind if I ask when?"

Thankfully, his question distracted her from the oddity I'd become.

She shrugged. "Maybe a hundred and fifty years ago."

Cole grinned. "Well...things are starting to make a lot more sense now."

Confused, I asked, "How's that?"

He turned to me. "Remember when I said a stranger came to town to stop those mercenaries?" I nodded, and he continued. "And do you recall me telling you that there were conflicting reports about it being a man or a woman?" He turned to Hayden. "That was you, wasn't it?"

Her gaze landed on him. "You were here?"

Cole nodded. "Yeah, and you saved a lot of people that day." He bit his lip and shrugged. "I've always been curious... Why were you here?"

She sighed. "I was doing a favor for Lazarus. It seems the old vigil—"

Cole cut in. "Samuel Estes."

She gave him a sad smile. "Yes. It appeared he'd been killed six or seven months before, and Lazarus wanted to see what I could find… which wasn't much. After a few weeks of investigating, the only thing that caught my attention was three asshole brothers trying to stamp out the locals by force."

I growled. "The Grants?"

She nodded. "I couldn't prove it, of course, but they hired a bunch of Spanish mercenaries to kill off the locals." Her fists balled up. "I offered the captain a healthy sum of cash to walk away, but he didn't care about money. All he wanted was to kill people, and he saw an opportunity to do that without much of a fight."

Cole nodded. "We did the best we could to move our people out of harm's way, but there were too many."

Hayden's expression darkened. "When it became clear he was more monster than human, I intervened directly."

Cole looked back at me. "And by intervened, she means she burned them all to ash over the course of an afternoon." He glanced back at her and hung his head. "We came to thank you, but you were gone."

She blushed. "I'd returned to Scotland to tend to another situation."

I sighed. "I still have a ton of questions."

"I can imagine." She gestured at the seat across from her. "Sit. We have much to talk about, and you have even more to learn."

Cole happily vacated the seat, and Hayden launched into a lengthy explanation of what she knew about who we were. She informed me of a host of powers I'd yet to discover, such as the ability to control separate elements—hers were fire and earth.

She eventually circled back to the constructs, explaining how they were separate from the Grim. It was almost as if we had two distinct personalities, one as the Reaper, and the other as…well, whatever we happened to be. Hayden went on to explain that controlling the Grim took a lot of practice, but it was possible to keep it in check. As for my teleportation ability, it would take me anywhere I'd ever been before.

All in all, it was a very educational few hours that made my head hurt due to information overload.

14

The first thing Hayden wanted to do when she finished the kindergarten class for yours truly was visit Sohio Mine. She probably wanted to handle the situation there properly. Which made sense—I'd just admitted to her that we'd only broken the necromancers' control over the undead but hadn't actually destroyed them.

We made the forty-minute drive, and Cole parked a bit further back than normal. I stepped out and held the door for Hayden. "I'm not sure what we'll be able to accomplish that Atsidi didn't."

She walked to the edge and motioned me over. "Come, and I'll show you."

Frowning, I shuffled over. "Yes, ma'am."

Hayden sighed. "If Atsidi is correct, a powerful necromancer could come along and do a mass raising. Granted, that would most likely leave that person drained for several days, but they'd still have a small army of the undead to do their bidding."

Cole shook his head. "Okay, what do you suggest we do? We already tried to dig them up...and let's just say that was less than effective."

She giggled. "Did you really?" He nodded, and she continued. "Don't worry, we're not going to try that again." She glanced over,

Dust Walkers | 109

placed her hand on my chest, and pushed me back a few steps. "You don't want to be that close."

"Okay." I shrugged. "So, what now?"

Hayden beamed. "Now it's time to show you what you're capable of without the Grim." She must've seen the blank look on my face, because she sighed. "Fire...remember, I'm a fire-based reaper, and if I had to guess, your element is ice."

I blinked. "Oh, that. Okay...how's that work anyway?"

She slapped her hand against her forehead, and probably counted to ten before continuing. "You'll need to quiet your mind. Afterward, search for the power reserves that reside deep in your being from the souls you've absorbed...and yes, that's separate from the Grim, no matter how much it tries to imply otherwise. Then it's a matter of tapping into that energy and allowing it to flow through you. For me, it's almost volcanic in nature." Shrugging, she chewed on her bottom lip. "I have no idea what it is you're looking for, but you'll know it the moment you find it."

As she pivoted to face the pit, her body transformed into living fire. Her eyes glowed blue, and she levitated several inches off the ground. The earth below us smoldered then became molten as a massive circular expanse filled with magma. The heat wafting out of the pit was enough to take my breath away and make my skin red.

Gasping for air, I choked out, "Holy shit."

The flames surrounding her slowly faded, and the temperature plummeted from that of the sun to something more tolerable. She turned to me with a big smile on her face. "Want to try to cool it off?"

Glancing between her and the gurgling earth below, I asked, "Just like that?"

She shrugged. "Pretty much. If you fail, no harm done, but if you can make it work then you'll be one step closer to understanding at least one of your abilities."

That was some hokey-sounding bullshit, but after witnessing her power, I was inclined to get on board. What was the worst that could happen?

Reluctantly, I moved forward to stand beside her. "Fine, I'll give it a shot."

At the edge of the mine, I closed my eyes, took several deep breaths, and relaxed. The sensation of being burned eventually left me, my chest cooled, and when I opened my eyes, the world was painted in shades of red. My arms were coated in thick ice backlit by blue flames beneath the surface.

The sight confused me, causing it to vanish in an instant.

Grumbling, I turned to Hayden. "Fat lot of good that did."

She stood there, mouth agape. "You'd be surprised."

Looking back, I found a thick layer of hardened black rock atop the lava field.

I gestured at the pit. "Did I...?"

Cole glanced between me and the onyx below. "That's some weird shit. Not as impressive as hers, but it's one hell of a first try." His gaze locked onto Hayden. "No offense, but the flaming ice monster he turns into is way more terrifying than your impersonation of a demon."

She nodded. "Couldn't agree more."

Cole walked over to his truck and leaned against it. "Just how many of you guys are there?"

Hayden sighed. "There can only be the two of us."

I glanced over at her. "Why is that?"

She shook her head. "Not a clue. Maybe the universe realized that the first Reaper was too powerful and decided to opt for two lesser versions... All I know is that we're designed to keep the balance."

I glanced down at the cooling pit and sighed. "Maybe it's because I'm young—comparatively speaking, of course—or maybe I'm just stupid, but I don't have a clue what that means." I gestured at myself. "Thing is, I'm barely out of diapers here, and the only balancing act I can perform is trying to stay upright."

She laughed. "The first few centuries are always the toughest. Once you get past those, it'll be second nature to you."

I ran a hand over my face. "If I live that long."

Dust Walkers | 111

She walked over and patted me on the shoulder. "Don't be so hard on yourself. You're making great progress."

I frowned. "Let me get this straight. You think that my inability to control any of my powers save for the Grim, which is iffy at best, is great progress?"

She gestured down at the pit. "I turned the ground down there into molten slag for at least two hundred feet. On your first attempt, you were able to cool it enough to place a dome over it. So, yes, it's pretty phenomenal. As for the rest of your abilities, you just don't know how to use them yet." She held out her arm, and a massive flaming scythe appeared in her hand. "In time, you'll be able to create one of these."

The sight of it sent a shiver up my spine. "Well, I guess we know where the legend came from."

Hayden shook her head. "Nope. Death carrying a sickle has been around longer than I have." She walked over and put a hand on my chest. "Just breathe. I'll teach you what I can, and show you the rest. After that, it's all on you. But don't worry, you've got time...hopefully."

I chuckled. "That's reassuring."

Hayden grinned. "Isn't it, though?" She pointed at Cole. "You said our next stop is a museum, right?"

He nodded. "Yeah."

She smiled. "All right, let's go."

Gesturing at her, I asked, "Are you sure you want to go dressed like that?"

She looked down at herself and sighed. "Goddamn it. I hate not being Ignatius sometimes."

I blinked. "What's that got to do with anything?"

She placed a hand on her hip. "Seriously? A guy can walk around wearing almost anything, and it's okay. But when a woman does it, people get all uptight. It's stupid." Chewing her lip, she turned to Cole. "Would you mind taking me back to the trailer for a few minutes?"

He shook his head. "Not at all."

Two hours later, we were nearly back in Grants, with Hayden

dressed in combat boots, comfortable jeans, and a t-shirt—a stark contrast to the body armor she'd been wearing.

We made a pit stop at Lotaburger since Hayden hadn't eaten. I was shocked, horrified, and more than a little impressed by the sheer amount of food she could pack away. She had five burgers, three orders of fries, and several other items on the menu just for kicks. The weirdest part was that she was still hungry.

She said that, given enough time, I'd have a similar appetite. Apparently, food didn't affect us the same way it did other people. Our metabolism was happy with an overabundance of sustenance or none at all. On a rather depressing note, she mentioned that it would take an ever-increasing amount of alcohol to get me buzzed as the years passed.

I wasn't exactly sure how it all worked, but it did explain my ravenous appetite lately. As it stood, though, I wasn't about to go on an all you can eat diet, or starve myself, to see if she was right...which she assured me she was.

After grabbing everyone's trash, I got to my feet, but when Steve, one of the Grants' goons, rounded the corner, I quickly emptied my hands. By the look on the man's face, he was painfully constipated...or maybe that was the look he was going for. Either way, this was going to be an exceptionally unpleasant meeting.

Just what I needed: a public altercation with the Grants' hired help.

The big man stomped over, but when his gaze fell on Hayden, he adopted an oily smile. "Are these two bothering you, ma'am?"

She frowned and leaned back in her chair. "Come again?"

Steve pointed at the two of us. "Are these *men*, and I use that term loosely, harassing you?"

She wiped her lips with her napkin, and her tone turned dangerous. "May I ask what makes you think that?"

His smug expression faltered. "Well...they've been harassing other women in town. I just figured they'd found a new target."

Hayden grinned. "Is this true?"

I shook my head. "Not a word of it."

Steve jabbed his finger into my chest. "You lying sack of shit."

Dust Walkers | 113

My gaze flickered down to the offending appendage. "Remove it before I do."

He raised his voice. "Do you realize who I am?"

The man's rudeness offended me on a primal level. "Does it look like I give two shits who you are? Now explain yourself before my patience runs out."

Growling, he jerked back his finger, balled his hand into a fist, and took his best shot. Steve's movements were so slow and exaggerated I easily blocked the punch. With my other hand, I slammed my palm against his chest and pinned him to the wall. "God, you're stupid. If you've got something to say, say it and leave before you get hurt."

Hatred burned in his eyes, but he nodded.

Stepping back, I eased up on the pressure, and he took a deep breath. I rolled my hand for him to get on with it. "You're burning daylight, and if I had to guess, you've got to run back to Lewis."

Steve growled. "That's Mr. Grant."

I flipped him the bird. "Fuck you. And him, for that matter. Either start talking or walking. You've got thirty seconds."

Blood rushed to his cheeks, and he glanced back at the wall. "You're going to pay for that."

I glanced down at my watch. "Twenty seconds."

He glowered at me. "It's come to Mr. Grant's attention that you've been badgering *certain individuals*. Not only that, he wants you to know that his business dealings are none of your concern. In short, you've overstayed your welcome."

Chuckling, I shook my head. "Your boss is about as dumb as a bag of rocks. All he had to do was let me finish my investigation, and there was a slim chance I'd leave without bothering him further." I slapped my hand against his chest again, hard enough to knock him into the wall. "But now, you can let him know he has my full attention—or will, once I've finished my current case."

When I released him, a black mist wrapped around his fist. He pivoted on the spot, hammered his fist into my chest...and nothing. I'm immune to magic, remember?

He staggered back. "What the hell?"

Tired of the man's shit, I backhanded him hard enough to take him off his feet. Steve crashed into the ground, and he flailed on the cement, groaning as he grasped his battered shoulder.

I took a knee and leaned over to whisper in his ear. "Maybe I wasn't clear earlier. Don't touch me." Grabbing the front of his shirt, I jerked him to his feet. "Go...while you still can."

Steve gritted his teeth. "This isn't over, freak."

I pointed back the way he'd come. "Never thought it was."

He stood there stupidly for a moment before slowly hobbling away.

Hayden snickered. "Jesus, I thought I had a short fuse."

Turning to her, I sighed. "You're assuming I was mad." I shrugged. "Annoyed, and a little irritated, sure. But not angry. Anger means a loss of control...and, trust me, no one wants to see that happen."

Her smile broadened. "Oh, we're going to get along just fine."

Cole frowned. "Lewis and his brothers are going to be pissed."

Hayden jumped to her feet. "Those assholes still run this place?"

He nodded. "Yep, and the only thing that's changed is that their hold on the area is stronger than ever."

She growled. "I should've killed them the last time I was here."

Cole closed his eyes and smiled. "If only you had."

I cleared my throat. "We can daydream about that later. For now, let's pay Ruth another visit."

She looked over at Cole. "Is he always this grumpy?"

Cole shrugged. "No idea. I've known him a grand total of three days longer than you."

Hayden laughed. "Guess we'll find out together then."

It took us about fifteen minutes to get across town to the museum, and, just our luck, Ms. Miller had called in sick. Her staff, such as it was, didn't exactly try to stop us from searching her office, not that it revealed anything of substance. I was dead set on visiting the nasty little hag at home, but no one knew where she lived, and a cursory background check wasn't any more informative.

On my way out the front door, another one of Lewis's thugs was leaning against the fender of the truck.

Glancing over at Cole, I asked, "Do you know this guy?"

He nodded. "His name is Allen Richards."

Hayden stepped past me and walked up to Allen. Her voice came out cold and hard. "Can we help you with something, young man?"

Allen gave her a once-over and pointed back at us. "You slumming it, lady?"

She shook her head and let out a long breath. "Only by speaking to the likes of you."

He pushed off the vehicle and smirked. "Miss, you have no idea what you're missing."

Hayden held her index finger close to her thumb. "I've got a fairly good idea." She grinned. "Unlike most of the women you disappoint, I'm accustomed to a better class of man."

Anger flickered in his eyes, and he raised his hand to slap her.

Her voice dropped to a whisper. "Please give me an excuse."

Clenching his jaw, he growled. "I don't hit women."

Hayden snarled, "Liar."

Allen towered over her. "Awfully brave with people at your back. I wonder how you'd do when you're all alone."

She huffed. "One day, I hope you find out."

Grunting, he sidestepped her and pointed at me. "You were told to leave Ms. Miller alone."

Sighing, I shook my head. "You people are some arrogant mother-fuckers. Not only that, but all of you need a reality check. Let me start by saying I don't answer to you, the Grants, or anyone else. The sooner you get that through your skull, the less painful things will be."

Allen wagged a finger at me. "Maybe you're stupid, so let me spell it out for you. Get the hell out of town. You've got until tomorrow night, or we'll ship you back to Lazarus piece by piece."

I folded my arms. "The last man who threatened me with that didn't survive the attempt." Shooing him away, I said, "Go back and tell Lewis that I'll leave when I'm damn good and ready."

Fire crawled down his arm to the tips of his fingers as he balled up his fist and swung for my head. Hayden stepped in and caught his hand in hers, snuffing out the flames. With a quick twist, she took him off balance, and he hit his knee, screaming in pain.

She slammed her palm into his chest, and he crumpled to the ground. "Tell Lewis that his interference isn't appreciated." Glancing back at me, she gestured to the truck. "We've got places to be."

Normally, I don't care to take orders from anyone, but in this case, I happily made an exception.

15

By the time we reached the far side of Highland Meadows, the temperature was rapidly dropping as the sun dipped below the horizon. When we neared Atsidi's place, our headlights shone on a beat-up 1970s era F-150 blocking the drive.

Cole groaned, eased off the gas, and pulled onto the shoulder. He threw the truck into park and glanced over at us. "If you thought the day's gone poorly up to this point, you're in for an unwelcome surprise." He pointed at the two-tone Ford. "That's Isaiah Jacob, and without a doubt, he's about to make our evening that much worse."

The name rang a bell, and I leaned forward to get a closer look. "Is this the same turd-nugget you've been telling me about"

Nodding, he said, "The very same."

Isaiah got out of his vehicle and stalked toward us as we piled out of the truck.

Cole raised his hand in greeting. "Evening. What brings you out this way?"

Isaiah was a slight man with short black hair, brown eyes, and dark skin. There were a few things about the man that were impossible to miss, such as his smug demeanor and the general dickishness wafting off the guy in waves.

The icing on the cake, however, was when the douchebag opened his mouth, because his tone grated against my last nerve. "Like you don't know."

Cole shrugged. "Actually, I don't."

He huffed. "You sent Atsidi to plead with the council to get involved in one of your messes again."

I cleared my throat. "That wasn't his doing. It was mine."

His gaze flickered over to me, and revulsion crossed his face. "I don't deal with outsiders, and neither do the elders. Now stop speaking, while the grownups talk."

Stepping past Cole, I pulled air in through my teeth. "Perhaps you don't know who I am—"

He huffed out a derisive snort. "It doesn't matter. You're white, and as I said, we don't deal with outsiders. Or are you too stupid to understand the concept?"

An old anger threatened to bubble up, but I forced it back down. "Again, you don't—"

Isaiah held up a hand to cut me off. "I'm quite aware of who you are, half-breed."

Unable to keep the annoyance out of my voice, I said, "Then you know that I'm a vigil."

He rolled his eyes. "I don't care what position you hold within the Archive. You're still an outsider, no matter who your grandfather is, and as such I have no use for you." Leaning to the side, he looked past me to Cole. "Whatever you're mixed up in, you'll need to handle it on your own. I've made sure the others won't get involved."

I moved to block his view. "Where is Atsidi?"

The disdain in his voice was impossible to miss. "That's none of your concern."

Cole growled. "Answer the goddamn question, Isaiah."

His face contorted in rage. "He sought to overrule my decision by seeking out Łééchąą'í."

Cole laughed. "That doesn't bode well for you."

Isaiah strolled past me and jabbed his finger against Cole's chest. "Don't test my authority, because you won't like how it turns out." He

Dust Walkers | 119

sneered. "I don't care who your parents are *supposed to be*, so tread carefully."

Cole batted the man's hand away. "I've always been respectful of your position, but if you step out of line, don't think for a moment I won't end you."

When he reached for Cole, I placed a hand against his chest, and an eerie sensation shot through me. It took me half a second to find my voice, but when I did, it came out flat and hard. "Easy now. You don't want me getting the wrong idea here."

Isaiah must've felt it too, because he jumped back and frantically brushed off his shirt. "Don't ever touch me again, or I'll be forced to do something about it."

The creepiness subsided, but the feeling lingered. I wanted nothing more in that moment than to wash my hands. "You might be someone important on the reservation, but here and now, you're just some strange little man standing in the way of me doing my job." I gestured at his vehicle. "It would be in your best interest to turn around and leave—now."

He rolled his eyes. "Or what? Do you think I'm worried about squaring off against the likes of you?" His gaze darted from me, to Cole, and finally to Hayden. Licking his lips, he ran his hand over the top of his hair. "Evening, Miss, I'm Isaiah Jacob, tribal elder and spokesman for the Navajo people." He straightened his shirt and offered her a pleasant smile as he gestured at me. "If I had to guess, this...pitiful excuse for a man has tricked you into spending time with him. You should be warned that he's been harassing redheads in Grants. So, if you're in need of a ride back to town, I'd be only too happy to accommodate." He thumbed over at me. "You never know what psychos will do once they have you alone."

Her eyes burned with blue flames. "You're right. You never can tell what a sociopath will do once you're alone with them." She stepped closer, and fire coated her right hand. "Which means I'll be turning down your *generous* offer."

Moving back, Isaiah shivered. "Suit yourself."

She folded her arms. "I think I will."

He stumbled, pivoted, and stomped over to his truck. It took him two tries to get the thing started. But when it did, the glasspack mufflers echoed in the early evening as he drove off into the distance.

Once he was gone, Hayden growled. "Goddamn it."

Confused, I turned to her. "What's up?"

Her fists clenched and unclenched in an odd rhythm. "It's jerks like him who remind me why my alter ego is so preferable."

I blinked. "Huh?"

Cole laughed as he shook his head. "In case you missed it, she's an attractive woman. You do realize she's a woman, right?"

I furrowed my brow. "Yeah, but what's that got to do with anything?"

Nodding, she grinned. "My point exactly, but did you see the way the guy looked at me?"

I gave the space he'd occupied a dismissive wave. "You cannot expect anything more from such a narrowminded piece of foreskin."

She sighed. "Eloquent, and true. But for some reason, anytime one of those types sees a female, they instantly treat us like a helpless child."

I sighed. "Well, that's just messed up."

She groaned. "No kidding."

Cole turned to Hayden. "On behalf of my people, I'm sorry you had to deal with that creepy little shit."

Hayden shook her head. "Not your fault, but we've got bigger problems to deal with than that asshole." She pivoted on the spot and climbed into the truck.

I followed quickly and closed the door.

Cole idled down the drive and parked next to the trailer. It took a few minutes for us to use the head and wash up. After that, we settled in around the table to figure out our next step.

Gesturing at Cole, I asked, "Why is Atsidi going to visit Łééchąą'í?"

Cole rolled his shoulders. "He's sort of the de facto leader of these parts. Not in the traditional sense, of course, but in times of dispute, the tribe will occasionally ask for his guidance. Whatever he decides is always adhered to by the tribe."

Dust Walkers | 121

I nodded. "Oh…okay."

He let out a long breath. "The only thing is it's one hell of a trek to get to him, which means Atsidi won't be back for at least a couple of days."

Hayden frowned. "Seriously?"

Cole grimaced. "Unfortunately." He leaned back in his seat. "Not that I've ever made the trek myself, but from what I've been told, he lives about fifty miles out in the badlands. He supposedly carved out a labyrinth underneath one of the plateaus. Once you've found your way to the heart of the thing, you have to perform a ritual of some sort and hope and pray that he comes out for a visit… If he doesn't, it's in your best interests to leave."

Shaking my head, I furrowed my brow. "Hold on—why leave? Wouldn't you just go deeper in?"

He shivered. "Not if you want to live. There's a story about two men who wanted to be chief, and the tribe couldn't decide, so they were sent to speak with Łééchąą'í. When they arrived, they followed the protocol…at first. One of them got tired of waiting and stormed into the cave, demanding to be heard. A few minutes later, his corpse came flying out." He turned to me. "So, no, you don't go looking for Łééchąą'í. He either speaks to you, or he doesn't. Simple as that."

I leaned forward and cupped my face in my hands. "Well, with manners like that, I bet the Jehovah's witnesses have him black listed.'

That made him chuckle. "They're pretty persistent, but probably."

I grinned. "Let me guess, he doesn't get out much either."

Cole flinched. "Not even a little. The old man, if that's what he is, hasn't been seen since 1803."

Furrowing my brow, I asked, "What do you mean if that's what he is?"

He shook his head. "He's supposed to have skin as dark as a starless night, violet eyes, and the head of a dog."

Hayden glanced between us. "He's a were?"

Cole pursed his lips and shook his head. "I don't think so. For one, he's too old, and he's got power…a lot of power." He placed his elbows on the table with a thud. "If I had to choose between going against him or the two of you at once...I'd ask you guys when and where, because there's no way I'm ever going to fight Łééchąą'í."

I scratched the top of my head and grinned. "Good to know." Falling back in my seat, I harrumphed. "But it makes me wonder what made him drag himself from his lair in 1803 if he hates people so damn much."

Cole winced as he bit his lip. "Well...that would be my fault."

Arching an eyebrow, I asked, "How's that?"

He pointed at himself. "That's when Łééchąą'í carried me out of the desert, delivered me to the elders, and asked them to watch over me."

Hayden dragged her nail around in a circle on the table. "I'm going to assume because of who your parents are." She thumbed over her shoulder. "Douche-O-Rama mentioned something about them."

Cole nodded. "Yeah, my mother is Na'ashjéii Asdzáá, and my father is Haashch'eezhini."

She blinked, and her mouth fell open. "If the legends are true, that's a pretty potent lineage."

Cole shrugged. "It is if you believe it. I think someone abandoned me, and Łééchąą'í felt sorry for me. He made up the story to ensure that I was well looked after, if I had to guess."

I shook my head. "There's no reason to make up such a story. They would've taken care of you just because he brought you in."

Cole glanced down at his hands. "I suppose, but since he did...all it's done is create issues for me."

Leaning my chin on my hand, I asked, "How's that?"

He craned his neck. "There are those who'd put me up on a pedestal to worship me as spirit made flesh. Then there are the Isaiahs of the world, who resent me because they think it's a lie. Any way you slice it, my world is more difficult because of Łééchąą'í's personal involvement, and the story he told."

I closed my eyes and opened them again as I let out a long breath. "I can see how that could cause problems."

Hayden flicked the table with her nail and sat back in her seat. "I've seen that type of thing fuck up a person's entire life... I'm sorry you have to deal with that."

Cole forced a smile onto his face. "Thanks."

She nodded. "You're welcome." Turning to me, she said, "With Atsidi out of the picture for a few days, that leaves the three of us to handle an untold number of undead, several badass necromancers, and this mysterious group they belong to."

The distraction of Cole's past had been nice while it lasted. "Thanks for reminding me... The way I see it, we need to deal with the local representatives of the Onyx Mind and their undead goons. As for the entire organization, I think that's going to take a combined effort...and maybe, with luck, you could sway Viktor into helping us with what's apparently a global problem."

She ran her hand across her forehead. "He's got his hands full for the next few days, but you can bet he'll want in on this. I'll make sure that the Pacis Gladius finds out as well."

Confused, I leaned forward. "What's that?"

Hayden chuckled. "They haven't contacted you yet?"

I shook my head. "Nope."

She grinned. "I'm surprised, especially with them trying to fold in as many of the older organizations under one umbrella as they can."

"Huh?"

Biting her bottom lip, she sucked in air loudly. "Well, are you familiar with the Krewe of Caesar?"

I nodded. "Isn't that the Archive's contribution to the Mystic Courts of Comus back in New Orleans?"

A smile crossed her lips. "Yes, and the MCC was created by Viktor in the guise of Comus, to help combat the darkness in the city. Over the centuries, other such unions were formed for the same purpose all around the globe. Thing is, their individual reach has always been limited. In an effort to combat this, they've banded together to form the Pacis Gladius, or the Sword of Peace. Under this new structure, they can share intel and resources, and thus respond to threats quicker than ever before."

I blinked. "Wow, okay... How does the Archive fit in?"

She shrugged. "No idea, but they've already contacted the Ulfr and Warden Global, so you guys can't be too far behind in line."

Cole frowned. "It's a shame they haven't been in touch yet."

Turning to him, I frowned. "Why's that?"

He spread his hands apart in frustration. "Because we could use the additional manpower right about now."

I shrugged. "Maybe, if it works as intended. Otherwise, it'll be a bureaucratic mess and more of a hinderance than a help."

Hayden ran her hand over her face and yawned. "Sorry. It's just that I've been up for nearly thirty-two hours now."

I checked my watch: 10:32. "It is getting late. Maybe we should turn in for the night." Gesturing at the back, I said, "I'll sleep out here, so you're welcome to my room for the duration."

She beamed. "Thanks, I really appreciate it."

Stepping past her, I rolled my shoulders. "You're very welcome. Let me get a few of my things, and it's all yours."

Ten minutes later, I had most of my things out, and she was quick to close the door. Cole had made himself scarce during the transition and, if I had to guess, was already asleep. That left me alone with my thoughts while I lowered the table to set up a third bed. I've never been fond of sleeping around strangers without a locked door between me and them, but tonight would have to be an exception.

My head was barely on the pillow when I fell asleep.

The first Reaper ruled over my dreams. He stood between this world and the next with violet flames covering his arms, with eyes to match.

He turned to me and whispered, "Greetings, child. I've waited an eternity for your arrival."

Trepidation filled me, and it took a moment to find my voice. "You've been expecting me?"

He nodded. "I have. Your counterpart has been waiting for you as well, even if she doesn't realize it yet."

My curiosity quickly overrode my nervousness—mostly. "What's that supposed to mean?"

He waved me over. "Come, child, and I will explain."

After moving up to stand beside him, I stared into the abyss. Before me was a vision of the multiverse, and that which could be. Many of the possibilities were filled with alien machines, hybrids made of shadow and advanced technology that ended with the destruction of all life. There were a few, however, where a balance was found, and organic life coexisted with the machine gods that were ruled by the Svartálfar and Álfheimr.

Unwilling to believe what I was seeing, I turned to him in the hopes that I was wrong. "What's this?"

Even though I couldn't see his face, I knew he was smiling. "You already know what this is. It's what could be. Much of how this turns out depends on you, and the choices you will eventually have to make."

In other words, no pressure at all.

A shiver ran up my spine as I glanced back at the abyss. "That's a lot of expectation to be heaped on one man, especially considering that I'm new to all this."

He placed a hand on my shoulder, and blue flames engulfed my body before being absorbed. "You'll be fine. Give yourself time and learn all you can from Hayden."

My curiosity once again overrode my good sense. "You know her?"

The billowing creature before me laughed. "Of course. I trained her, after all, and I'll do the same for you when the time is right." There was a deep sadness in his voice. "Her path is different from yours, and her fate is tied to this universe, but you are what is to come...the birth of something new."

Like an idiot, I mumbled, "If you say so."

He tapped one of the violet claws against my skull. "Listen to the little dragon inside you."

Shuddering, I asked, "You mean Kur?"

The light in his eyes glowed brighter. "Really? You carry Kur's essence?"

I nodded. "Yeah."

His voice was full of wonder. "Fascinating..."

The First Reaper pointed out at the abyss and began telling me the story of how we came to be.

Long ago, something in this realm triggered a catastrophic failure in the dominion of the Machine Gods. While he wasn't sure what had occurred, the Svartálfar and Álfheimr were infected with a virus. Their sickness caused a war to break out between their supporters, who'd been tainted by the plague, and those who'd proven resistant to its influence.

Even worse, the dragon lords—some of the oldest and most powerful beings among the machine gods—were partially affected by the disease. As the eldest, Kur was their leader, but he was betrayed by one of his most trusted allies, Zmey Gorynych. Because of that, the war created by the Svartálfar and Álfheimr raged on for untold eons. After they defeated Kur, the Idunn, and many others, they banished the fallen to this land to be trapped forever in stasis.

In time, Kur and the others were forgotten, but this didn't stop the war, it just created a new enemy—themselves. The Svartálfar and Álfheimr fought one another for absolute power, and in the end consumed all their resources.

In order to survive, they sought out new allies, the first of whom were those in the land of mist. The Álfheimr gave them form, allowing them to exist as pure energy, or as physical beings known as the wraiths.

At one point, they attempted to strike a deal with the mad god, better known to some as the gray wanderer. But even they were repulsed by the depths of his depravity...he'd perverted the Idunn with a parasitic version of the virus that had consumed the Svartálfar and Álfheimr to create the vampires.

Eventually, the machine gods grew desperate and forged an alliance with the other Children of the First. To seal the pact, the Svartálfar created the nine lich lords for Ankou, and Álfheimr brought forth the seraphim for Lugus. It was through this union that they gained a solid foothold in this universe. And now it was up to me to fight this war, win...or at least hurt them enough to broker a peace.

This was why Kur had celebrated when he'd bonded with me...I was a warrior, a reaper, and—according to this guy—what would be.

Whatever that was supposed to mean.

The first Reaper turned to me. "It's time for you to go. There's so much more for me to tell you, but I think you've had enough for one night.

He reached out and tapped my forehead, and the world before me faded in an instant.

16

February 27th

My mouth was dry, my head hurt, and I was queasy. I'd never had a hangover in my life, but if I had to guess, this was what it felt like. When I reached up to wipe the sleep out of my eyes, I had to scrape away several chunky bits before I could open them. Even after brushing most of it away, it was like running fine-grit sandpaper over my corneas. Which meant that no matter how hard I tried, the world wouldn't come into focus.

Grunting, I swung my legs over the edge of the makeshift bed and vigorously rubbed my face. The next time I opened my eyes, Cole stood there with a mixture of concern and horror on his face. When I turned to Hayden, her expression wasn't much different.

Massaging the top of my head in the hopes the throbbing would stop, I asked, "Was I snoring or something?"

Hayden frowned, picked up her phone, tapped the screen, and handed it to me. The recording showed a mass of black mist and blue flames hovering above where I'd been sleeping. Strangely, I was nowhere to be found.

I held it up to her. "What's this?"

She gestured for me to look at the screen. "Keep watching."

A few seconds later, the swirling mass slowly lowered to the bed and vanished, leaving me behind.

I did my best to shake off the brain fog. "Oh. Ah...okay."

She snorted. "That's all you've got to say?"

"Pretty much." My answer didn't appear to satisfy either of them. Shrugging, I said, "I was having a dream about the first Reaper...then I wasn't."

Cole gave a nervous laugh. "If that's how you dream, I'd hate to see what your nightmares are like."

Handing the phone back to Hayden, I sighed. "That makes two of us."

She waved her hands back and forth in front of her. "Wait a minute, you were dreaming about the first?"

"Yeah."

Considering how crazy it sounded, even to me, I thought it best to give them a carefully edited version of the vision. It wasn't so much a matter of trust as it was that I didn't want to wind up in a padded room. During the course of the discussion, I returned the table to its rightful place while Cole made breakfast.

Hayden leaned against the wall of the trailer and stretched her legs out across the bench. "So, he claims to have taught me."

Doing my best to play it off, I grinned. "It was a dream. You're acting like I was somehow communicating with an ancient being that hasn't been seen in eons...if ever."

Granted, I did believe the vision was real, but as I said, it was a bit out there. Plus, I'd left out a lot of information, such as the *Svartálfar*, *Álfheimr*, Kur, and his allies, which wasn't helping my half-assed story. But, going around talking about living machines, dragon lords, and some weird virus that had corrupted them made me sound nuts.

She didn't appear convinced, though. "I get that, but...it's pretty weird that the dream was so specific. Was there anything else in it?"

I bit my lip and nodded. "Yeah, but I'd rather not talk about it just now if that's okay."

Dust Walkers | 129

She let out a single chuckle. "Suit yourself, but if it's got anything to do with you being encased in darkness and flames, you might want to share sooner rather than later."

Wanting nothing more than to shift this discussion off me, I did my best to deflect. "Can't see how it could." I waved my hand at her. "If it did, I'm sure you'd know."

She jerked her head back. "Why's that?"

Bewildered by her response, I stared at her blankly for a second. "Because I'm sure you've experienced this at least once or twice over the years."

Hayden cocked her head to the side. "Ah...no, I haven't."

My chest tightened, and I shifted uncomfortably in my seat. "Really?"

She nodded. "I'm fairly certain I'd remember."

"Are you sure? Because I can't be the only one he's chosen to speak with."

She offered me a comforting smile as she reached out and patted my arm. "The fact that you've been contacted by the first just goes to show the many differences between us."

I blinked. "Other than me being taller, male, and the opposite element...what's so different?"

She tapped my right hand. "You have an onyx gauntlet, and I don't. It's one of the reasons I'm almost always in full armor." Reverence worked its way into her tone. "And it would appear you have a connection to the first."

When she put it like that, I did sound a bit dense for not noticing. "Umm, okay. But if he didn't teach you, how did you learn to use your abilities?"

Hayden grimaced. "As far back as I can recall, this was just the way things were."

Cole placed a plate in front of her. "Even as a child?"

Her cheeks turned crimson. "I was never a child...or if I was, I have no memory of it. One day, I just was."

Cole handed me my food and turned to her. "Everyone has a beginning. Are you sure that was yours?"

She bit her lip and shrugged. "Mostly."

This was getting a bit too deep for me, and Hayden was obviously uncomfortable with the turn we'd taken. "While I'm sure we'd all like to get to the bottom of this, we should probably focus on our current problems. And that's the three of us trying to hunt down several necromancers." Cupping my forehead in my hands, I massaged it gently, hoping to rid myself of my headache. "Thing is, I haven't got the first idea where to start today. I mean, it isn't as if we're awash with leads."

Cole grinned. "I might be able to help with that."

Hayden took a bite of her eggs. "I'm all ears."

He snickered. "How do you feel about visiting some of the local bat caves?"

She laughed. "What, are we going to meet Bruce Wayne?"

I glanced up at her and frowned. "Who?"

Cole's mouth dropped open. "Dear God, you *do* know who batman is, right?"

I dropped my forehead back into my hand and nodded. "Oh... yeah. The comic book character."

He ran his hand over his face. "Jesus, man, have you lived under a rock your entire life?"

Pushing my plate to the side, I grumbled, "No, but it wasn't like I read them as a kid, and most of my adult life, I've been busy."

Hayden blinked. "Doing what?"

Blood rushed to my cheeks. "I worked for the DoD for twenty-eight years, and this job has kept me rather busy for the last nine months."

She giggled. "And to think, someone recently told *me* I need to get out more." Glancing at Cole, she asked, "Why are we visiting these caves?"

His expression soured. "The local bats have been acting weird for the last few months." He gestured at the two of us and said, "I figured, while I had some backup, this would be an excellent time to check Mount El Malpais for chindi."

Caves filled with bats weren't my favorite places to visit. I'd been

Dust Walkers | 131

in a few in the course of my duties, and, partially due to their stench, they hadn't been the most pleasant experiences. The added risk of disease, and having shit smeared all over me, made this lead less appealing by the second. But it was the only one we had at the moment.

With that thought, I lost all interest in what remained of my breakfast. "Great. When do we leave?"

Cole checked his watch. "It's six now. I figure by the time we get cleaned up, it'll be after seven…so maybe eight?"

Hayden nodded. "Sounds good to me." She got to her feet. "Anyone mind if I hit the shower first?"

We shook our heads.

She snickered. "Suckers."

Cole laughed. "It's an instant water heater, so we'll all be fine."

She grinned. "Good to know." And with that, she ducked into her room to grab a few things then into the bath she went.

Forcing myself to finish the last bite of my breakfast, I asked, "How far away is it?"

He paused for a moment then shrugged. "Probably about an hour from here. Why do you ask?"

"Mostly curious. It seems that no matter what's going on we're an hour from where it's happening."

He chuckled. "Welcome to the great southwest. Most people live here for the isolation, and believe me, you can get plenty of that in these smaller towns."

I nodded. "I bet." Gesturing at my bags, I said, "After I finish the dishes, I'll get my gear in order."

Twenty minutes later, Cole took his turn in the shower while Hayden changed into what appeared to be modified hiking gear. As for me, I dressed in jeans, a t-shirt, and a pair of work boots.

Hayden took one look at me and frowned. "That's what you're wearing? Did you forget that we're hunting a bunch of undead and a small pack of necromancers?"

I laughed. "I didn't forget."

She frowned. "Your getup seems a bit…I don't know…civilian?"

I gestured at myself. "Just because I'm not decked out in tactical gear doesn't mean I'm not protected."

She reached out and pinched my shirt. "Enchanted clothing?"

I nodded. "Yep."

A big smile crossed her lips. "In all my years, I've never found one who's a tailor."

With a dismissive wave, I chuckled. "Neither have I. Andrew, my uncle, supplies all the enchanted material to a man named George—who I might add, is a phenomenal tailor. If you're interested, I'd be happy to put you in touch with him."

She furrowed her brow. "Andrew Randall?"

I nodded. "Yeah."

She blinked. "He's an enchanter?"

Ever say something and suddenly realize you probably shouldn't have? That was how I was feeling right about now. "Yeah. I guess that isn't public knowledge."

She shook her head. "No, no, it's not. For future reference, most enchanters hide their talent to keep themselves safe." She must've seen the confusion on my face because she continued. "Due to them being so rare, and their skills so sought after, someone might try to take advantage of them...or enslave them." Shivering, she shook her head. "But no one in their right mind would try to turn that man into an indentured servant."

I rolled my eyes. "He's not that bad. In fact, he's a pretty nice guy."

Hayden grimaced. "Right up until he's not." She held out a hand to stop me. "But, I've heard good things as well...look at what he did for the weres in North America. But given my...*our* abilities, being around a telepath makes me nervous."

I blinked. "Why's that?"

"Because they can read our damn minds, that's why."

Unable to stop myself, I let out a chuckle. "That's what's got you so worked up?"

She nodded. "Well, yeah...doesn't it bother you?"

Shaking my head, I grinned. "Telepaths are just like anyone else in the Archive—their powers don't work on us."

Her mood instantly lightened. "Really?"

"Yeah."

She threw her head back and laughed. "Oh, that's fantastic."

I shrugged. "Glad to make your day."

Hayden snickered. "And you have. I've spent most of my life purposely avoiding telepaths." Her voice dropped, and she blushed. "This might sound silly, especially given the revelation, but I have an irrational fear of them."

I patted her on the back. "Well, you can put that to bed now."

Her smile returned. "Thanks, I needed that."

Chuckling, I said, "You're welcome."

Cole stepped out of his room and pointed at the door. "Are we ready? We've got a long trip ahead of us."

Without any further discussion, we piled out of the trailer and into the truck. It appeared we had an appointment with a bunch of flying rodents.

17

It turned out our destination was about fifteen minutes from where we'd found the skinless chindi. Or, as Hayden had started calling them, deadites... Apparently, she was a big Evil Dead fan. Or maybe she just loved Bruce Campbell's chin.

It took us several minutes to make our way from where we'd parked to one of the many sheer rock faces of El Malpais. Cole guided us down a well-worn trail before veering onto a less popular one. A little later, he climbed halfway up the mountain to a spot not meant for your standard tourist. There, on a little outcropping, we found a dozen or so tubes that led into the dark interior of the extinct volcano.

I removed my pack before taking point and climbing in ahead of the others. Using my enhanced vision, courtesy of the Grim, I scanned the area for bats—we didn't want to spook them with lights unnecessarily. As it turned out, it was a needless precaution since they were nowhere to be found. I cracked a couple of glow sticks and tossed them into the gloom. As they fell, they highlighted small mountains of guano in heaps on the floor.

The climb down wasn't too tough, given the numerous natural handholds, shelves, and the slope of what had once been a massive magma chamber. Granted, I was still at about a thirty-degree angle with my back toward the floor, but it was doable without a harness and a ton of rope. While there weren't any bats in the vicinity, their stench lingered. Once on the ground, I flashed my light several times to give the all clear signal then looked around.

The cavern was massive, with a domed ceiling and a large tunnel at the far end. Since it was the only exit down here, I had to guess that was where we were headed. It took them a couple of minutes to make their way down to me. Hayden had secured a rope at the top, so it'd be somewhat easier to get out of this hellhole when we were finished.

Cole shone his light against the far wall. "We'll be making our way through there. The passage narrows in a few places, but you should be able to make it easy enough."

I pointed my flashlight at the ceiling. "No bats."

He nodded. "That's what I was afraid of. This place used to be filled with them. But over the last year, they've stopped nesting here. I can't be sure why, and without backup, venturing into the unknown seemed unwise."

I patted him on the shoulder. "Given how the last few days have gone, that was probably a wise choice."

Hayden glanced between us. "How in the hell would this be tied to the walker problem?"

I chuckled. "No idea, but if you'd told me a week ago that I'd find several hundred undead buried in an old uranium mine, I would've thought you were nuts."

She frowned. "That's true." She pointed at a nearby pile of droppings. "Plus, it'd practically take an act of god to make the bats leave a home they've had for so long."

Cole's voice hardened. "Agreed."

Her frown deepened. "I'd really like you to be wrong about this. The last thing I want is to be caught in a confined space with a ton of deadites." She glanced up at me. "I'm not sure if you know this or not, but most of our abilities are worth dick against zombies."

I nodded. "Yeah, I've noticed."

Her gaze landed on Cole. "I take it that you've been in here before?"

His eyes lit up. "Yeah. I was a kid at the time, but I'm familiar with the tunnel system." He gestured at the opening. "There are several offshoots in there, most of which are dead ends, but if we follow the main path, it'll take us to a small grotto. If we don't find anything there then this is just a weird coincidence."

Eyeing the pile of crap, I grumbled, "Have I mentioned how much I hate this?"

Hayden snickered and walked past me. "Only a few dozen times. But do tell us again, because I'm sure we've forgotten."

I flipped her the bird. "No need to get snippy. I'm just making sure my concerns have been heard and noted."

Cole snorted. "I think we get it. You're afraid of bats."

I shook my head. "Not at all. I just hate the things. And the only thing I dislike more than that is walking through a mountain of their crap. It's disgusting."

Hayden spun on her heel and gawked at me. "It can't be any worse than charbroiling some random guy during the first triumvirate meeting you attended...can it?"

I held up a finger to stop her from going any further. "Let me be clear here, nowhere in that story was I ever forced to wade through his shit."

Cole blinked and staggered back a step with laughter. "Wait... wait...so in your mind, it's all okay until there's feces involved?"

I gave him a thumbs-up. "Bingo. We have a winner."

Hayden chuckled. "Oh God. You're worse than Viktor. He can't stand being covered in blood—even though it happens more often than you might think—but he doesn't whine about it." She pointed at the tunnel. "The sooner we get going, the sooner it'll be over...along with your whimpering."

Grr. "Fine, but I still hate this."

Her tone became highly sarcastic. "Really? We hadn't noticed." She pointed ahead. "Now, move it before *I* start flinging shit at you."

I sighed, and my gaze hit the floor. "Fine, let's get this over with."

Dust Walkers | 137

We traipsed into the darkness, following Cole's lead. There were several twists and turns that forced me onto my knees while the others merely had to stoop. This was one of those times when being short was a bonus.

Several minutes passed before we reached the end of the passage and stood on the edge overlooking a lava tube that traveled up to the sky and down about thirty feet. There was no need to go any further since the bottom of the tube was packed with a small horde of undead. Not only did they fill the cavern below but several of them lined the ledges like gruesome statues.

Why on earth did the necromancers need this many undead? Between the mine, bridge, and here, they probably had enough to take over a small country. Granted, we'd turned some of them to ash, but given the semi-trucks and now this, the losses hardly seemed significant.

I whispered, "Turn off your lights."

The moment it was dark, my vision changed spectrums, allowing me to scan the cavern for signs of life. But as I'd already guessed, there weren't any. Which meant all we had to deal with were the undead below. That made it sound easy, but the reality was it would be anything but, since my and Hayden's superpowers were useless. And given how tightly packed the chindi were, it would be impossible to get down there to chop off their heads without being crushed to death ourselves.

I gestured down at the undead. "There isn't anyone here to tend to these things."

Cole gave me a puzzled expression. "How can you tell?"

Hayden frowned. "We can see life...and he's right. Other than the three of us, we're alone with those...things."

Kneeling, I glanced over at Cole. "Do you know if this cavern is connected to the tourist site further up the trail?"

He thought about it for a moment then shook his head. "None of the tunnels large enough for me to squeeze through do, but I can't speak for the smaller ones. Why? What's on your mind?"

I swung my pack off my shoulder and pulled out a healthy sized block of Symtec. "This."

Hayden took a step back. "Have you lost your goddamn mind?"

I wobbled my hand back and forth. "Depends who you ask."

Cole frowned. "You just carry that shit around?"

I sighed. "Considering I don't have an ounce of magical ability, I compensate by bringing guns and explosives to any given party. Sue me."

Hayden chuckled. "Christ, you are nuts." She put a hand on her hip. "So, what's your plan?"

I shrugged. "Attach a detonator to it, set the timer for ten minutes, and run like hell."

Horror filled her eyes. "I take back what I said earlier. You're not crazy, you're fucking stupid."

I rocked back on my heels. "Hey, it's a solid plan."

She folded her arms. "Only if you want to blow yourself up. Goddamn idiot. What the fuck is wrong with you?"

I stood up. "For the record, I've set a lot of these charges over the years, so I doubt this will be the one that kills me."

She groaned and shook her head. "You can teleport, you idiot. Running seems a bit stupid when you can just appear outside with loads of time to spare."

I blushed. "Ah…you can teleport. I…I can't yet. I mean, I've done it, but I haven't got a clue how to make it work when I want it to."

A snicker escaped her lips before she clamped her hand over them. It took a few seconds, but the silent laughter subsided. "Oh, okay. Ah, yeah, maybe you should hand that stuff over to me, and I'll let you two get out of here." Her lips started to twitch again as her gaze landed on me. "Sorry. I'm not laughing at you, I'm laughing *with* you."

I gestured at myself. "Does it look like I'm laughing?" Handing her the Symtec and a couple of detonators, I said, "Maybe I'll find it funny later, but right now, I just want to get out of here."

She shooed us back into the tunnel. "I know, sorry." Checking her watch, she set the timer. "You've got ten minutes, starting…now."

Taking a deep breath, I nodded. "Okay."

Dust Walkers | 139

She tapped the glass face of the watch. "This would be a good time to start running."

Cole tugged on my sleeve. "Let's go. She's got this."

I took off at a sprint with Cole close on my heels. Of course, he overtook me in the smaller places where I was forced to crawl. By the time we climbed up the rockface and out the opening, we had about two minutes to spare. We used that time to make our way over to the trail to wait for the inevitable. Not long after, Hayden appeared a bit further down the path.

She looked at her watch and turned to face the opening. A moment later, a low rumble shook the earth beneath my feet, and long tongues of flame spewed out of dozens of spots along the mountainside.

After the inferno stopped, I turned to Hayden. "It shouldn't have done that."

She shrugged. "My guess is it ignited the bat droppings, and that magnified the blast."

Cole snickered and patted me on the back. "Guess you won't have to worry about stepping in shit when you go and check on them."

Hayden smiled. "He has a point. I did set off the explosion. It's only right that you assess the damage and make sure I got them all."

Shaking my head, I said, "I don't think that'll be necessary."

Grinning, she placed a hand on her hip. "Oh, I think it is."

I glanced up at the mountain and sighed. "Then you go do it."

She folded her arms. "Nope, this isn't my gig. You're the vigil."

Cole nodded. "She's right...you are the one in charge."

It was clear I'd already lost the battle. Groaning, I let out a long breath. "Fine, I'll go. No need for either of you to bother yourselves. I've got this."

Cole patted me on the back. "Glad to hear it." He gestured at Hayden. "We'll wait here for you."

I flipped them the bird before climbing back up to the opening. The explosion had dislodged several rocks, which made the entrance we'd used earlier impassable. It wasn't until I reached the third opening that I was able to make my way back inside. While the mountains of shit may have helped fuel the explosion, there were more than a few slimy chunks lying about to hinder my progress.

Each and every step caked more of the foul-smelling stuff onto my boots. Stumbling, I put my hands out to catch myself on the nearest wall only to have my hands covered in shit...not like it mattered at this point, I was practically coated in the stuff. I was pretty sure they were having a good laugh at my expense right about now, but the joke was on them. They had to ride back with me.

Eventually, I made it to the alcove where the zombies had stood. All that was left was a mess of broken bodies, dirt, and rock. I searched the area thoroughly to ensure none of them remained intact. Finding nothing, I turned back the way I'd come, and my stomach twisted at the thought of having to wade through that again. I closed my eyes and thought about being outside. A moment later, a brilliant blue light filled my vision, and when I opened my eyes again, I was standing a few yards away from the others.

Hayden beamed. "Well done."

I flicked my hand in an attempt to shake off some of the goo. "For the record, there was still plenty of crap. But the good news is all the zombies are...well, they were already dead, so how about dismembered?"

Cole gave me a thumbs-up. "Works for me."

Hayden's stomach growled loudly. "I'm starved."

I shook my head. "There's no way we're eating while covered in walker goo, bat shit, and dirt."

She laughed. "Maybe you won't, but I sure as hell will."

Dumbfounded, I asked, "Seriously? You're that hungry?"

She bobbed her head. "A girl has to keep up her strength. Besides, do you think looking this good comes from eating salads?"

I rolled my eyes. "Fine, but can it be to go?"

Cole appeared a bit horrified by the idea. "You two aren't eating in my truck."

I folded my arms. "I don't think us eating in it will be any worse than me sitting in it."

Dust Walkers | 141

He shook his head. "Hell no, that's never going to happen. You reek…and is that blood?"

I glanced over at my shoulder. "Probably—I did just traipse through a bunch of corpses."

Cole's hand came up in an instant. "Nope, you're sitting in the back until we can hose you off."

I rolled my eyes. "Okay, fine, but—"

His stance shifted, and he folded his arms. "No buts. You're riding in the back, and we're not eating in my truck."

"Christ, okay, but if we're going to stop somewhere, let's make it quick. I don't feel like making a public spectacle of myself any longer than I have to."

Hayden shrugged. "I'll do my best, but it'll depend on how fast they can get the food out."

My shoulders slumped. "Fine, but could it be an outside venue? I really don't feel like getting us thrown out."

He nodded. "That I can do."

It took us about half an hour to work our way back to the truck, and another twenty-five to get to Grants.

18

Thankfully, lunch was uneventful, but instead of going back to the trailer to let me shower, we stopped at the Gems Home Center. Unsurprisingly, the owner completely refused to speak with us...well, he refused to talk to Cole and myself.

Hayden, on the other hand, was an entirely different story. The old man was tripping all over himself attempting to flirt with her. When she asked to see the surveillance footage from the day Mikhail bought the containers, he was forced to admit the cameras didn't work. He only left them up as a deterrent to thieves, which put us back at square one.

Yippee.

By the time we made it to Highland Meadows, it was nearly sundown. I was sitting in the back, watching the highway fall away behind us, nearly half asleep. We'd turned onto the road that led out to Atsidi's place when the sound of screeching tires filled the air. The truck jerked to the left, causing me to skid across the bed and slam into the opposite sidewall.

As we careened into the ditch, I slid forward, my head hitting the cab hard enough to make me see stars. After we came to a jarring halt, I quickly squeezed my eyes closed and shook my head, trying to

Dust Walkers | 143

regain my senses. It worked. Don't get me wrong, I still hurt like hell, but the pain could wait till we'd dealt with the problem at hand. I pushed myself upright and launched myself over the side with Hayden appearing right beside me.

The tire marks on the highway belonged to Charles's Cadillac, which was a little shocking since I hadn't thought the heap capable of attaining enough speed for that to happen. Before I could make sense of what was going on, both front doors popped open, and Charles stumbled out. A moment later, I was forced to do a double take when a man who looked remarkably like Mikhail stood, seemingly more than a little pissed off. As Mikhail was missing his soul, not to mention a good portion of his chest, I doubted it was him. Nevertheless, Mikhail's doppelganger leveled his pistol at the truck and fired three rounds through the windshield.

Hayden darted toward him and slammed her shoulder into his gut, pinning him against the car. Before Charles could lift his revolver, I blinked across the distance, appearing behind the man. I twisted his gun arm around behind him, snapping it at the wrist and elbow. His scream was cut short when I smashed his skull against the roof of the car with a nasty crack. Honestly, I wasn't sure he'd wake up from that, but getting shot at really pisses me off.

Cole still wasn't out of the truck, and for a split second, I was torn between helping Hayden or checking on him. But she looked to be holding her own against her opponent. I rushed over to find Cole gripping his left shoulder. Blood oozed between his fingers, and his head lolled forward as he started to lose consciousness. After scrambling down the embankment, I reached for the door, only to be thrown back several feet when a brilliant silver light materialized between the two of us. The glow became brighter and brighter, until I had to shield my eyes. A few moments later, the brilliance faded, and an elderly woman stood there with a disapproving look on her face.

She turned, calmly strode over to the truck, lifted the front end, and pushed it back onto the road. A moment later, she popped the door and placed her hand over Cole's wounds as she kissed him on the forehead. "Rest, my son."

144 | KEN LANGE

Cole's eyes closed, and he leaned back against the seat. A metallic thread wrapped around him, cocooning the unconscious man in seconds.

She held out her hand to me. "I am Na'ashjéii Asdzáá, and you are?"

There was a crash of a body impacting the car behind me, and when I turned, the new guy was lying on the ground, bleeding from several cuts. His chest was still moving, which meant he was alive—probably more than I could say about Charles at this point.

Na'ashjéii Asdzáá cleared her throat. "It's impolite to ignore an old woman when she's speaking to you."

Returning my attention to her, I stammered, "Ah, sorry...I'm Gavin Randall. Pleasure to meet you."

She nodded and flicked a finger at Cole. "I'd appreciate it if you'd stop trying to get my son killed."

I shook my head. "That wasn't my intention."

Her grin told me she'd tried to make a joke. "The young are always so serious."

"Sorry."

Na'ashjéii Asdzáá's gaze fell on Hayden. "It's good to see you in your true form."

Hayden approached us cautiously. "Do I know you?"

Na'ashjéii Asdzáá waved her hand, and the world seemed to stop. "Not anymore, but you did." She pointed at the eerily still night sky. "I played my part in helping you and the Star Born tilt the scales against the mad god." A tear ran down her cheek. "Because of the two of you, the rest of us have a glimmer of hope now... Thank you."

Hayden stammered. "You...were there?" Na'ashjéii Asdzáá nodded, and Hayden took another step closer. "Then you have the answers I've been seeking all my life."

Na'ashjéii Asdzáá offered her a weary smile. "I do, but you're not ready for them."

Hayden blinked, and her expression hardened. "I've waited for so long, and I've done everything that's been asked of me—"

Na'ashjéii Asdzáá cut in. "That's true, and we're all so very grateful,

Dust Walkers | 145

but knowing too much, too soon, could tilt the balance." She offered Hayden a sad smile. "You've only won the battle, not the war, and with what's coming, none of us can risk altering the plan."

Hayden opened her mouth to argue, but Na'ashjéii Asdzáá bowed her head. The gleaming light returned then she was gone, allowing time to resume its natural course.

The man lying beside the car groaned. I promptly walked over to him and slammed my boot into his face.

Glancing back at Hayden, I frowned. "Who is this Star Born?"

Her expression faltered, and she suddenly found the pavement at her feet very interesting. "It's not my place to tell his story." She lifted her gaze to mine. "But I have a feeling you'll figure it out soon enough, or he'll tell you."

I wasn't happy with the answer, but we had a wounded companion, a prisoner, and, most likely, a corpse to deal with. Shaking my head, I said, "That was weird as hell."

She nodded. "Yeah."

Leaning over the side of the truck, I reached into my pack, pulled out a couple of zip ties, and got to work restraining our prisoners. Hog-tying them before tossing them into the back of the truck might've been overkill, but I'd rather be safe than sorry, or possibly dead. It took us a minute to maneuver Cole into the passenger seat, before Hayden drove the truck down the drive. That left me to move the heap that Charles called a car off the road and park it out of sight on the other side of Atsidi's place.

Once that was done, I carried Cole into the trailer and placed him on his bed. When I stepped out, Hayden was strapping each man into a metal patio chair. She'd tossed their IDs on the ground at their feet. Curious, I stooped over to pick up the new guy's wallet. His name was Timur Ivanov, and given his birthdate, he was Mikhail's twin. Guess that explained why he was here trying to kill us. When Hayden opened his shirt, there was an exact copy of the tattoo we'd found on his brother. The Grim desperately wanted to perforate the bastard, but with a great deal of effort, I resisted the urge.

I gestured at Charles. "Guess that thick skull of his is useful after all."

Hayden arched an eyebrow. "And how's that?"

"He's still alive."

She chuckled. "Barely. You did a number on him."

I shrugged. "He was trying to shoot us, so you'll have to forgive me if I don't get all broken up about it."

Rolling her eyes, she said, "I wasn't implying that you should, but it's going to be difficult to question him with a concussion."

Irritated, I nodded. "True."

My previous employment hadn't required me to be gentle, which meant that survivors were frowned on. This was something I'd have to get used to. But with Assholes-R-Us in play, it made ignoring my instincts difficult.

It was a good half hour before Timur stirred. Granted, he was blindfolded, gagged, and strapped to a chair, but he was awake...for the moment. He let out a muffled scream then what I guessed was a string of Russian curses. After about twenty seconds of that, Hayden strode over and slapped him hard enough to topple the chair onto its side.

She knelt beside him and whispered, "Shut up already."

Timur grunted out a fairly audible, "Fuck you."

Her boot clipped his forehead. "In your dreams."

The impact was enough to make him stop mouthing off. I took the liberty of sitting him upright before Hayden decided he wasn't worth talking to and caved in his skull. It hit me that her impulse to kill the man was probably as strong, if not stronger, than my own. In which case, I was sure Timur had no idea how bleak his immediate future was going to be if he didn't cooperate.

Over the course of the next three hours, we learned that there were three more in his team: Diana, Erik, and Artur. They'd moved the plethora of undead to somewhere in the badlands, and there were still more strongholds we hadn't discovered. But when pressed on that, the Black Circle, or the Onyx Mind, he refused to give us anything further.

It was getting late, and if Charles was going to make it to sunup, he would require a hospital. That took some doing since Hayden had to remake her Ignatius construct before returning to Scotland. There, the Ulfr could tend to their wounds while they were being questioned.

That left me on my own to check in on Cole, who was still recovering. The cocoon had started to fade, leaving him encased in a soft, glowing silver light. The only thing I could gather without burning out my retinas was that he wasn't bleeding any longer. Other than that, I hadn't a clue.

19

February 28th

When I fell asleep, the first Reaper was quick to overtake my dreams.

We were standing on the edge overlooking the abyss once more when an enormous double-headed axe materialized in front of me. It had deep grooves along the blade that wound their way to the face, creating a Celtic shield knot in its center. A moment later, four symbols shimmered into view: the crossed swords of my office, a glowing red scarab with gold highlights, the interlocking triangles I'd seen at Viktor's place, and the wagon wheel design we'd found on Mikhail's chest... Except this one was slightly different, with ten spokes instead of nine, and the extra one didn't have a symbol carved into it.

There was a gentle wind, and the Celtic knot glowed. The four symbols leaked power—red from the scarab, blue from the triangles, black from the wagon wheel, and silver from the swords. Each of these touched the axe and followed the grooves to its heart to fill the knot.

Pointing, I asked, "What are those?"

The Reaper gestured toward the axe. "The crossed swords represent you, the triangles belong to Odin, as for the scarab...I do not know." He waved a hand, and everything save the wagon wheel vanished. "This, however, is the symbol of the lich lords." Tapping two identical symbols inside, he said, "This one is repeated."

"Why?"

He sighed. "In the beginning, there were only nine, but one of them accidently created a copy of himself when he performed an unholy ritual to steal something from a dead man." He pointed at the blank spoke. "This was one of the originals. He was killed about ten years ago by the Storm Bringer, which is why it's no longer marked."

I blinked. "Okay...I wish that this made some sort of sense to me, but it doesn't. How exactly is any of this supposed to be helpful?"

He laughed. "No idea, child. I am what was, Hayden belongs to the now, and you are the future. This is your mystery to ferret out. Maybe Kur can help you."

I shook my head. "Perhaps in time, but he's been hibernating due to an injury...probably from when he was banished."

The old Reaper tapped the ring Atsidi had given me. "This will help him heal. I can speed the process along, but you won't like it."

He cupped my face in his hands and blew black mist with blue flames into my mouth. My body tensed, and Kur writhed in my mind. Pain flooded my senses, my knees buckled, and my vision narrowed.

The Reaper whispered, "There is yet much to do in the now to reach what will be."

Darkness took me, and there was nothing more to hear or see.

My head pounded, and I felt sick to my stomach as the vision faded. When I opened my eyes, I was more than a little grateful to find myself alone. The last thing I needed at the moment was people gawking at me. There was only one thing I could think of that would help with my foul mood and that was a shower. After that, maybe some breakfast would be in order...maybe.

An hour later I'd eaten, washed dishes, and gotten bored sitting there. On that note, I decided to step outside and watch the sunrise. Just as the first rays of light broke over the horizon, the Aquila on my shoulder burned. The shock of it caused me to stumble back against the trailer. I clamped my hand over my shoulder and massaged it, hoping the pain would subside. After a while it either felt better or I'd adjusted to the discomfort.

Frustrated by all the weirdness over the last few days, I made my way inside to check on Cole. When I stepped into his room, he was sitting up in bed, trying to check his shoulder.

I motioned for him to sit back. "Take it easy. If you're that curious, I'll find you a mirror."

He grimaced. "Did you fix me up? Is that something you can do?"

Not knowing what to say, I shook my head. "That wasn't my doing." Hesitantly, I sat on the edge of the bed. "It was your mother. Na'ashjéii Asdzáá showed up and placed you in a cocoon of sorts."

Cole poked at his new scars and winced. "My mother? You're sure it was her?"

I shrugged. "Ah, that's what she said, and I'm inclined to believe her. I mean…there aren't a lot of people who'd pop in out of nowhere, save your life, and chastise me to boot."

Irritation flashed in his eyes as he let out a long breath. "Well, that's just fucked up."

That was a weird response to finding out that your mother was who you thought she was, and that she'd saved your life. "Huh?"

His expression was one of joy, and sadness. "Nothing…I just can't believe you met her before I did." Running his hand over the three fresh scars, he sighed. "But I'm grateful for her help."

I grinned. "Me too." Gesturing for him to follow, I got to my feet. "Come on, I'll make you something to eat."

Cole shook his head. "That's not going to happen today." He gently tapped the new tissue. "They may be sealed, but it took me half an hour to work my way into this position. I don't see me walking anywhere unless it's really necessary."

Rubbing my side, I nodded. "Being shot sucks. I had four slugs pulled out of my chest twenty something years ago, and it still bugs me from time to time."

He stifled a laugh. "Thanks for the pick-me-up."

I gave him a big smile. "No worries. Sit tight, and I'll bring you something to eat."

Before I could get food out of the fridge, there was a knock at the door.

I turned, picked up my pistol off the counter, and aimed it at the door. "Come in."

While it was doubtful the bad guys would announce themselves first, I wasn't taking any chances.

The door swung open to reveal Hayden. She jerked back and gave me the finger. "Seriously? That's how you're going to greet me after the night I've had?"

I shrugged and returned the weapon to its holster. "Sorry, but I don't want to get caught off guard."

She nodded. "Fair enough." Blowing out a long breath, she shook her head. "Apologies for being grumpy. It took a lot longer to get those two assholes stowed away with the Ulfr than I'd anticipated."

I gestured at the table. "Take a seat and fill me in while I cook."

After making breakfast, I brought Cole some food. A few minutes later, I was about to step out and assess the damage to the truck when there was another knock. Glancing over at her, I leveled my gun at the door and stepped over to open it.

To my great surprise, Alexander was standing there with a big smile on his face. His voice was gruff, and the bags under his eyes said he hadn't gotten enough sleep. "Morning."

Blinking, I put the weapon away. "Not that I'm unhappy to see you, but how did you find me?"

Alexander tapped the Aquila on his wrist. "When I stepped through the gate this morning, I realized I didn't have a clue where you were staying." He shrugged. "That's when this little fella started to burn like hell. Once it cooled off, it guided me here."

Hayden glanced between me and Alexander. "I've seen a lot of shit in my life, but I've never seen a brand guide someone. How is that possible?"

I shrugged. "No idea." Stepping back, I waved him in. "Hayden, this is Alexander, a friend." Turning to Alexander, I said, "And this is Hayden. She's a new acquaintance, and someone who can be trusted."

She stepped over to the counter and held out her hand. "Pleasure to meet you, but I'd still like an answer."

I nodded. "So would I."

Alexander squeezed through the opening and shook her hand as he made his way over to the table. "Bear with me. I know this is going to sound nuts, but after my mark stopped burning, I just had this sense of which way to go. The closer I got to this place, the stronger it became."

Turning to Hayden, I pulled up my sleeve to reveal the Aquila. "Mine started burning just after sunup."

He nodded. "That's when I arrived."

Hayden frowned. "I don't get it. Isn't that just a brand?"

I shook my head. "Nope, it's one of the marks of my office."

She leaned over and ran her nail along the lightning bolts. "Okay, but...how?"

Pulling my sleeve down, I rolled my shoulders. "No clue. If I had to guess, there's more to the coin than even I know."

She arched an eyebrow. "And just what do you know?"

Kur whispered in my mind, *"If she'll reveal the name of the Star Born, you can tell her about me."*

Puzzled, I asked, *"Why, what does that matter?"*

Kur's tone carried hope. *"Because the Star Born is allied with the Idunn."*

Understanding came to me. *"Your old allies in the war against the Svartálfar and Álfheimr."*

He squirmed in my mind. *"Yes. Our only hope of standing against them is with the aid of the Star Born and the Idunn."*

I folded my arms and eyed Hayden. "I'll be only too happy to share if you tell me who the Star Born is."

She bit her lip and shook her head. "I've already said it's not my place to tell you about him."

I nodded. "You did, but that's the deal."

She frowned. "Then hold onto your secrets for now."

Kur sighed. *"Patience, we will learn the truth one way or another."*

An uneasy feeling came over me. *"How did you guide Alexander here. That was your doing, wasn't it?"*

"It was. I think it's in your best interests that your centurions are able to find you in times of need. This is only one of many abilities bestowed on you and your people."

Grimacing, I said, *"I'm not sure I like it."*

Kur chuckled. *"If you don't wish to be found, that can be arranged, but given the current situation, I thought it prudent to guide him here expeditiously."*

"You were right, but maybe give me a heads-up next time."

His form wriggled inside my brain. *"I'll try."*

I had to wonder what other special gifts I'd unknowingly given to those under the centurion banner. It would be pointless to ask Kur at the moment; I sensed he'd gone back to sleep.

Hayden thumped my chest. "You all right?"

I nodded. "Yeah, sorry…I was distracted."

She snickered. "No shit."

Alexander shrugged. "He does that. I've gotten used to it."

Shaking my head, I asked, "Are you two finished?"

Hayden shrugged. "For now."

The three of us moved into Cole's room, and I spent the next hour going over what had happened since we last spoke—minus the part where Hayden was actually a drag king who'd adopted the Ignatius persona for the last fifteen thousand years. I did my best to gloss over the fact that she was a reaper, and I was a flaming ice monster.

It turned out Alexander's team wouldn't be here for another two or three days, so it was just the four of us. Well, three; Cole was in no condition to get around. Thankfully, Alexander had rented a massive SUV when he arrived, which meant we wouldn't be crammed into the front seat of a truck that had recently been ventilated.

Cole sat up in bed. "Would you guys mind if I got some rest? I'm still pretty whipped."

I nodded. "Yeah, sorry about the intrusion."

He gave us a dismissive wave. "It's cool. If I'd wanted you gone, I would've said something."

Hayden grinned. "I think you just did."

He chuckled. "Yep. Now get."

Alexander stopped at the front door and asked, "Do you think you could show me where Mikhail was staying?"

"Sure. Let me grab a few things first."

Hayden checked her watch. "While you two do that, I need to check in on Timur and the boy."

I frowned. "You literally just got back from there. Can't that wait?"

She shrugged. "I'd rather do it now while we have some downtime. Who knows when that'll happen again."

Reluctantly, I agreed. "True."

Hayden gestured at Alexander. "Besides, it looks like you'll be in good hands while I'm gone."

Alexander beamed. "Absolutely."

She grimaced. "Plus, it's been several hours, and there's a chance the others may have some new information for us. They are very efficient."

Alexander furrowed his brow. "Who's *they?*"

Her eyes glowed blue. "The Ulfr."

He blinked. "Seriously?"

She nodded. "Yeah."

He turned to me. "Let her do her thing. If anyone's going to get something out of those two, it'll be the Ulfr."

There was no point arguing; she was going regardless. "All right, but could you hurry back? I'd like to have all hands on deck if things go haywire."

She sighed. "I'll do my best, but it really depends on what happens when I get there."

I frowned. "All right."

Without another word, she walked back to my room and disappeared in a ball of flame. Alexander and I made the half-hour trek into the desert to Mikhail's home-away-from-home. Now that we weren't in a rush to fix the truck, I took my time and sifted through the place with a bit more care. Alexander, on the other hand, went straight for the bed, pulled off the blanket, and stepped outside.

I searched through the books in shelves made out of wine crates. Most of them were written in Russian, but there were a few popular fiction pieces in English. The box near the center was loose, and with a little coaxing, I was able to remove it. There, in a cubbyhole carved into the rock, was a black, leather-bound, handwritten journal.

Paperclipped inside were a few photos of Mikhail, Timur, and three others I didn't recognize. After leafing through several pages, it became clear that this wasn't a diary, but possibly notes for a book... or so I hoped.

The main character was a woman named Jade Baker. She was an oddity, being the child of one of the lich lords and an archangel, with the powers of both. According to the myth he was creating, this was an impossibility somehow turned reality.

She was sent to America to be reared by a prominent member of the Onyx Mind. A special team of handpicked individuals were sent to ensure not only her safety but her education. This was where Mikhail had inserted himself into the story as the leader of this group. The first few chapters were a little off-putting, but then things turned downright disturbing, as he developed an interest in the young girl.

Unable to read any more of that section, I skipped ahead several pages to Jade's twenty-sixth birthday. She'd been sent to Siberia to train under Ke'lets, one of the nine lich lords. After spending ten years under his tutelage, there was a great battle against the mad god that ended with Ke'lets's murder at his hands.

Leave it to a necromancer to make a lich lord out to be the good guy in this scenario.

Anyway, that was when Inna, the leader of the Onyx Mind and Jade's honor guard, scooped her up, saving her from certain death. Once they were safely away, Jade returned to America, where she was to stay until she was ready to take her rightful place as one of the nine.

There were hundreds of pages of notes, sappy passages, and a shitty love story that would've made even the worst romance author cringe. The further into the text I got, the more deranged Mikhail's writings became. While I couldn't be certain, I really hoped this was a work of fiction. Because if this were real, the necromancers had themselves some sort of messiah on their hands, and that would make them all the more dangerous, which was the last thing anyone needed at the moment.

Alexander tapped me on the shoulder. "Did you find something?"

I shook my head. "Not unless you're into bad fiction." Stuffing the book into my bag, I gestured at the small treasure trove of personal items. "There are some photos, drawings, and other stuff in here that may prove useful in the long run. But for now, it's mostly junk." I gestured at him. "How about you? Did you turn up anything useful?"

He held up the blanket. "I think so."

I eyed the filthy thing. "Care to elaborate?"

Tossing the bedding onto the cot, he said, "There were at least five different people staying here."

I glanced over at the bed, and sighed. "And?"

He tapped his nose. "If I get close to one of them, I'll be able to identify them."

That made me laugh, even though I couldn't say why. "Okay...and how does that help us?"

Shrugging, he sighed. "Maybe we should visit Grants and let me poke around to see if I pick up their scent."

It wasn't like I had any better ideas. "Sure, why not?"

20

Not having a clear target made things difficult. Which meant that we spent the morning stopping at every gas station and grocery store we came across, hoping that Alexander would randomly pick up a scent he could track. That went about as well as you'd expect. It was nearly noon, and we were both grumpy, hungry, and more than a little tired.

We'd passed a sign for La Puerta Steak House earlier, and that was when I'd decided that we were having steak for lunch. Mainly due to the fact I wasn't up for another round of fast food. No matter what Hayden said, I couldn't see how clogging my arteries with grease was a good idea. According to the sign, they were just opening, and the lot was empty, so I pulled up next to the long, tan adobe building. It had a strange, lifeless vibe to it, but the brightly colored mural on the front promised steaks and booze...and as they said in Jerry McGuire, they had me at steak.

The downside to sitting in one place for any length of time was that it significantly raised our chances of meeting one of Lewis's thugs. Which was a bad thing, because with the necromancers, a pile of undead, and God knew what else, my nerves were wearing thin. Hopefully, Alexander's rental would make finding us a bit tougher, and maybe allow us to eat our meal in peace.

Even so, I warned Alexander about the possibility, and asked him to refrain from killing anyone. With him working on little to no sleep for the last several days, he agreed to try, but couldn't promise anything.

Unfortunately, my expectations of the place were met the instant we walked in. Everything inside the restaurant was straight out of the late seventies, with mauve chairs, dim lighting, and poorly done dark wood paneling. I guess for a steak house in the middle of nowhere, it wasn't that bad, but it certainly wasn't my style... Call me crazy, but I liked being able to see what I was eating. To make matters worse, the hostess kept us waiting several minutes before seating us, even though the place was empty.

After she left us, I scanned the menu and settled on a ribeye, baked potato, and an ice tea.

Setting the menu aside, I sighed. "At least we'll have something in our stomach for the second half of the day."

Alexander chuckled. "Don't be so quick to give up. If they're in town, we'll find them."

I put my elbows on the table and shook my head. "But what if they're not?"

He shrugged. "One way or another, they'll turn up. I've got two of my best trackers joining us." Leaning back in his seat, he shrugged. "On my best day, I'm little more than an amateur compared to either of them."

"If you say so." I held up my hand to cut him off and greeted the waitress. "Ma'am."

She grinned. "Afternoon, gentlemen. My name is Estella, and I'll be your server today." Her eyes flicked over me and landed on Alexander, and her smile grew. "What can I start you off with today?"

He pointed at the back of the menu. "I'll take whatever's on tap, and a water."

Estella turned to me. "And you?"

With a finger, I edged the menu toward her. "Ice tea."

She frowned and scribbled it down. "I'll be back shortly with your drinks."

Alexander chuckled. "She doesn't seem impressed with your drink selection."

I smiled. "She'll get over it."

Estella arrived a couple of minutes later with our drinks and took our orders. After the first steak, I was still hungry and ordered a second. I guess hanging around Hayden was doing weird shit to my appetite. But it was unfair to blame her; I'd already noticed a steady uptick in my food intake over the last several months, but this was getting ridiculous.

I'd just paid for our meal when the door opened, and an attractive brunette stepped in. She was all of five-two, thin, and she wore a grim expression as she strode toward the bar. Normally, she wouldn't have caught my attention for more than a second or two, but the way Alexander's eyes fixed on her told me she was important.

He glanced over at me and nodded. "She was there."

I returned the gesture. "Okay." Getting to my feet, I motioned for him to do the same. "Time to go."

His eyes narrowed, and he whispered, "What?"

Frowning, I gestured at him to hurry up. "Come on. I'm not going to accost the woman in public, for God's sake."

I pulled out my phone and took a couple of photos before walking out to the parking lot. In an attempt to keep from spooking her, we moved our SUV down the block and waited. Fortunately for us, she'd ordered takeout and was carrying several bags of food. I kept a respectable distance between us when she made her way across town to a tourist trap...I mean art studio-slash-memorabilia shop on Route 66.

We found a place to park in a lot across the street. It may not seem very discreet, but the four lanes of highway between us took care of that. It was our good fortune that a large plate glass window spanned most of the front. The small woman carried the bags in and was quickly out of sight. A few minutes later, the asshole who'd shot me stepped into view.

I leaned my forearms against the steering wheel. "Well, it appears we've found all of them."

Alexander cocked his head at me. "How can you be sure?"

I pointed at the man through the window. "See that blond guy there?"

He nodded. "Yeah."

Touching the sore spot in the center of my chest, I said, "That's the dick who tried to put me down the other day."

His eyes narrowed as he turned back to the man. "You killed one, captured another, and we've spotted two more...that leaves one left to find."

I frowned. "Yeah, and I'm betting they're inside." He gripped the latch, and I held my hand out to stop him. "Wait...I want to see if they go anywhere."

Grumbling, he asked, "Why?"

I leaned back in my seat. "I find it hard to believe they're here randomly. And if I'm right, there's a good chance they'll lead us to whoever's in charge."

Alexander glanced up and down the street. "Really? You think they're answering to some sort of criminal mastermind...in this shit-hole of a town?" He shook his head. "It's way more likely they're just a bunch of assholes using this town as a cover to build their undead army."

"You might be right, but there's no harm in waiting to make sure." He didn't seem convinced, and I sighed. "Tell you what, let's just hang out for a while, and if they don't give us something by morning, we'll do it your way. Sound good?"

Frankly, I wanted nothing more than to go over there and stomp their faces in. But that wouldn't solve the problem, especially if they had helpers, or answered to someone else.

About twenty minutes later, my phone rang. "Hello?"

Hayden's voice was full of curiosity. "Where did you guys duck off to?"

I kept my gaze locked on the window of the shop. "We're following up on a couple of leads. How about you? Are you back?"

She grunted. "Not yet, but I can be there in seconds if needed."

Dust Walkers | 161

Nodding, I massaged the side of my head. "We're fine for now. Please tell me that they've given you something useful."

She blew out a long breath. "Not a lot. From what I understand, they're there to oversee a project called Dust Walkers."

I groaned. "In other words, zombie central."

She chuckled. "Pretty much. Other than that, he hasn't given us much of anything else."

Closing my eyes, I asked, "When should we expect you back?"

Her voice tensed. "I'm not sure. There's a situation in New Orleans that needs tending to—which means I could be a bit. But in the meantime, this is my direct number. If something comes up, call me, and I'll be there."

I glanced at the phone, and sure enough, her number was there. "Okay, no problem."

She ended the call.

Turning to Alexander, I said, "Guess we're on our own for now."

Concern crossed his face. "She is coming back, isn't she?"

I nodded. "Yeah, but it might be a day or so."

Shortly after dark, I managed to convince him to go check on Cole and pick up some stakeout food on the way back. It left me on foot, but I was hoping I'd be able to keep up with them if they left the place. Then again, they may've spotted us and used an atman stone. In which case, we were all sorts of screwed.

Eventually, those fears were put to rest when the brunette made her way to the front to lock up and turn off the lights. The wait was the toughest part of any job, but I'd had plenty of practice. I would've normally spent the time finding the best way in and out of the situation after I pulled the trigger or extracted the target. Tonight, however, I was bored.

My greatest hope was that this wouldn't turn into a massive firefight, because I had no idea how to fight necromancers. Walter had been my first, and last, experience with them, as far as one-on-one went. And his fight had been a little anticlimactic because he'd used his stone to try to murder me. All that did was allow me to drain him and his stone of power. I didn't know how I'd stack up against one of the members of the Onyx Mind. While magic wasn't an issue, I wasn't so sure about necromancy.

As it stood, specters could hurt me, even if it was temporary, and zombies had all my powers stumped. I wasn't sure what other abilities a necromancer might possess, so it was difficult to plan accordingly. Nights like this made me miss the times when all I had to worry about were things that went boom.

It was a little after ten when Alexander showed up with plenty of snacks and a bedroll in the back, ready to take the next shift. But I insisted he get a few hours shut-eye. A little after one, he woke up, and I crashed out.

21

March 1st

What little sleep I'd managed had been fitful at best. My dreams were fragmented, and I couldn't tell if they were figments of my imagination or Kur's memories. The only positive was that I'd been comfortable. Which was probably more than a little messed up. Who in their right mind preferred the back of an SUV to a soft, cushy mattress?

I rolled back the blanket and crawled up to tap Alexander. "You want to catch a few more zees?"

He shook his head. "Nah, I'm good for now, but thanks."

I patted him on the shoulder and snaked into the passenger seat beside him. "Anything new?"

Alexander yawned. "Nope. As far as I can tell, they haven't left the building." He leaned forward, placing his elbows on top of the wheel. "I want to get a closer look once they open."

That idea didn't sit well with me. I didn't want to send him in there on his own against three uber powerful necromancers, and I couldn't go with him since one of them knew my face. In the end, that left me little to no choice in the matter.

"As much as I dislike the idea, it's probably our only option." Turning to him, I sighed. "You realize you'll be on your own over there, and it'll take me several seconds to get to you if things go wrong."

He nodded. "I know, but we need to find out what we're up against."

I wiped the last of the sleep out of my eyes. "Agreed."

His tone was entirely too cheerful given the hour. "Besides, with a little luck it'll go smoothly, and I'll be in and out before they're the wiser."

Choking back a chuckle, I shook my head. "Yeah, right...when's the last time something worked out that well for you?"

He rolled his shoulders. "There's always a first time."

I covered my mouth to stifle a yawn. "Sure there is."

His laughter was deep and rich. "Has anyone ever told you you're a real grouch in the morning?"

I grunted and rubbed my face. "The time of the day has nothing to do with it."

Alexander grinned. "Oh, and what does?"

Thumbing over my shoulder, I stretched. "Waking up...especially after a shitty night's sleep."

He frowned. "Yeah, you were tossing and turning back there."

My cheeks burned. "I was?" He nodded. "Sorry about that."

He shrugged. "No worries. But back on topic, if anything goes wrong, you can be across the street in less than a minute. I should be able to hold my own until you get there."

I gestured at his phone. "Keep the line open when you go. That way I don't have to guess when things go sideways."

He nodded. "Sounds simple enough."

Leaning my head against the seat, I chuckled.

It was nearly half an hour before the brunette strolled in from the back, turned on the open sign, and unlocked the door. That was Alexander's cue. He got out of the vehicle, dialed my number, and dropped his phone into his shirt pocket before walking across the street.

Dust Walkers | 165

All I could do was answer the call and wait for whatever came next. Yeah, it was exactly as exciting as it sounds. Not only did I get to watch him cross the four-lane highway, there was also the audio to go along with it...which was mostly his mobile jostling around in his shirt pocket.

Lucky me.

A chime sounded when the door opened, and silence quickly followed. A few seconds later, a soft female voice with a thick Russian accent came across the speaker. "Good morning. Is there anything I can help you find?"

Alexander's voice was pleasant. "Maybe...I'm looking for something for my niece as a housewarming present. Could you suggest something she might be interested in that isn't too big...or small, for that matter."

The woman spoke again. "*Da*. I'm Diana, and you are?"

He cleared his throat. "Alexander."

Diana's voice grew louder. "Pleasure to meet you. Are you looking for a painting or a sculpture?"

His voice was flat. "What would you suggest?"

She clucked her tongue. "Hmmm. Does she have a lot of floor space?"

There was rustling as the phone scraped against his shirt. "Not really."

She chuckled. "Painting... If you'll come this way, I have just the thing." There was silence for a few seconds then she spoke again. "Erik."

A male voice responded. "*Da?*"

Diana spoke again. "Would you bring me Artur's latest work?"

Erik mumbled something I couldn't understand then said, "He isn't going to like you selling that one."

Her voice hardened as she started speaking Russian. "The other one is across the street in the SUV. Get Artur and bring him to me." In English again, she said, "Sorry about that. It sometimes takes a bit of convincing for my people to do what they're told. But I'm sure you'll love this piece. It's a sunset in the desert near an abandoned stretch of Route 66."

Apparently, the jig was up, and had been for some time. But why had they waited for us to make the first move? Whatever the reason, it only left me a couple of options: stay put and let her lapdogs fetch me, or pop across the street and start raising nine types of hell. The way I saw it, I had the advantage here as they didn't realize that I knew what was up. With that in mind, I took option one.

Alexander was quiet for a moment. "That's an awfully big gun for such a little lady."

She laughed. "Sit tight. We'll have your friend here in a moment."

Her goons were coming up behind the truck. Which was an interesting turn of events since I hadn't spotted them crossing the road. I ended the call and stuck the phone in my pocket.

The blond knocked on the driver's window. "Out."

Ah, this was Erik. Good to put a name to the man who'd tried to kill me. After opening the door, I kept my hands up in the hopes that he wouldn't shoot me in public—I wasn't sure there was enough time for my armor to materialize if he opened fire at close range.

I stepped out of the vehicle and held up the keys. "Mind if I lock up? I'd hate someone to steal it while we're inside."

Erik rolled his eyes. "Not like you'll need it again, but sure, go ahead."

I clicked the button on the keyring, and the doors locked. "Thanks." Gesturing across the street, I sighed. "If it's okay with you two, let's take the direct route. I'm not going to try to get away."

The other man, who I was guessing was Artur, was a few inches shorter than me, but made up for that by being massive everywhere else. He sauntered up to me and gripped my shoulder. "Try anything stupid, and I'll snap your neck. Understand?"

I nodded. "No problem."

His eyes narrowed. "Keep your mouth shut."

They perp-marched me across the highway and in the front door, which Erik quickly locked. He pointed toward the back of the shop. "Keep going."

We made our way through the main shop, past the storeroom, and into the next building, which I hadn't realized was connected. This place was a cross between a boardroom and den. I guessed that the upper level contained their sleeping quarters, but they probably weren't going to give me a tour of the place to confirm.

Alexander was on the far side of the room, casually leaning against the wall. His gaze fell on me, and he smirked at Diana. "My boss is here. Any questions you might have can be directed to him."

She huffed. "You're making yourself more expendable by the second."

He snickered as he pointed at me. "I'm a betting man, and my money's on him."

Diana sneered. "You expect me to be afraid of Lazarus's latest lackey? His first one wasn't much of a challenge, and I suspect this one will be less so."

Anger coiled inside me, and I glared at her. "You knew my predecessor."

She scoffed. "I had the pleasure of being there when Chandra cut Naevius's throat and ripped out his soul to be used as her plaything."

Could this be the same necromancer Viktor had told me about? Well, there was an easy enough way to find out.

Keeping my gaze on Diana, I asked, "Would that be Chandra Raghnailt?"

The lot of them stood stock-still, which more or less confirmed that it was.

Diana was the first to regain her composure. "How do you know that name?"

I smirked. "I've got a friend who'll be thrilled to find out she's still alive."

Erick roughly shoved me toward Alexander. "Answer the question."

Diana held out a hand to stop him. "Easy now. He only thinks he knows something about us. Truth is, he's fishing."

Chuckling, I shook my head. "Then I'm one hell of a fisherman."

Her eyes narrowed. "Oh, really?"

"Yep."

She gestured for me to continue. "Then tell me, what is it that you think you know?"

I suppressed a snicker. "More than you'd like, I'm sure."

She rolled her eyes. "Such as?"

"If I had to guess, you three are part of the Onyx Mind, which is a subset of the Black Circle."

My only hope here was to piss them off enough that they'd slip up and make a mistake that would give Alexander, and me, a chance to escape.

Her cheeks darkened as she stared daggers through me. "You are very well informed. It puzzles me, though. If you know who we are, why would you ever agree to step into the same room with us?"

I shrugged. "Curiosity, mostly."

Artur snorted. "Are you stupid?"

Cocking an eyebrow at the man, I said, "That's a bit like the pot calling the kettle black."

He stepped forward and swung, trying to take my head off.

Alexander was quicker and caught the big man's fist. "In case no one's told you, it's rude to interrupt."

When he shoved Artur backward, Diana and Erik lifted their weapons. On instinct, I raised my arm, and a massive sheet of ice formed between us. The bullets slammed into the barrier, which cracked, but held. When they'd emptied their clips, I charged Diana. Alexander slammed his knee into Artur's groin as I passed. I pushed my hand forward, and the makeshift shield shattered, sending shards of ice hurtling toward Erik.

Putting all my weight behind the blow, I hit the tiny woman square in the chest, knocking her off her feet. My body bent weirdly when a bloody Erik drove his shoulder into the side of my chest, tackling me. He scrambled atop me, alternately hammering one of his fists into my gut and the other into my kidney—over and over again.

There was a thunderous roar when Alexander shifted into his werebear form. One swipe from his enormous claws tore long gashes across Artur's chest.

Dust Walkers | 169

Diana's voice became panicked. "Goddamn it, he's a fucking were-beast." She held out her hands to create a massive sphere of fire. "Erik, move."

He rolled off me, and I got a good view of Diana's malevolent smile as flames sped toward me. Her celebration was a bit premature as the ball of flames audibly popped and died out on impact.

I got to my feet slowly and dusted myself off. "That was stupid."

Diana stumbled and fell against the wall, panting. She glanced over at Erik and Artur. "Time to go."

Erik threw something dark at Alexander, and he staggered back, but otherwise seemed unharmed. But it was enough for Erik to grab his friend, clasp something in his hand, and vanish. Unfortunately, Diana did the same.

I slammed my fist into the bar, shattering the marble countertop. "Goddamn it!" Glancing over at Alexander, I managed to rein in my anger. "Are you all right?'

After transforming back into his human form, he nodded. "Yeah...I think so."

I gestured upstairs. "Let's see what we can find. Maybe something up there will tell us where they'll be holed up."

Alexander grimaced. "You don't think they're gone for good?"

"No, they've invested too much into collecting a small army of zombies." I rubbed my forehead. "They'll be close by...but that can be a relative term. Especially considering how wide open the area is."

He nodded. "Agreed." Gesturing at the pool of water on the floor, he said, "That was pretty damn cool...no pun intended."

"Thanks."

It took nearly an hour to search the place. Oddly enough, we found a couple of blow torches and a bunch of other heavy equipment used to work on railroads. On top of that, we acquired five laptops, all of which were encrypted, and two floor safes—locked, of course. If we ever managed to get into them, we might have something to work with. For now, all we had were possibilities.

22

After searching the building, Alexander cleaned up, moved the SUV, and dropped the shades to ensure we weren't disturbed. I thought it was strange that with all the equipment in here, they didn't have an alarm system, or cameras to keep an eye on the place. I guess when you summoned the spirits of the dead and played with zombies, thieves weren't your main concern.

While Alexander checked the perimeter, I dialed Hayden in the hopes she'd be able to lend a hand. Instead, I was greeted by her voice-mail asking me to leave a message...which I did, reluctantly.

Alexander meandered over to the fridge, popped the door, and scrounged around.

Tucking my phone away, I got to my feet. "What in the hell are you doing?"

He shrugged. "I'm hungry."

Dumbfounded, I blinked. "Have you lost your goddamn mind?"

He shook his head. "No...I'm just really hungry."

Holding my hands out, I said, "You need to slow down, stop thinking with your stomach, and realize that you're digging around in a necromancer's icebox."

Dust Walkers | 171

He didn't move for a full five seconds then he stood up and eased the refrigerator closed. "You know what, that's a damn good point."

I pulled out my wallet and grabbed a hundred. "Tell you what, go get some food, check on Cole, and come back when you're done."

Apprehension crossed his features. "I'd rather not leave you alone."

Shaking my head, I sighed. "Unfortunately, or perhaps fortunately, I don't think they're coming back to claim the shop."

His voice tightened. "How do you figure that?"

My gaze locked onto his. "You ripped open one guy's chest, another is a bloody mess, and Diana's totally freaked out by you...or maybe weres in general."

Alexander's frown deepened. "You noticed that?"

I nodded. "Yeah, it was impossible to miss. You worried her way more than I did."

He laughed. "Maybe at first, but that quickly changed."

I took a seat at the bar and handed him the money. "It really doesn't matter anymore. Fact is, if they were coming back, they would've been here by now. Besides, if they do show up, I don't need a vehicle to escape."

He furrowed his brow. "That's what you say, but—"

Brilliant blue flames surrounded me, and I was suddenly across the room. "But nothing."

Alexander didn't move for several seconds then, slowly, he found his voice. "How is that even possible?"

I arched an eyebrow. "You just witnessed three people vanish on the spot, and you weren't fazed. But the moment I do something similar, you're all freaked out. What's up with that?"

He shook his head. "You warned me about their atman stones. But whatever you just did was different." He shivered. "It was like the world warped around you, and just before you reappeared, I knew where you'd be."

That was new.

I ran my hand over my head. "Come again?"

His features contorted as he searched for the words. "I don't know how else to say it, other than it felt like reality was being reshaped, and when you moved from where you were to where you are now...I could almost feel the movement. It's some seriously creepy shit."

Resting my chin in my hand, I considered the implications. "If it's that pronounced, why hasn't anyone else said something about it?"

He shrugged. "No idea. Were they weres?"

I shook my head. "No, but—"

Holding out his hands for me to stop, he continued, "That's probably why. If you haven't noticed, we aren't like the rest of the folks in the Archive. It's one of the reasons we were enslaved."

I jerked my head back in revulsion. "Because you're different?"

He nodded. "Yeah." Seeing the blank expression on my face, he continued. "No one truly understands our abilities, or how they allow us to shift from one form to another."

Curious, I asked, "Do you have any idea how it happens?"

He laughed. "Not a clue, but I do know we're more sensitive to certain types of magic, such as nature and blood. The type of energy a person taps into to use those is something we can...feel, or sense, or however you want to describe it."

I leaned my forearms against the counter. "Do you think that's why necromancers are afraid of weres?"

He shrugged. "I don't think so."

I gestured for him to continue. "But...?"

Alexander grimaced. "But...what I'm about to tell you is probably going to sound a little out there."

Stifling a laugh, I gestured around the room. "It can't be any more farfetched than a bunch of high-level necromancers hanging out in the middle of nowhere creating a zombie army. Seriously, whatever you've got to say has to make more sense than what's actually happening in this town."

He wobbled his hand back and forth. "Debatable."

When he realized I wasn't going to let it go, he told me about his grandfather, the secret keeper for his clan. Once Alexander was of age, his grandfather told him that there would come a time when the weres would wage war against the Children of the First. It was his grandfather's belief that weres were the foot soldiers needed to end the war between the darkness and the light since they were immune to their powers. Because of this, angels, necromancers, and their ilk couldn't harm weres directly—which was most likely the reason they were afraid of them.

Alexander shrugged. "Of course, it isn't as if I've had an opportunity to test my grandfather's theory until today."

I nodded. "Well, whatever Erik threw at you earlier didn't do shit to you, so maybe your grandfather had a point."

Rolling his eyes, he said, "Maybe, but let's not put too much stock in the ramblings of an old man."

"I'm betting he's onto something." Pointing at the door, I grinned. "But now that you know I'll be fine, would you mind grabbing us some food and checking on Cole?"

He leaned against the wall. "Yeah, I can do that. What are you going to do in the meantime?"

I held up my phone. "Wait for a call back."

He pushed off the wall. "I hope she gets in touch soon. With her connection to the Ulfr, she should be able to access the laptops and maybe get us a few more boots on the ground."

The first part, yes, but the last was never going to happen as long as she remained in her true form. "That's the plan."

He grinned. "All right. Is there anything you need me to do before I go?"

"Actually, there is."

It took us a few minutes to gather up some of the more miscellaneous items, such as handwritten journals, several notebooks, and a bunch of ledgers. In addition, I had him take two of the laptops with him as insurance. Not that I didn't trust Hayden, but if I was wrong and Diana and her crew showed up randomly, there wouldn't be any time to save this stuff.

Once Alexander took off, I puttered about the place in an attempt to keep myself busy. I was on my third trip through when Hayden finally called.

I did my best to be upbeat when I answered. "Hello."

She sounded exhausted. "You phoned?"

"Yeah, we met three more of the gang."

She instantly sounded more awake. "I'm taking it you survived the encounter."

With a great amount of effort, I didn't say, "Duh," but there was no mistaking the sarcasm in my voice. "No, this is my voicemail."

She grumbled, "Don't be an ass."

I let out a low groan. "Fine, but just so you know, that is my specialty."

She yawned. "Great, just what I need: another smartass in my life."

I chuckled. "You sound wiped."

Hayden was quiet for a moment. "I am… It's been a long few days."

Sitting up in my chair, I sighed. "Sorry about that. I'll get to the point. After our encounter with the three remaining assholes, we found a bunch of their stuff…including several computers, but they're encrypted. Do you know anyone who could hack them?"

She snickered. "As a matter of fact, I do."

"Fantastic. Mind if I ask who it is?"

With a laugh, she said, "Viktor has a guy. His name is Mir, and he's a genius when it comes to technical stuff."

Finally, something was going in my favor. "All right, now all I have to do is figure out how to get it to him while the information is still useful."

The exhaustion returned to her voice. "Not to worry. I'm on my way back to New Orleans, so I'll pop in shortly and pick them up." That was great news. "Is there anything else?"

Smiling, I sat up straight. "Yeah, there are two floor safes here I can't crack. Any ideas?"

She blew out a long breath. "Have you tried shattering them?"

"Huh?"

Her tone was slightly amused. "You know, freeze the lock and hit it with a hammer?"

Now that she'd said it, the solution was pretty freaking obvious. "Ah, that never crossed my mind…"

She snickered. "Try it, and I'll be there soon."

Ending the call, I walked to the storage closet, pulled a hammer out of the toolbox, and knelt by the first safe. I placed my hand on it, closed my eyes, and focused on freezing the metal. There was a loud groan, and when I opened my eyes, a thick layer of frost coated the entire room. Shrugging, I raised the hammer, slammed it into the dial, and the door cracked. I grabbed the handle and slowly pulled it open.

Inside were some old pamphlets about temporary housing for the Jackpile-Paguate Mine. According to the paperwork, there was a doctor on staff, a bowling alley, tennis courts, pools, etcetera. These were supposed to convince people back in the fifties, sixties, and seventies to come work for them to pull ore out of the world's largest open-pit uranium mine.

There was also a ledger for what they called a spur, an additional nine miles of railroad track laid to move the ore to the main line outside Grants. If they were trying to repair that section, it would explain the heavy equipment. Why would they bother, though?

I opened the second safe and was rewarded with a portable drive, but nothing else. That would have to be placed with the other three laptops to be decrypted by Viktor and his people. There was a bright flash of orange, and Hayden appeared.

Arching an eyebrow, I asked, "You've been here before?"

She shook her head. "Nope, but you're here. As I said, a strong connection to another person is just as good as having been somewhere before."

I nodded. "Good to know." Gesturing at the electronics, I said, "That's the stuff I need Viktor to look into... Are you sure he'll be able to help? I thought he had some sort of problem."

Hayden grinned. "He did, but my alter ego helped him solve it."

Intrigued, I asked, "So, Lamia's no longer an issue?"

She frowned. "No, but her death did bring up a whole new set of problems."

I grimaced. "What's that supposed to mean?"

Her expression hardened. "Are you familiar with what makes a vampire a vampire?"

I frowned. "Not exactly. From what I gather, some sort of parasite takes hold and changes a person."

She blinked. "Well, for someone claiming not to know exactly what's going on, you actually do. Yeah, it's a combination of the Idunn, an organic nanite, and a parasite that's more machine than biological...but the technicalities aren't that important. What is, however, is that when Lamia died, it caused a catastrophic failure in the others like her... So, while vampires like Ms. Dodd weren't affected—because they aren't directly linked to Lamia—the rest died the moment she did."

Leaning forward in my seat, I rested my elbows on my knees. "You said the Idunn were involved?"

She nodded. "You've heard of them?"

I wasn't sure how much to tell her, but she had information I needed. "Only by name. So, they're nanites?"

Her eyes glowed blue as she nodded. "They are. Why do you ask?"

Shrugging, I said, "Just trying to put a puzzle together. Someone once told me a story about a war the Idunn were involved in, and how the mad god used them in conjunction with a corrupted parasite in an attempt to manufacture a super soldier. In the end, all they managed was to create vampires."

She closed her eyes and shook her head. "I've never heard that story before. Who told it to you?"

I lifted my gaze to hers. "It was part of my dream the other night... the one with the first."

She huffed out a laugh. "That's an awfully specific dream about some very classified information for it not to be true."

"I suppose."

She smiled. "Seriously, whatever you were told is starting to sound less like a dream and more like reality. Is there anything else you'd like to share?"

I shook my head. "Not really. How about you?"

Hayden got to her feet. "Same..." She picked up the laptops and portable drive. "I know we've only just met, but I've got a good feeling about you." Her gaze met mine, and she said, "You asked me the other day who the Star Born is."

"Yeah, and you said it isn't your place to tell me."

She grinned. "It still isn't, but if it's okay with you, I'd like to tell him what you just told me."

I gave her a dismissive wave. "Feel free to tell him whatever you like."

She nodded and glanced around the room. "Do you have a bag I can load this crap into?"

I stepped into the storage room and grabbed a couple of duffle bags. It didn't take long before we had them filled with what would hopefully be a treasure trove of information. As it was, I'd learned that the Idunn were real and that the first had been correct about vampirism. All that should've been good news...but then there was the rest of what he'd told me. And I wasn't sure how to deal with an imminent war between beings of such power.

Still, I did my best to paint a stoic expression onto my face. "Any idea how long it'll take them to crack these things?"

She shrugged. "Not long. Is there anything else you need?"

I shook my head. "Nah, I'm going back to the trailer for a bit. A little later, I'll be heading to yet another abandoned mine not far from the one we took you to. After that, I'll let you know what the plan is."

Smiling, she said, "Okay. Stay safe."

Red flames encapsulated her, and she was gone. That left me to go check on Cole, and hopefully Alexander.

23

It was after ten when I got back to the trailer. Once we had a bite to eat, I helped Cole step outside to get some sun while we discussed what was next on the agenda. Turned out Alexander needed to return to Santa Fe this evening to pick up his people. Given how little he'd slept over the last few days, he was beat. I offered him my room to get some rest, which he happily accepted, so that essentially took him out of the equation for the rest of the day.

Cole was on the mend, but it was clear he wouldn't be in the field for a few days yet. As for Hayden, she was an unknown factor since she was splitting her time between New Orleans and here.

Which meant I was on my own for reconnaissance this evening. I wasn't keen on popping out there in the middle of the day; it'd be too easy to spot me moving in the distance. My main objective was to figure out why they wanted their own personal railway, even if it was only nine miles of track. I was hoping they didn't have enough undead to require a freight train to move them around.

Over the course of the afternoon, I picked Cole's brain for some background information. From what he said, my destination was several times larger than the Sohoi mine. For the life of me, I couldn't understand why they were using abandoned uranium mines to store their meat puppets. Was it the wide-open space they needed, or the low-grade radiation, or the privacy, or what?

It wasn't as if Grants was heavily populated, or some sort of tourist hotspot, and with Lewis's death grip on the area, I doubted they had to worry about scaring people away. Something about the way they stored their—what did they call them?—Dust Walkers had to make sense to someone, just not to me. Not yet, anyway.

I'd hoped Kur would help, but he'd been unusually quiet. Even as I tried to contact him, it was obvious he either didn't have answers or simply wasn't going to share them. I was leaning toward the not having them, since he seemed just as confused about the subject as I was. Eventually, after a lot of prodding, he took a wild guess that the necromancers were using the radiation to mask something else.

On a totally different front, Kur was worried about an unusual transmission that had originated in New Orleans and terminated somewhere outside Mexico City. According to him, the information contained within the signal was encoded on a frequency that shouldn't have existed in this world.

When I pressed him on the issue, all he managed to do was give me a headache by playing the screeching white noise inside my brainpan. It goes without saying that I didn't understand what had him so worked up. The harder he tried to make me understand, the more frustrated he became. That, and the exorbitant amount of energy he'd used to try to decrypt the information, had worn him out, so he bedded down to take another nap.

That was just great. A bunch of mumbo-jumbo from my imaginary friend. If he was right about the low-grade radiation being a cover for something, there was nowhere better suited in the world than where we were standing. Which meant that not only was the Black Circle a massive organization with its own elite forces, those who were running it were exceptionally clever. That made them so much more dangerous than I'd originally anticipated...and that was saying something.

To be honest, I couldn't fathom how they'd been able to go untold millennia without being discovered. Hell, until a few days ago, their organization wasn't even a blip on the radar. With the resources Hayden, Viktor, and Lazarus had at their disposal, that should've been an impossibility.

Another mystery was how the memories of Samuel Estes and Naevius Sutorius Marco's deaths had been erased. What power or magic did the Black Circle have at their disposal that could remove their final moments from the coin, or Kur, for that matter?

I'd searched his memories of Naevius's last few weeks. While he'd been in Hastings in October of 1066, Kur had no clear recollection of his actual death. It was becoming clear, though, that he hadn't died in the battle as everyone had been told.

No, he'd been killed by Chandra Raghnailt, and she'd torn out his soul to be used for some darker purpose. I wasn't sure if she'd intended to cripple the Archive for the next thousand years or not, but it'd certainly worked out that way.

The more I found out about these guys, the more they concerned me. My biggest worry was that they'd somehow infiltrated us. If Walter was any indication, they were close, even if they weren't actual officers within the Archive itself. I'd have to put an end to letting prefects induct their own vigils until I could be sure. The thought had no more than crossed my mind when four denarius coins formed in my palm.

Well, shit.

Then again, I had an idea for one of the coins. Pocketing them, I stepped into the trailer to find Cole seated at the table and a freshly showered Alexander cooking. I slid into the seat across from Cole. "How are you feeling?"

He grumbled, "Like I got shot."

"Fair enough." Pausing, I took a deep breath. "Remember the first night we met?"

His eyes narrowed. "Yeah...what about it?"

I placed my palm on the table with the denarius underneath it. "You and your lovely wife Danielle commented that it was nice to have a vigil who understood your point of view."

Cole nodded. "Uh-huh. What's your point?"

I slid the silver coin toward him. "We need someone who can serve locally. My better half pointed out recently that I couldn't keep doing this job on my own forever. And I thought you might be interested." Shrugging, I said, "It's obvious you already go out of your way to look after the area. If you accept the offer, you'd have the authority to back it up. Besides, it'd be nice to have another vigil who'd have my back."

Alexander placed a plate in front of each of us. "This should be interesting."

Cole didn't move for a long moment. Eventually, his gaze traveled from the coin to me. "Are you serious?"

"Absolutely."

He glanced back at the coin. "Why me?"

I folded my arms. "Because it's becoming apparent that there's a major threat to our survival out there, and I'm not entirely sure the Archive hasn't been infiltrated."

He hesitated. "And if I refuse?"

"Then you do, but I sure as hell could use the help." Thumbing over at Alexander, I said, "He can't do all the heavy lifting for me, and I think you're the man for the job."

Cole's expression hardened. "Are you sure?"

Sitting back in my seat, I nodded. "Yeah, I am."

He bit his lip. "Okay, I'm in. What do I need to do?"

I pointed at the coin. "Pick it up. It'll do the rest."

Cole's hands shook as he reached for the small piece of silver, and he tentatively picked it up. In that moment, a sharp pain shot through my temple, my eyes slammed closed, and my body went rigid as agony tore through me.

After what felt like an eternity, the world around me gradually brightened, and when my vision cleared, I wasn't in the trailer any longer. Instead, I stood atop a massive disk of onyx that was floating in the vastness of space. A large crack ran the breadth of the thing, but other than that, it was unmarred.

Dozens of galaxies swirled in the distance, and a small moon hung over the far edge. A few seconds later, Cole slowly materialized beside me.

I reached out and caught him when his body crumpled. "Easy. Are you okay?"

He gasped for breath and pulled himself upright as he glanced around in awe. "Where are we?"

I shook my head. "Not a clue."

A thunderous roar shook the platform, and when I glanced up, there was Kur. He was massive, his black, armored scales were backlit with blue light, and his eyes glowed violet.

He circled us once before softly touching down in front of us. In his true form, he towered hundreds of feet overhead. He tilted his head, and his gaze landed on me as he smiled, revealing gleaming silver teeth. "It is good to see you again." He turned his attention to Cole. "I am Kur, and it's a pleasure to make your acquaintance."

Cole bowed. "Likewise. Any idea where we are?"

Kur chuckled. "This is a junction between your reality and my own. It doesn't have a name, as far as I know."

Clearing my throat, I frowned. "Why are we here?"

Kur ducked his head to keep me from breaking my neck as I looked up at him. "Because this is the only place we can truly speak to one another. In my current state, it's so very difficult to form words, but here...it's as if I'm whole once more." He cut his eyes at Cole. "When you added his power to the collective, I was able to pull you both here to have this conversation in person."

Cole glanced between the two of us. "So, you two know one another?"

I scrunched up my shoulders. "Sort of, but this is our first face-to-face meeting."

Kur winced.

Stepping forward, I reached out for him. "Are you all right?"

A low growl escaped his lips. "No, my injuries are making it difficult to maintain this reality, which means we can't stay here long...but know this: there are more from my realm here. If what the other Reaper said was true, it would appear the Svartálfar and Álfheimr gifted the Children of the First abilities from my realm, which makes them more dangerous than you realize."

Shrugging, I asked, "What can I do to help?"

He staggered to the side and stifled another moan of pain. "Fill the

*remaining positions within the collective. Once it's complete, I can assist you
in my true form and help drive these polluted avatars of the Svartálfar and
Álfheimr from this realm. And if we're able to find the Idunn, they'd likely
lend their strength to the cause and hopefully ensure our victory. That's why
it is so important that you find out what Hayden knows. Our very existence
could hinge on what she's hiding from us."*

"Okay then...so no pressure." I held out my hand to stop him from
pounding the point home. "She did say she'd talk to the Star Born, and maybe
with his help, we can find the Idunn." Curious, I asked, "Why are the
Svartálfar and Álfheimr coming to this world? I thought this would be more
of a punishment for them than a prize."

*The realms controlled by the machine gods of light and darkness filled my
mind. A massive wave of shadowy energy emanated from this world and
traveled through a portal that had been created by the Dvergr—the machine
gods version of blacksmiths crossed with engineers and scientists—back into
their realm. At first it was ignored, but in time, Kur determined that this one
act had caused the corruption of the machine gods. The resulting war had
depleted their resources and lives, not to mention driven them mad. With
their realm in tatters, the only thing left was to find a new one to inhabit...
and that was the world of organics—the very source of the original
corruption.*

*The vision vanished, and I was on my knees with Cole doing his best to
keep me off the ground.*

He leaned over. "Are you all right?"

I shook my head. "I'm not sure."

*Kur groaned, and his form wavered. "I cannot keep us here any longer. Be
well, and stay safe."*

The world rushed back to me, and I screamed.

It took a moment to realize we were still seated at the table. Blood
ran from Cole's nose and eyes, but otherwise he appeared to be okay.

He grimaced. "That was unpleasant."

I was weak and wanted nothing more than to vomit, but otherwise
fine. "No shit."

He glanced down at his hand to see the vigil symbol carved into
his flesh. "Looks like it's official."

"Apparently." Hesitating for a moment, I said, "I'm sorry about that. If I'd known..."

His laughter was dark. "You would've still done it."

I couldn't disagree. "Probably."

He patted my arm. "I think it was the right decision, and a small price to pay if you're right about the necromancers possibly infiltrating the Archive."

Alexander handed me a towel. "You two look like hell. Maybe you should clean up before you eat."

Getting to my feet, I passed the cloth to Cole. "Here. I'll be back in a minute."

I headed for the back and stopped in the bathroom. Not only was my face covered in blood, so was my shirt. I stripped, washed up, and grabbed some clean clothes before returning to the others. Needless to say, breakfast was eaten in silence.

24

It was a little after three in the afternoon when Alexander excused himself and headed off to Santa Fe to pick up his team. After our excursion to the far reaches of God knows where, Cole was exhausted. I had to help him back to his room, where he fell asleep almost instantly.

As for me, I was still itching to visit Jackpile Mine, but as I'd already decided that getting shot was a bad idea, I opted for something a bit safer. I popped back to the shop in Grants, hoping to find something I'd missed earlier. That, and I needed to make a call. If I was lucky, Viktor's guy had broken the encryption, and Hayden would have an update for me.

I made another pass of the place in an attempt to keep myself busy, and not appear so impatient. That lasted all of five minutes before I pulled out my phone and dialed Hayden.

She picked up on the first ring, but the voice that came over the line was Ignatius's. "Hello. I was just sitting here talking to Viktor about your predicament."

My hopes were lifted for a moment. "That's great. Is he able to help?"

Ignatius sighed. "Yeah, but it'll take a few days to get his people mobilized. It would seem you're not the only one with problems. Over the last few months, rival syndicates have been taking shots at one another."

I shrugged. "Why does he care if a bunch of criminals try to tear each other apart?"

He snickered. "Do you recall the shakeup in the MCC a few months ago?"

Shakeup was putting things mildly. From what I gathered, Viktor had tossed the former leader of the MCC out on his ass. "Yeah, some guy named Leonard found himself unemployed."

Ignatius chuckled. "Essentially. Thing is, when he vacated the premises, a lot of people went with him. Ever since then, he's been causing a ton of problems for a man named Nigel, who's grown tired of the inconvenience and is currently in the process of dismantling Leonard's crew. To be totally honest, it's making a mess here in town. Add to that the general spike in craziness with Lamia having been on the loose since January, and there's a lot of cleanup going on. If this situation were contained to the city, I'd be more inclined to let Viktor's people handle it, but as it stands, a lot of my forces are tied up as well. Which means all hands on deck at the moment. Sorry."

I sighed. "In short, I'm on my own for a bit."

He lowered his voice, sounding slightly embarrassed. "I'm afraid so. If we could do more right now, I promise we would."

Plopping into a nearby chair, I grumbled, "I get it. This is just one more fire in the middle of an inferno."

He laughed. "That's as good a way of putting it as any. Look, I've got a couple of things to do here, but with luck, I'll be back in a day or so. Hopefully by then, Mir will have accessed the laptops." He paused for a moment and took a deep breath. "Apparently, the encryption is unbelievably complex."

I clasped my hand over my forehead. "Of course it is."

"Anything new to report on your end?"

I shook my head. "Nothing solid yet, but there's a lead I want to track down."

He paused. "You got help?"

Dust Walkers | 187

Shrugging, I said, "Probably, but they won't be available till later this evening. But honestly, once things start going bad, I'd like to have you around for backup."

His voice dropped to a near whisper. "I know, but this is just as important right now. You'll have to trust me on this. I'll be there as soon as I can."

I thunked my head against the wall. "Fine, but I can't promise that the zombie apocalypse won't start without you."

Ignatius groaned. "I know, but you're not the only one dealing with apocalyptic shit."

Sitting upright, I sighed. "I'll take your word for it."

His voice turned serious. "If something comes up, try to get a message to me."

The situation didn't make me happy, but there wasn't anything I could do about it. "I'll do my best. Talk soon."

I ended the call and stuffed the phone in my pocket. Then the chime of the front door opening sounded through the back of the house.

Well, that couldn't be good news for me.

A soft female voice called out, "Don't get twitchy. I've come in peace."

Not recognizing the woman, I unholstered my pistol and made my way to the stairs. "Not that I don't believe you...but I don't. Would you mind moving very slowly to where I can see you?"

She stepped into view with her hands held out in surrender. "Good enough?"

It took me a second to place her, and then I remembered the young woman who'd been at the Grants when I first arrived. "Jessica?"

She nodded. "Yeah."

I waved for her to put her hands down. "Okay...what are you doing here?"

"I came to see you." She pointed at the bar. "Do you mind?"

Stepping back, I shrugged. "Be my guest."

Jessica knelt and pulled one of the panels away then there was a sharp click as she flipped a switch. "Good. Now we can talk in peace."

I facepalmed myself. "Christ, how many others know I'm here?"

She shook her head. "No one. I hijacked the feed shortly after things went south between you and the others." Pointing at the pistol, she said, "Mind putting that away?"

If what she said was true, she'd done me a favor, and if it wasn't, it wouldn't take a second to put a bullet between her eyes. I holstered the weapon and gestured at the chair next to her. "The obvious question is why you would do that, and why you even have access to this equipment in the first place."

Jessica grinned. "Short answer, I'm not a fan of Diana and her crew...what's left of them anyway. I'm guessing you're responsible for that."

I frowned. "Yeah, but I'm still confused. How are you involved with them?"

Her tone turned hard. "Look, it's a long story, but they, along with 'my dad' and his brothers, seem to think I'm the second coming, or some shit." She glanced up at me and smiled. "I'm not, but they sure as hell believe it."

"I don't get the air quotes. Isn't Lewis your father?"

She growled. "No." Taking a deep breath, she calmed herself. "Sorry, but that freak has been telling me and everyone who'll listen that he's family...and his nut-bag mother isn't much better."

"Huh. I'm surprised he has a mother. He seems like the type who would've killed her at an early age."

She shook her head. "Ruth's far too crafty to let something like that happen."

I blinked. "Wait...Ruth Miller is his mother?"

She nodded. "Yeah. And she's a blood witch on top of being a necromancer, which just makes her that much crazier...and probably evil to boot."

I gestured for her to continue. "Okay...ah...think you could back up a little and tell me what's going on?"

She checked her watch and sighed. "Sit. This is going to take a second."

I did, and she sat on the sofa across from me. She leaned her

Dust Walkers | 189

elbows on her knees and started talking. When she was a little girl, she'd believed the story that her mother had died during childbirth, and that Lewis had raised her on his own. He'd dedicated his life to educating her in all things, especially the art of necromancy and combat. When she turned twenty-six, Lewis sent her to Russia to learn from one of the masters of the craft, Ke'lets.

At that point, I started reconsidering the journal I'd found in the cave.

When that ended in violence, she'd been sent back to Grants, but something Ke'lets had told her made her believe that Lewis wasn't her father and that her mother was still alive.

Irritation flashed in her eyes. "Not that I know who they are."

I held up a hand to stop her. "Were you close with Mikhail?"

She looked queasy for a moment. "Not really...but he was obsessed with me. The only break I got from his *adoration* was when he was tending the herd out by Highland Meadows."

I frowned. "Ah...I've got a book you need to read. There are parts of it you won't like, but maybe something in there will help you find your real parents."

Jessica's gaze hit the ground. "I'd be very grateful."

The idea of telling her that her father was a lich lord and her mother an archangel made me uncomfortable. "I'd reserve judgment until you read it."

Jessica nodded. "I have a request."

I gestured for her to continue. "What's that?"

She lowered her voice. "When this is all over, I'd like to disappear." Grimacing, she fought back tears. "I'm not asking for help with that part. I just want you to let me go. Can you do that?"

I blew out a long breath. "I'd certainly like to, but—"

She held up a hand. "Before you finish that statement, I have something to offer in trade for my freedom."

I shook my head. "Please, I'm not trying to bargain with you. But understand, I have a job to do, and while you seem innocent in all this...it would be a bit careless on my part to just let you walk away."

Jessica frowned. "I understand, but what if I find out where they're holding their massive undead army?"

Now, that was one hell of a choice: avoid a major conflict with an undead horde, or hope for the best and tell her no.

"Fine, but—"

She got to her feet and handed me a card. "My number's on the back." I gave her one of mine, and she pocketed it. "I need to get home... Oh, John's gone missing. It's a safe assumption that he's going to try to kill you and your friends at his first opportunity."

I walked her out. "Good to know. Thanks."

She grinned. "You're welcome." Turning to me, she said, "Try to stay alive."

Patting her on the shoulder, I said, "I'm sure it'll all work out."

Trusting a stranger wasn't something I was accustomed to doing, but she had warned me about John, and she did seem genuinely interested in my wellbeing...even if she had an ulterior motive for it.

25

It was just before dusk when I got back to the trailer to check on Cole. Unfortunately, my intrusion woke him, so I spent the next several minutes going over what Jessica had told me. He was just as shocked as I'd been to learn that Ruth was Lewis's mother.

Shaking his head, he sighed. "I can't believe that woman is their mother...especially since she only moved to town about ten years ago. Maybe she's from Canada too."

"Huh?"

He leaned back in his chair. "That's where the Grants came from— or at least that's where they were before moving here back in the 1800s." Glancing up at me, he grimaced. "If I'd given it a little thought, I probably could've pieced this all together."

I arched my eyebrow. "What do you mean?"

Cole gestured at the door. "Think about it. They have this place on lockdown, which means nothing happens here without their approval. The only thing that doesn't really fit is the flesh-walker."

I let out a rueful chuckle. "Really? As sickly as John looks, I would've laid money on it being him."

He frowned. "I have to admit, the thought did cross my mind for a second, but there's something about that scenario that doesn't feel right."

When I craned my neck, it snapped a few times. "If you say so, but it doesn't really matter in the end."

Cole furrowed his brow. "Why not?'

I shrugged. "Because he's neck deep in this necromancy bullshit, and the law is clear when it comes to that."

He nodded. "You make a good point."

I got to my feet, and Cole held out a hand to stop me. "Where are you going?"

Gesturing outside, I said, "It's curious that they know where we're staying but haven't bothered to come visit us in person. In fact, the closest they've come to us is Atsidi's driveway, and I'd like to know why. I'm going to search the property and see what turns up."

He rubbed his chin. "True—but what do you expect to find out there?"

I rolled my shoulders. "No idea, but I'd like to walk the perimeter to make sure we're not being lulled into a false sense of security."

He gave me a thumbs-up. "Probably a good idea. Let me know what you find."

"Back in a bit."

With that, I stepped outside and walked toward the edge of the property. There I found an intricately carved corner post, and I knelt to inspect the massive piece of silver inlayed with a number of unusual glyphs.

Kur whispered in my mind, *"This is the language of my people."*

A tingling sensation ran through my fingers as I touched them. *"These?"*

Their power seemed to soothe him. *"Yes. It's been so long since I've seen such beauty. Atsidi is a talented and well-versed man."*

"How can this be the language of your people? I thought you were from another dimension or something."

He laughed. *"I suppose that's as good a way of putting it as any. As for how it can be...I don't have an answer."* The ring Atsidi created for me warmed. *"I'm not sure how it's possible, but it would seem Atsidi has an unconscious connection to my people."*

I got to my feet. *"Has something like this happened before?"*

Kur sighed. *"It has... Long ago, we were contacted by the Telchines."* His voice became distant. *"Against the council's better judgment, the ruling body of the Svartálfar and Álfheimr allowed the Dvergr to forge tools to be sent through the portal."*

"Why would they do that?"

His tone dropped. *"I'm unsure...but in exchange for the Dvergr's help, the Telchines were required to build an altar. Think of it as a gateway between realms. Later, the Svartálfar and Álfheimr used this portal to banish their enemies...like me."*

I sighed. *"I'm sorry."*

His voice dropped to a near whisper. *"Thank you."*

By the time I'd finished walking the property, I'd found a total of nine of the silver posts. According to Kur, the glyphs would prevent anyone who wasn't invited from crossing the threshold. A very helpful trick, and one that explained why the attacks had taken place on the road.

All in all, it took me about an hour and a half to make my way back to the trailer. When I stepped inside, I found Cole sitting at the table.

Gesturing at him, I asked, "What are you doing up?"

He shrugged. "Got my beauty rest, I suppose." Tugging his shirt to the side, he pointed at the scars. "It seems I did some healing as well."

I leaned over to get a closer look. "Your mother's work?"

He shook his head. "I don't think so. My money's on the coin."

Kur squirmed inside my head. *"It was the least I could do, considering the odds we're facing."*

"It was...or so I'm being told." Standing upright, I shook my head. "I had no idea it could do that."

When he moved around in his seat, he winced. "I'm not back to one hundred percent, but I'm not bedridden anymore."

I smiled. "That's great news."

There was a knock at the door then Alexander pulled it open and stepped inside.

Leaning to the side, I asked, "Where are the others?"

He grinned. "Don't worry. I dropped them off at the shop in town. I figured this place was already a little crowded."

"Good point." Keeping my gaze on Alexander, I pointed at Cole. "Would you mind staying here while I go check on something?"

Alexander didn't move. "If it's all the same to you, I'd like to tag along."

I sighed. "Thing is, we've got some new information. Do you recall the three brothers I told you about?"

He nodded. "The assholes who think they run this place?"

Letting out a small groan, I closed my eyes. "Yip, the very same. It seems they're neck deep in this shit, and one of them has gone rogue."

He scowled. "All the more reason I should go with you."

I shook my head. "No, it's not. I can take care of myself, but Cole's still hurt, and leaving him alone before we know what we're up against seems a bit...I dunno...stupid."

Grumbling, he said, "But—"

My tone hardened. "This really isn't a request."

He growled and folded his arms. "Fine, but could you make it quick? There's something in this place that makes me edgy."

"You and me both. All I'm going to do is check out another mine and see what's there. Then I'll be right back here. Promise."

Alexander flipped me the bird. "You're a royal pain in the ass. I hope you understand that."

I smirked. "I've been called worse."

Not long after, I figured it was late enough to make my way to Jackpile Mine without getting myself shot.

26

It was nearly dark by the time I reached the outskirts of the mine. Once I found suitable cover, I reached into my pack and pulled out a pair of binoculars. After nearly a minute of scanning the rugged terrain, I located their base of operations in the southwest corner of the pit. From what Cole had said, all the structures built by the Anaconda Copper Company were demolished years ago.

But that was hardly a deterrent for a bunch of whacked-out necromancers—they'd taken the liberty of erecting a temporary structure made of tin. They'd positioned themselves a few dozen yards away from a set of newly restored tracks. It appeared they'd put the equipment I'd found in the shop to good use. Sitting atop the rails was a modern locomotive with three container cars behind it.

The oversized oaf, Artur, was hobbling from one car to the next, ensuring that the padlocks on the doors were secure. He was sweating profusely, and his chest was wrapped in bandages. Apparently, the wound Alexander had given him hurt like hell.

Good. With a little luck, Artur's injury would turn toxic and he'd die.

It took him several seconds to work up the courage to climb the ladder to speak with the conductor. After Artur disembarked, the train slowly pulled out and headed south toward the main line. I really didn't want to think about what they were transporting, because the only thing that came to mind was zombies.

Artur lumbered off toward the metal structure, opened the door, and disappeared inside. Given its poor construction and lack of amenities, they couldn't be happy about being forced out of town. Their inconvenience was hardly my concern, though. My main worry was how to get closer without being spotted. After I'd run through a half-dozen scenarios in my head, the door opened. Artur, Erik, and Diana made their way to the old SUV parked around back and drove off.

That was fortunate...unless there were more of them inside, but it was a risk I was willing to take.

When no one else exited the building, I climbed out of my hidey-hole and hiked over. I stopped at the small loading dock but found nothing of interest. Turning to the building, I shrugged, took a deep breath, and approached with caution.

With the way my week was shaping up, it wouldn't be out of the question to find that the place had been rigged to blow.

That feeling doubled when I put my hand on the knob, and it turned. How polite of them to leave the place unlocked for me. Hesitantly, I pushed the door open and let myself in. I had to say, it was a lot nicer inside than I'd assumed. There were two sofas against the far wall, three sets of bunk beds on the next, and a table in the center. It wasn't much, but it was better than the cave they'd been staying in out by the bridge.

Unfortunately, there wasn't anything of interest in here either. This was clearly just a staging area. All I found in the foot lockers was a generic change of clothes that would've fit almost anyone...except maybe Artur. Hell, the only thing that even resembled a clue was the whiteboard on the wall that had today's date and the number seven hundred and fifty-two on it. I guess that settled how many zombies they'd pulled out of the mine the other day. Fantastic.

Irritated at the lack of anything helpful, I stepped outside to see the last rays of the sun dip below the horizon. A moment later, I was

Dust Walkers | 197

hit by a vomit-inducing stench that sent a chill up my spine and made my skin want to crawl off my body.

Kur writhed through my mind, intensely alert.

There was the sound of footsteps behind me, and I turned to find John Grants standing at the far corner of the building. Maybe it was a trick of the dying light, but I could've sworn his skin bubbled for a second…maybe two.

He smiled. "Good evening, Gavin."

I nodded. "John."

Craning his neck from side to side, he shook his arms. "You know, it was very kind of my brother to offer you a chance to leave. You really should've taken him up on it. But not only did you ignore his request, you went and harassed our mother."

There was a weird energy in the air, and it made my stomach twist in on itself. "I'm pretty sure the message I sent with your brother's lackeys was clear. I don't answer to you, and I'll leave when I'm done. Not a moment before." Shrugging, I said, "As for your mother…I'm starting to think you three mama's boys are still attached at the nipple." I cracked my knuckles. "Where is the hag anyway? I'd like to pay her a visit once I'm done with you lot."

He twitched as he took a half step forward. "Careful, boy."

I smirked. "Why—I've already discovered that the three of you are necromancers."

John grinned. "Figured that out, did you? Congratulations. Would you like a gold star?"

Cocking my head to the side, I sighed. "Christ, you're stupid. You do understand that I'm a vigil, and admitting to the practice is an automatic death sentence…right?"

The whites of his eyes glowed yellow, and his voice became husky. "I understand the Archive's law." His fingers elongated into talons, and his stomach growled. "But since they're irrelevant, and I'm so very hungry…you'll understand if I don't concern myself with such regulations." His teeth stretched out into fangs. "Be a nice boy and don't fight. The adrenaline makes the meat taste funny."

Kur whispered, *"Wendigo."*

With his transformation nearly complete, he sprinted toward me as he morphed into an emaciated, nightmarish creature. Hardened shadows wrapped around me as I sidestepped the grotesque thing. He was quick, turning on the spot and raking his nails across my shoulder blades.

My back erupted in agony, and a tingling sensation shot down my arms to my hands. While the armor had kept me from losing my spine, it hadn't stopped the pain. The blow left me off balance, ready to puke, and dizzy. Falling forward, I tucked my shoulder in and rolled back to my feet.

There was enough moonlight overhead for me to get a good look at the wendigo. He was slightly taller than John had been, and very thin. So much so that the remnants of his clothing hung oddly off his withered frame. His skin was an off yellow, an aesthetic highlighted by his funky golden eyes. Last, but certainly not least, he was sporting some serious death-breath.

Christ.

Sweat ran freely down my torso, and when John grinned, I couldn't control the shiver that ran up my body. The moment he moved, I tugged the gladius from its scabbard but barely got it up in time to deflect the next blow, which was meant to take my head off.

He howled in frustration at having to work for his meal. I, on the other hand, was a little freaked out that the sword hadn't actually harmed the wendigo. Hell, it hadn't even chipped one of his overly long nails. While it worked wonders against the undead, and harpies, it had zero effect on this guy. I might as well have been holding a glorified toothpick for all the good it was doing me.

Opting for plan B, I pulled the pistol and fired three rounds, all of which landed dead center between his eyes. All that managed to do, though, was make him stagger back a couple of steps before he laughed and dove for me again. His long talons raked across my torso, carving out gashes in the shadow armor that quickly filled themselves in.

Even so, my chest spasmed, and it was difficult to breathe as agony coursed through me. While the blow hadn't pierced my breastplate—

Dust Walkers | 199

yet—it was only a matter of time, given his strength. At that point, it would be all over…for me. The wendigo, however, would have a nice, hardy Gavin snack.

John growled then feinted with a left swipe. I moved to avoid that, and his right landed hard against my face. My head twisted violently to the side, and my body spun on the spot before I hit the ground with a resounding thud. The resulting headache made it hard to think, or move, or generally exist.

This wasn't going according to plan. Then again, who goes into a fight wanting to get their ass handed to them?

Before I could get to my feet, he kicked me hard in the ribs, and I hit the side of the building, denting it. His leg cocked back for another go, but this time I caught it and wrenched it to the side, taking him off his feet. It took a great deal of willpower to get back on mine, wobbly as I was.

The moment he was upright, he grabbed me by the shoulders, and his bottom jaw unhinged as he pulled me closer. In a moment of pure desperation, I summoned ice and flame to replace the shadowy armor. When the ice touched his hands, he howled in pain, releasing me as smoke and mist trailed from his palms.

I slammed my fist into his dislocated jaw, snapping it and leaving a burn mark in the shape of my knuckles on his jaundiced flesh. But it wasn't there for long before his skin returned to its sallow, unmarred state. Shit, who was I fighting? Wolverine? That was highly unfair.

Blue flames coated my left hand and the onyx gauntlet my right. When he came for me this time, I caught his arm, and the blue flames licked his flesh before quickly spreading across his torso.

To my surprise, it took very little time for the wendigo to be engulfed. He thrashed about, trying to stop the inferno from spreading, but the more he flailed the stronger it became. Eventually, he stopped screaming. Then moving. And after several minutes, all that was left was a pile of white ash.

I staggered, collapsed to my knees as nausea overwhelmed me, and lost the contents of my stomach. It was all I could do not to tumble face-first into my own vomit. Rolling onto my back, I stayed there for a long while, panting hard.

Eventually, I worked up the energy to get myself onto my knees. Blue flames wrapped around me, and I was at the trailer in an instant. My vision darkened as Alexander sprinted toward me. My body rocked back, and I couldn't keep my balance as the moon came into view for a split second before I fell unconscious.

27

March 2nd

The thudding of my pulse in my head was excruciating, but that paled in comparison to trying to open my eyes. I was lying on the bed in the back of the trailer, stripped to the waist, and generally feeling like dog shit. My arms weighed a ton, but eventually I got them to move and checked to make sure all my bits and pieces were still attached. Despite my discomfort, everything seemed to be in its proper place, other than the four large welts stretching from my abdomen to my chest.

Since I was an absolute moron, I thought it was a good idea to touch them...which was when I screamed. The pain was so intense that I nearly fainted, but somehow, I managed to stay conscious. Trust me, not by choice.

Alexander was the first through the door, followed closely by Cole and Atsidi.

When I tried to sit up, Alexander placed a hand on my shoulder and forced me back onto the bed. "Easy now."

Grunting, I choked out a breath. "How long have I been out?"

Atsidi stepped into view and frowned. "About ten hours." He pointed at my chest. "Care to tell us how that happened?"

I closed my eyes. "John Grant."

Cole blinked. "He's a sorcerer. I thought you were immune to magic."

I shrugged. Or tried to, anyway. After I caught my breath, I cleared my throat. "I am. But he didn't use magic against me."

Cole folded his arms across his chest. "Then what did he use?"

The memory of John's face as he transformed nauseated me. "He changed into a wendigo."

The others went silent. Atsidi shook his head. "You must be mistak—"

Alexander cut him off. "If he says he fought a wendigo, he did."

Atsidi shook his head. "If that were the case, he'd be dead."

Alexander chuckled. "There was a time, not that long ago, when I was saying the same thing...but since then I've seen him survive a host of specters, deal with an ancient werepanther, a powerful necromancer, and a harpy. By the sound of things, we can add a wendigo to the list."

Atsidi frowned. "It would explain the marks."

Even though it was excruciating, I used all my strength to push myself up into a sitting position. "How so?"

He took a deep breath. "They injure the soul more than the flesh. They don't want to mar the meat too much, since that's what they hunger for."

Well, that made sense. The wendigo hadn't broken through my armor, but it had wounded me nevertheless. "Okay." I glanced up at Atsidi. "So they're cannibals?"

Running his hand over his head, he sighed. "From what I've read, they're like a snake, eating their victims whole."

Guess that explained the unhinged jaw.

I pointed at my chest. "Any idea how to fix me up?"

He scowled. "Not a clue."

Cole walked over to the window, pushed back the curtain, and opened it. The bright noonday sun blinded me, and my chest started to burn. When my vision finally cleared, I wished it hadn't. White smoke trailed from the welts, which were pulsating weirdly. After what had to be an eternity, weakness overtook me as I grew numb and the pain faded away. In a matter of seconds, I drifted off to sleep...or fainted, possibly.

When I awoke facedown, the sun was considerably lower in the sky, and Atsidi sat in the corner, watching over me. This time when I tried to move, my body was a little more responsive. While I was sore, weak, and generally trashed, the unrelenting nausea had passed.

Atsidi held out his hand. "Don't push yourself too hard."

Slowly, I sat up, and swung my legs over the bed. "What the hell happened?"

He grimaced. "Cole tested a theory."

My head swam slightly as I wavered on the spot. "And that was?"

According to legend, the wendigo can't step into the sunlight, so Cole thought exposure to the sun would cleanse me of John's influence—which, apparently, it had.

I rubbed my forehead. "Next time, maybe he should give me a heads-up before doing something like that."

Atsidi laughed. "Would you have agreed if he had?"

I shrugged. "I'm not sure."

He grinned. "Then it was best he did it this way. I'm not sure even you could've survived your wounds for another night."

The red marks on my chest were gone, mostly, and I was sore as shit. But I'd live.

Running my hand over my torso, I sighed. "Fair enough." I picked up my bag and pulled out a set of clothes. "I'm off to the shower, and after that, you can fill us in on what you learned from Łééchąą'í while I eat."

His voice hardened. "That'll be a short conversation."

Tempted as I was to delve further into that comment, I shook my head. "After."

I got to my feet and slowly made my way into the bathroom. Once I was clean, dressed, and reasonably presentable, I stepped out. Alexander, Atsidi, and Cole sat at the table.

Cole pointed at the food on the counter. "Take what you like. The rest of us ate earlier."

I filled my plate, sat, and ate, while the others spoke. Atsidi hadn't had any luck with his pilgrimage. Łééchąą'í's sanctuary was guarded by several large, heavily armored worms. Even after he'd rung the bells, the only one to come out to see him was an overly large, dark-skinned man with a bald head, who hadn't said anything before ducking out of sight. The long and short of that story was, we couldn't expect any help from the tribal elders.

Alexander's people—all two of them—were holed up at the shop in town. They were doing their best to recruit a few more foot soldiers, but that was looking unlikely with the conference still going strong.

As for Cole, he was back on his feet with only minimal discomfort.

Good job, Kur.

After finishing what was essentially a very late lunch or early dinner, I stepped outside and soaked in the rays of the sun. It wasn't long before I felt normal...well, nearly anyway. I couldn't shake the deep-down sick feeling in my gut. But thanks to Cole, that wouldn't last long. I hoped.

Alexander clapped me on the shoulder. "I'm about to head into town. Care to join me?"

I nodded. "Yeah, I'd like to see what type of shit storm I've unleashed with John's death."

He looked over at me. "How did you manage that anyway?"

I frowned. "Burned him to death. His ashes are probably covering half of Grants by now."

Laughing, he shook his head. "You're a very interesting man."

28

At the shop, I found Samantha Wilson, Alexander's second, and Dean Branscomb. Sam was a small woman with long blond hair, and fit hardly began to describe her. While she wasn't unattractive, she wasn't what you'd call a knockout either. All the parts were there, but they didn't seem to work well together.

As for Dean, he was average height, heavily muscled, dark haired with hazel eyes. His most pronounced feature, however, was his southern drawl. When he started rattling things off, it was difficult to understand him at times. But he was exceptionally polite, and one of the nicest people I'd ever met.

I locked the door behind me. "Evening, and thank you both for coming here to help. I know you guys have things that need to be tended to elsewhere."

Sam cracked her knuckles. "Think nothing of it. After the last few weeks of sitting on my ass and talking about my issues, I'm ready to knock someone's block off."

I laughed. "Guess therapy isn't for you."

She grimaced. "That isn't therapy. It's a goddamn bitch fest." Annoyance crossed her face. "Why didn't you just push the law through?"

Alexander chuckled. "If he had, the old guard within the Archive would've tried to skirt the new laws." He paused and lifted his gaze to hers. "If that happened, there'd be a lot of pushback from our kind. Eventually that could lead to a war...and none of us want that. Going about it this way allows them to voice their opinions and gives them the illusion of having input."

She harrumphed. "We'll see how well this works out. I have a feeling there'll be bloodshed no matter what."

I nodded. "I'm sure you're right, but in the end, I hope we'll keep it to a minimum."

Dean raised his glass in a toast. "That would be awesome."

Sam cut her eyes at him. "Not all of us are pacifists here."

He frowned. "Obviously, neither am I, otherwise I wouldn't be here, would I?" She started to interrupt, and he held out a hand to stop her. "I've fought in more wars than I like to think about. So, if there's a chance for peace...or at least less fighting, you can count me in to do whatever it takes to make sure lives aren't carelessly wasted."

Sam's gaze hit the floor. "I know, but—"

He grinned and patted her on the shoulder. "But, you're impatient."

She shrugged. "At times. I just want my kids to grow up in a world that doesn't view them as slaves."

Dean nodded. "You need to have kids first."

Grinning, she said, "You offering?"

He shook his head. "Not today, but get back to me when this is all over, and we'll see what we can work out."

She smacked his ass and winked. "That's my boy."

I smiled. "You two finished?"

Dean snickered. "You'll have to forgive her. She's wound a bit tight."

Alexander sighed. "I can't take you guys anywhere."

Sam shrugged. "What did you expect? You've had me negotiating with those knuckleheads in Europe for weeks now."

He shrugged. "A little appreciation for getting you out of there."

She folded her arms. "Please. I'll be appreciative when I cave in a few necromancers' skulls. Do you have any idea how frustrating the French representatives have been?"

Alexander rolled his eyes. "You act like you've been there all on your own. Have you forgotten that I was there with you?"

She frowned. "No, but you're always too fucking nice."

Alexander chuckled. "Okay, but I did manage to get the Germans to allow the weres full rights...and how far have you gotten with the French again?"

Sam's expression soured. "Their representative is a royal pain in the ass. Do you have any idea how arrogant the man is? I mean, it was all we could do to get him to sit down with the weres in the first place, and then to have me, a woman, discuss the details infuriated him."

He shrugged. "Maybe next time unbutton your shirt a little more, or God forbid, flirt. He's a man, for God's sake. Show some skin, and he'll do whatever you want."

She put a hand to her mouth and made a choking noise. "Please stop. You're making me ill."

Dean shook his head. "Christ, this isn't about you. It's about our entire community. Swallow your goddamn pride, and get it done."

She hung her head and nodded. "You're right. Sorry. I'll do better when we get back."

Taking a seat, I said, "Hopefully, that will be soon. Right now, we've got a host of problems."

Alexander grimaced. "That we do. We're dealing with a bunch of necromancers, a horde of undead, and," he pointed at me, "Gavin put a wendigo down last night."

Dean ran his hand over his face. "Christ Almighty. That's one hell of a list of bad guys."

I nodded. "It is, and the sad thing is I'm not sure we know who all the players are yet. This town seems to be a haven for some really sketchy characters."

He clenched his fist, and several of his joints popped. "I'm sorry to hear that."

Not as sorry as some of these assholes were going to be. Dean was one of the strongest, if not *the* strongest, in the clan. He'd never challenged Alexander for leadership since that wasn't something he was interested in. Add to that that he'd been a highly decorated soldier in several different conflicts over the centuries all around the world, and you wind up with one truly badass individual.

An explosion rocked the store, sending shards of glass, bits of steel, and chunks of brick hurtling our way. I brought up a shield of ice that kept most of the shrapnel from slicing us to pieces. When I lowered the barrier, Steve, along with several of his buddies, plowed through the shattered façade. Sam was the first to react, transforming into her were—a massive light brown bear on two legs—and charging the intruders. Steve ducked out of the way and dashed toward me. Shadows formed around his fists, and his eyes glowed red.

That was just freaking great. The last asshole whose eyes had lit up nearly killed me. But this jerk wasn't a wendigo…or at least I hoped not. Alexander and Dean transformed as they made their way to the entrance, stemming the tide of unwanted guests. That left me and my new dance partner alone to finish the conversation we'd started at the restaurant the other day.

He clasped his hands together, and the dark ichor between them solidified into a dozen specters. They were different from the ones I'd faced previously, as they appeared to be more substantial…almost solid.

The Grim wrapped around me in an instant and tore large, gaping holes out of them. Even though the attack staggered them, they remained upright…until the strength I'd absorbed from them pulsed through my body with a power unknown to me and ripped them apart in an instant. My vision turned a dozen shades of crimson, and my form expanded.

Steve stood there, dumbfounded. I slammed my onyx hand into his throat and snapped his neck. When I pulled back, I removed his soul and tore it to pieces before consuming its remains. Hovering several inches above the floor, I floated to the doorway, waved my hand, and the dozen men before us fell dead. The building groaned as their essence poured into me.

Dean was quick to react, grabbing Sam and Alexander before

forcing them out ahead of him. A moment later, the building shattered. Some of the debris fell in, but most was blown out into the desert and street. It took several seconds for me to regain control of myself and force the Grim back into his cage.

Alexander cocked his head to the side. "I'm surprised there aren't any sirens." He turned to me. "You weren't exactly subtle just then."

I shrugged. "Sorry."

He stepped out into the street and looked both ways.

Tapping him on the shoulder, I asked, "What are you looking for?"

"Cops." Thumbing over his shoulder, he said, "The last thing we need is to wind up in jail this evening." He gestured at the devastation. "It isn't like this will go unnoticed for long."

I pointed at the SUV. "You guys head back to the trailer. I'll clean up the mess and any fallout that follows."

Sam shook her head. "No way."

Glancing at her and then Alexander, I tilted my head. "I'd really rather you go with them. Trust me, I'll be fine."

Alexander put his hand on her shoulder. "Come on, let him tend to this. And if that fails, it isn't like they can hold him."

Dean's expression turned dark. "No, I wouldn't think they could."

She didn't care for the idea, but she relented in the end, and they piled into the rental. It took them a few minutes to negotiate the rubble before they were able to make their way down Route 66 to the safety of Atsidi's place.

29

It'd taken me a while to get all the bodies inside what was left of the building, which was little more than broken walls and rubble. Honestly, I was surprised the police hadn't shown up. Now that I thought about it, there hadn't been any cars in the last few hours either.

The hairs on the back of my neck stood up, and I couldn't shake the feeling of being watched. Turning, I scanned the area and found nothing.

"I know you're there. You might as well come out...or don't. But decide quickly so I can get on with my day."

Jessica rounded the corner of the shop across the street and slowly made her way over to me. Shaking her head, she sighed. "You made a mess."

Snickering, I said, "You didn't see it earlier. I've cleaned up."

She rolled her eyes. "If you say so." With a wave of her hand, she cleared the rubble out of the street. "We can't have the tourists wrecking their vehicles when the detour ends."

I blinked. "Come again?"

Jessica extended a finger toward the far end of town. "Lewis has the sheriff diverting traffic this evening, presumably to avoid any prying eyes when Steve killed you and disposed of your corpse." She cut her eyes at me. "Speaking of which, where are they?"

I gestured at the broken structure. "In there. Fifteen of them in total."

Her gaze tracked over the shattered remains. "Did they do that?"

Shaking my head, I sighed. "Nope, that was…an accident."

She grinned. "I'm really glad you're okay. It took longer than expected to get away."

I smiled. "Why are you helping me anyway?"

Placing her hand on her hip, she sighed. "Weren't you listening earlier? You're my golden ticket out of this hellhole. But you've got to survive, and the Grants and all their minions need to be dealt with. I don't care if they live or die, as long as they can't stop me from leaving."

"Why not just run away?"

Her laugh was bitter. "Because Lewis, John, Angus, and what's left of the Onyx Mind are tied to me via blood magic, thanks to Ruth. As long as they're alive, or free, it will take them a matter of minutes to find me and bring me back." Anger rolled through her eyes. "The only edge I have is that they don't know that I hate them. This is my one and only shot at freedom."

"You are getting out of there." Revulsion coursed through me at the thought of what they'd done to her, and I had to shake it off. "Speaking of Ruth, where is she? I'd like to have a word about her boys being necromancers."

Jessica shrugged. "No idea. After you questioned her, she stopped by the house and said she had to go out of town for a few days."

Well, shit.

"Thanks. As for John, you don't need to worry about him anymore."

Her expression went blank. "Why?"

"He's dead."

She blinked. "Seriously? He didn't come home…but we were working under the assumption he'd found a meal elsewhere since you were still around."

Confused, I leaned against the corner of the building. "Did he have a habit of disappearing?"

She nodded. "Yeah, whenever he transformed into that...thing, he'd go on a bender, eat a few people, then hibernate for a week or two before coming home."

I grinned. "Well, that's fantastic luck for me."

She furrowed her brow. "How's that?"

Rolling my shoulders, I pushed off the wall. "It keeps them off my ass for a while."

Her eyes went wide. "You do realize they just sent one of their top guys, along with a dozen men, to kill you and your friends, right?"

"Yeah."

Rubbing her forehead, she asked, "How do you figure that's them staying off your ass?"

I patted her shoulder. "He's sending pawns. If he were really pissed off, Lewis, Angus, and the other members of the Onyx Mind would be crawling all over me."

She shook her head. "No, they wouldn't."

"Huh?"

Jessica let out an exasperated breath. "Diana, Erik, and Artur are doing their best to save the rest of their undead horde."

I held out my hands to slow her down. "What the hell is that supposed to mean?"

Annoyance flashed across her face. "It means you destroyed their major staging area. So, now there are thousands of the things out near Ambrosia Lake."

I blinked. "Wait...there's a lake in the middle of the desert."

She gave me a *you must be stupid* look. "It's not an actual lake. It's a uranium mine."

"Oh..." Scratching my head, I asked, "Why do they keep using the old mines to store their zombies?"

She spluttered, "Zombies. That's what you call them?"

I nodded. "Yeah...is there a better name?"

Jessica thought about it for a second then sighed. "Not sure if it's any better, but we call them revenants. And there are two reasons they're hidden in such places. First, most people are frightened of radiation poisoning, so they stay away."

"And second?" I asked.

Her gaze hit the ground. "That's a bit more complicated, and you're probably going to think I've lost my mind."

I chuckled. "Seriously? After all the shit I've discovered in the last nine months, you're going to have to try real hard for me to think you're nuts."

She lifted her gaze to me. "Okay...you asked for it." Taking a deep breath, she blew it out slowly. "There's a separate world apart from our own called Niflheimr. The people who live there, better known as the wraiths, are little more than a shadow, and when they come into this world, they need a vessel. People are difficult since they have a soul, but once their spirit leaves the body..."

Realization hit me. "They could pop in and take over their corpse."

Nodding, she shivered. "Basically, yeah. But, when you expose that corpse to low doses of radiation, that's no longer possible."

"Am I to take it that the necromancers and the wraiths aren't friends?"

Shaking her head, she said, "Normally, no, though they've been known to cooperate once in a while. But I think that's because necromancers outnumber them."

A shiver ran up my spine at the thought of wraiths pouring into this world. "But if they were to get their hands on a few thousand zombies, that would change the odds."

She nodded. "Pretty much."

I rubbed my temple. "God, the more I learn, the bigger my headache becomes."

Her voice was hollow when she spoke. "Think how I feel. I'm stuck in the middle of these crazy fuckers, with a host of revenants not far away. And there's nothing I can do about it."

My stomach clenched at the thought. "Where did you say they were again?"

She gestured out toward the north. "Ambrosia Lake, and I'd suggest taking care of them before trying to deal with Lewis."

I laughed. "And how am I supposed to wipe out an army of undead?"

She shrugged. "No idea, but I doubt you want to be overrun with them at the compound."

"Good point."

She glanced over her shoulder. "I've got to get back before they realize I'm gone."

"Okay. Stay safe."

She grinned. "You too."

She quickly made her way behind the building and was lost to the night. I looked around and shrugged. The rubble and bodies were out of the street. Jessica had made it clear that the authorities weren't coming anytime soon, which meant I had a little more time to try to fix things before the mortals got involved.

In short, my night was far from done.

30

March 3rd

It took us a couple of hours to decide on a plan, and even then, it wasn't much of one. Basically, it boiled down to us hoping Diana, Erik, and Artur were out there on their own, so we could work our way in and dispose of them before they knew what hit them. As for the buttload of undead...well, we'd have to cross that bridge when we got there.

The lone holdout on the plan was Atsidi. He was less than thrilled with the odds, and that went double for our lack of backup. Thing was, we weren't exactly spoiled for choice. The longer we waited, the more likely it became that we'd lose any advantage we had, and we'd all die without making a damn bit of difference. With that in mind, we packed up and headed out.

It took us nearly two hours to make our way around the detour in Grants, and another thirty minutes to get to our destination. Ambrosia Lake District looked much the same as the other mines we'd been to over the last week.

We parked about a half mile out, deciding it was probably best not to show up as a single target. As we got closer, the sound of several generators running filled the air, and harsh florescent lights lit up the night sky. It took us several minutes to climb the last hill overlooking a large rectangular pit with layers and layers of earth peeled away. If the work lights were any indication, during the day, the scene would turn a few hundred shades of tan, gray, and black. But this evening, it was just varying tones of darkness between highlighted sections of desert.

Near the center, there were maybe a couple dozen rail cars full of what I had to guess were zombies. To make matters worse, Erik, Artur, and Diana weren't alone. Over the course of the next five minutes, I counted twenty-four armed guards patrolling the area, which made things that much more difficult...especially since we didn't know if they were necromancers or just the hired help.

Sam and Dean headed out toward the east. Alexander and I went west, leaving Cole and Atsidi to hold their position until we were ready to make our move.

We really needed to have this wrapped up by dawn, because that was when the detour would be taken down. Which meant that the police would find a bunch of dead bodies stuffed into the smoldering remains of the local arts & crafts store.

At that point, other agencies would get involved, and I'd likely lose my chance to stop Lewis's plan...whatever the fuck that was. Plus, I wanted to have his head on a pike by sunrise as a warning to all other necromancers. Not that I thought it would stop them, but it might give them pause...especially when they lose control of Jessica.

Alexander and I were about halfway around when he slipped, catching the attention of a couple of nearby guards.

Guess we were about to find out what these guys were made of.

He lifted his weapon, but before he could pull the trigger, Alexander crossed the distance and hit the man hard enough to snap his neck. While he hadn't been able to shoot us, his broken body rolling down the hill into his buddy wasn't at all helpful.

The startled guard sent up a hail of panic fire in our direction, which missed us by a mile. That was where the good news ended.

Everyone looked at him, and then at us… The game was up, and we were about to go a full ten rounds with these assholes.

I raised my arm to create a thick barrier of ice between us and the idiot gunman. Nevertheless, we'd hit the hornet's nest with a stick. On the upside, everyone down below was focused on us, and no one was paying attention to the others.

Seconds later, the sound of giant soda cans being crushed rang out as three container cars caved in on themselves. In the broken mess of metal, blood and other bodily fluids leaked from the wreckage. The godawful stench of the dead filled the air, nearly making me gag. Just as my mind caught up with the carnage, a massive fireball shot out of the darkness crashing into a clump of six guards. They didn't even have time to scream before their bodies were torn apart and their flesh burned to ash.

There were a few random shots across the way, which, if I had to hazard a guess, was the work of Sam and Dean. I charged the barrier, shattering it with a thought, and the shards tore through four more. Suddenly, out of nowhere, there was a sharp impact in my ribs as Diana drove her shoulder into me.

She rabbit-punched me in the gut several times before jumping to her feet and smashing her boot into my midsection. Not to be outclassed, I kicked out, and my foot landed against her chest, knocking her onto her back. I pulled a knife off my hip, blade down, and slashed out, carving a thin red line across her thigh. She grunted in pain and flicked a fistful of flame my way.

It fizzled on my chest, and I stood. "Thanks for the pick-me-up."

Diana scrambled to her feet and backpedaled away in an effort to put some distance between us. Before I could skewer the wench, someone hit me from behind, and I was eating dirt again. A forearm caught me hard in the back of the skull, and my face bounced off the rocky ground. I swung the knife back and lodged it in their thigh. They screamed and rolled off me. I was able to push myself upright, while Artur was occupied with trying to remove the blade from his leg.

I spun and punched Diana in the face. Last thing I needed was for her to have a free shot at my back, but with that in mind...where the hell was Erik? Artur grunted, and the earth underneath me shook. A moment later, I was airborne as the ground exploded. The one good thing about being this high up was that I spotted Erik—he was unlocking one of the box cars. That couldn't be good.

As the old saying goes, it wasn't the fall that killed you, it was the sudden stop, and while I wasn't dead, a part of me wished I were. When I caught my breath, all I wanted to do was rip Artur's head off his shoulders, but he and Diana were nowhere to be seen. What was visible, however, was a veritable sea of undead bastards heading my way.

Fucking fantastic.

Cole, Atsidi, Dean, and Sam came up beside me to stand against the horde of revenants. Even with them at my side, I didn't like our odds. My stomach churned, and I clenched my jaw. If this was the way I was going out, they would have to pay for the privilege. I summoned the ice armor, and my vision turned crimson. Trying one of the things Hayden had taught me, I stepped forward, clenched my fist, and a massive column of blue flames came down from the sky to burn a hole through the ranks of the undead, but it did nothing to slow them down.

The horde was maybe fifty yards away when the night sky above us lit up and turned gold. Massive shafts of yellow light burned through the flesh of the nearest group of zombies, and they fell, unmoving, to the ground. A huge, dark figure flew out of the brilliance on silver wings, and a moment later, Gabriel landed beside me.

He grinned. "Sorry I'm late."

Dumbfounded, I shook my head. "I didn't know you were on the way."

He swept his arm out in front of him, and a wide arc of golden light spilled out of his hand, felling a dozen corpses. "Lazarus said you needed me...so, I'm here. We can discuss the details later."

Patting him on the shoulder, I nodded. "Sounds good."

While he was handling the flood of undead, the rest of us went in search of the three remaining rats...and with luck, Alexander. I hadn't seen him since my encounter with Diana and Artur.

Taking point, I guided us through the maze of dirt, rail cars, and empty cargo containers. When I rounded the last corner, Erik stood there, holding a knife to an unconscious Alexander's throat. Diana was dabbing her nose with a handkerchief, and Artur had tied a tourniquet around his leg.

Erik's voice shook with anger. "Stop, or I'll slit his throat."

Gesturing at him, I frowned. "That threat is only good as long as he isn't hurt. The moment you do anything moronic, I'm going to tear you three to pieces."

Diana placed her boot in the small of Alexander's back. "You've got a big mouth."

Atsidi glared at her. "And you are going to die here today."

She laughed. "I very much doubt that, old man."

He waved his hand, and the blade against Alexander's throat transformed. Several spikes protruded from the metal and through Erik's hand. Screaming, he stumbled back and yanked the offending steel from his hand before dropping it. Dean was on the wounded man in an instant. With one swipe of his claws, he removed his throat and most of his neck.

Artur brought up a wall of shadows to protect him and Diana, but I sprinted through the barrier. There was a tingle as the magic touched my flesh, and then it was gone...both the barrier and the sensation. Even though they'd only been out of sight for a few seconds, Diana was nowhere to be found. Artur reminded me of his presence with a fist to the temple. My vision blurred, and I staggered to the side.

Before I could get myself together and mount a suitable defense, Sam was on the man. Her claws raked across his already wounded chest, ripping through flesh and bone. Another swipe of her paw opened up his abdomen, and the next tore out his heart. That only left Diana, but that bitch was playing hide and seek.

To make matters worse, there were more undead than before, and they were quickly closing in on Gabriel. I had to make a choice: save my friend or keep hunting the woman... Guess which one I picked? With a wave of my hand, another column of cobalt fire fell from the sky, obliterating a large number of the zombies in front of Gabriel.

When the rest of the team saw the horde behind us, they charged into the fray. Atsidi placed his hand on the nearest container, and large chunks of steel tore free and launched into the mass of shambling corpses. While it seemed like they'd lost their direction, that hadn't slowed them down, or stopped them from wanting to tear us limb from limb.

We fought with fire, ice, steel, light, and claws. But we were outmatched, surrounded, and it was only a matter of time before we were overwhelmed by their numbers.

Using so much of my power was leaving me winded and weak. In a moment of desperation, I decided to try something new...if I failed, we'd be in the same position we were already in, which was neck deep in undead.

"Everyone on me." They fell back to me, and I placed my hands on them. "Grab onto one another."

I focused on being back at the trailer, blue flames encased us, stuttered, and quickly vanished, leaving us right where we were. The exertion took me to my knees.

Panting, I coughed out, "Shit."

The earth at our feet buckled, and everything rumbled as the ground shook. Rocks shattered, huge plumes of dust erupted as giant pits opened to swallow groups of the undead. To my right, something massive, gray, and inhumanly fast shot out of the embankment to tear through the ranks of the zombies. Before I could get a good look at the thing, it burrowed into the dirt and vanished from sight. What was left behind was a wide swath of destruction that left half eaten or crushed bodies in its wake.

If that wasn't enough, an ungodly howl came out of the north. The dim light of the moon showed a massive violet dust storm heading our way. Not wanting to have our flesh stripped from our bones, I created a dome of ice around us a few seconds before the wind and sand ripped through the remaining undead. In the haze of ice and

Dust Walkers | 221

dust, we watched as the revenant army was decimated in a matter of seconds. Violet flames consumed the revenants by the hundreds.

When the storm died down, a strange figure stepped into view. My mind stuttered over the sight of the being before me, struggling to comprehend. He had the body of a human, but the head of a jackal, and stood well over seven feet tall. He was bare chested, wearing only a purple shendyt around his waist, and leather sandals with gold straps on his feet. The stars in the night sky above were reflected in the onyx skin that covered his heavily muscled form. He stood there for a moment, inhumanly still, as his lavender eyes scanned the horizon. When he appeared to be satisfied with his handiwork, he strode over. Extending a finger, he tapped the ice, and it shattered.

Kur whispered, *"Anubis."*

Atsidi took a knee. "Łééchąą'í, I didn't think you'd heard my call for help."

Anubis frowned. "I didn't, but the Loki did."

His voice was one I recognized instantly. This was the man who'd pulled me out of the pit my grandfather had stuck me in, healed my wounds in Iraq, and again in New Orleans last year. Łééchąą'í, or Anubis, was the first reaper.

After several seconds, I found my voice. "Thank you for your assistance, Łééchąą'í. Or would you prefer Anubis?"

He grinned. "Either will work. It's been a long time since anyone's called me by my true name."

I shivered. "This is the third time you've saved me."

Anubis chuckled. "It is becoming a habit, but a worthwhile one." With a wave of his hand, time stopped. "We have but a moment. It isn't our time yet. But soon, Hayden, myself, and you will need to sit down and talk. You know where to find me now."

I blinked, time resumed its natural course, and he was gone.

Alexander woke and pushed himself to his feet. "What the hell happened here?"

The violet flames had turned a large portion of the pit to glass. Nothing was left of the undead horde other than the occasional body part sticking out of the now barren landscape. And the stench. There

222 | KEN LANGE

was nothing on this planet viler than the smell of burned rotten corpse.

All of us were spent, but this was hardly the time for a nap. We had one more stop to make before we could call it a night. Reinforcements were on the way, but they were still several hours out, according to Gabriel. Andrew, Heather, and even Lazarus himself would be through the gate in Santa Fe sometime after dawn. But what we had to do couldn't wait.

As we trudged back to the truck, I sent Jessica a text. *We'll be there soon.*

31

On our way to the Grants, the hand of God did a spectacular job of painting the sky in shades of purple, red, and orange. When we arrived half an hour later, the gate to the compound was haphazardly ajar. Black smoke trailed out of the rear building, and people were scrambling to help or get the hell out of the way.

Either Jessica had gotten the party started without us, or this was just some really convenient timing.

After parking, Alexander, Dean, and Sam went left to clear the buildings there, while Cole, Atsidi, and Gabriel took the right. That meant I was on my own to contain the main house...or at least try to. The first guard caught sight of me when I stepped through the door. He went to pull his gun, but I was quicker and slid the gladius through his chest.

Quickly moving forward, I eased him to the ground, and quietly proceeded to the study, dispatching random guards along the way. When I pushed open the double doors, I found Angus rifling through the desk.

Clearing my throat, I asked, "Looking for something in particular?"

He snapped his head up. "You... I should've known this was your fault."

I wasn't sure what he was talking about, but if it pissed him off, I was only too happy to take credit. "Probably. What did I do this time?"

He pointed toward the back of the house. "You did something to Jessica's mind... Tell me what you did, and I'll make your death quick."

Okay, so it wasn't my fault. "Sorry, dude, that wasn't me, but how about we renegotiate the terms? Surrender, and I'll let you live. Mind you, you'll be in a cage for the rest of your life, but that's got to beat death."

Fire wrapped around his hand. "Fuck you. Now, I'm going to ask this one more time. What did you do to her? Tell me the type of magic you used, and I won't let Lewis torture your soul."

I gestured at the fire he held. "Put that away before you hurt yourself. I don't have a clue what happened to Jessica. Maybe she realized that you freaks aren't her real family. Not that she's going to enjoy finding out the truth, but I'm fairly certain she hates you all, and has for quite some time."

With a snarl, he pulled out a pocket knife and slit his palm. "You're going to die now."

The blood mixed with the fire, and it transformed into an inky darkness that he flung my way. I wasn't sure why, but this new mixture of magic made me nervous. As I turned to the side, the black sphere grazed my shoulder. Instead of fizzling on contact, it burned a hole through my shirt and seared my flesh.

Thank God it had been a glancing blow, or I would've lost an arm.

Okay, so I wasn't immune to all forms of magic. Whatever that was could hurt and even kill me. My shadow armor wrapped around me as I darted across the room. When I was a few feet from the desk, I launched myself over the top and speared him in the gut, taking him off his feet. We crashed into the books behind us, and I brought my fist up into his solar plexus. He doubled over. I picked him up and slammed him into the hardwood floor with a resounding thud.

He spun on the spot and swept my feet out from under me. Fire poured out of his hand and caught me full in the chest. The force of it

Dust Walkers | 225

knocked me into a nearby wall, but this time he'd forgotten to include his blood, and I felt better than ever. Flames continued to pour out of the man, and he grunted under the strain of it. I stepped forward, and the inferno engulfed me, obscuring him from view.

This went on for several more seconds then they flickered and died. Angus lay there in a winded heap, sweating from the strain of using so much of his magic. I leaned over, slammed my hand against his chest, and pushed until it collapsed under my weight. His body convulsed then he went still as the life faded from his eyes. The Grim was quick to pull his soul from his corpse.

After ensuring the first level was clear, I made my way up the stairs to what appeared to be an exact duplicate of the floor below. Weird. But that was becoming commonplace with the Grants. When I opened the door, what I thought would be the study turned out to be a massive library. Jessica stood in the far corner with a bloody nose and bruised cheek, looking a little worse for wear. Diana and Lewis were apparently trying to convince her to calm down.

Diana turned, and blinked. "Who the hell are you? Where's Angus?"

Huh? Why didn't she recog— Oh yeah. Helmet.

I raised my arm, and a shard of ice darted across the room. The point tore through her eye socket and out the back of her skull before wedging into a row of books.

Lewis whirled on me and threw a bolt of black lightning my way. I tried to dive to the side, but I wasn't quick enough, and it caught me full in the chest. The impact shattered my armor and flung me into the wall, nearly knocking me unconscious. My enchanted shirt was shredded, and the extreme heat had burst the blood vessels under my skin. I tried to move, but my body wasn't having any of it.

He howled in rage. "You? What the hell are you?"

Wish I could say I had a witty quip on the tip of my tongue. Instead, I was lying in a pool of my own drool and twitching in an odd rhythm.

Lewis wrapped lightning around his hand, and it trailed out behind him like a whip. He raised his hand overhead and brought it down, allowing the tip of the lightning to encircle my leg. Pain coursed through me, and all I could do was try to scream—the high voltage locked my muscles, so I only managed a single *ack* before my body convulsed.

It stopped the moment he pulled back his hand in preparation for another swing. But before he could bring it down, he froze on the spot. His head jerked back, and a long black blade protruded from his throat. With a nasty twist, his head came loose from his shoulders. Lewis's head remained suspended in the air, while his corpse flopped onto the floor.

Jessica tossed the thing to the side, and it hit the wall with a wet *thwap*. She knelt beside me and placed a hand on my chest. White light poured out of her. While the pain eased, I was graced with a new set of scars across my chest and a burn mark on my shoulder.

She staggered back and fell on her butt. "You'll live."

I rolled onto my side and nodded. "Thank you."

Jessica smiled. "Glad I could help." She glanced over at Lewis's leaking body and scooted to the side. "I take it Angus is dead as well."

I nodded. "He's in the study downstairs."

She wiped the sweat from her brow. "I can feel it. I'm free."

An instant later, her wounds healed.

I pointed at her face. "That's convenient."

She grinned. "Now that the blood curse has been lifted, I'm able to heal. They've held me captive my entire life...or in their words, *ensured my safety*. But now I'm free of them." She glanced up at me. "I'll help you with the remnants of those left behind, but after that, I'd really like to be allowed to leave in peace."

I wasn't keen on letting her go without some conditions, but she had helped me with her *family*. The least I could do was permit her to live her life as she saw fit. "Where will you go?"

She shrugged. "North. I'd like to see a proper winter. Beyond that, I haven't decided."

It took several hours to clear the last of the Grants' forces from their positions. Once we were finished, I was shocked that there weren't any survivors. Jessica explained that the Black Circle forbade capture, and it was up to each of them to fight to the death—most likely the reason so little was known about them.

While Jessica packed up to leave, I teleported to the trailer to pick up Mikhail's journal. When I returned, I handed it to her. "You might want to read this."

She frowned. "Is this the book you were telling me about?"

I nodded. "It is, and you might find some useful tidbits tucked in between some less desirable parts. You can read Russian, right?"

"Yeah, I can." Reluctantly, she slipped it into her backpack. "Thank you again."

I held up a hand to stop her from leaving. "Do you still have my card?" She nodded. "Good, it has my number and email should you ever need me."

Shaking her head, she blew out a long breath. "No offense, but all I want to do is to lie low and live in peace."

"I understand that, but they think you're pretty important, so I'm betting they're going to try to track you down. When that happens, call, and I'll show up to help."

Jessica gave me a curt nod as she mounted her motorcycle and started the engine. "Take care, Gavin."

Stepping back, I waved. "Thanks."

She idled out the gate and was gone. A few hours after the fact, the cavalry arrived, and I couldn't have been more grateful that Andrew and Lazarus were there to handle the legalities of essentially wrecking the place...oh, and killing a bunch of people.

Heather had the unflattering job of trying to stuff Alexander, Atsidi, Cole, Sam, Dean, Gabriel, and myself into a small passenger van she'd rented. It wasn't that we put up much of a fight, but the six of us in one spot made things a bit tight.

Instead of driving back to Atsidi's place, Heather found the nearest hotel, got each of us a room, and handed out keys. Once she got everyone else settled into their rooms, she helped me to mine.

Using the keycard, she unlocked the door. "Shower or bed?"

I leaned against the wall and pointed. "I need to get clean."

228 | KEN LANGE

She helped me out of my clothes and did her best not to flinch at my new scars. "What happened?"

I shrugged. "Not sure. The Grants were using a new type of magic, and as you can see, it hurt like hell."

Frowning, she did her best to examine me without actually touching the marred flesh. "Any idea what it was?"

My ruined shirt fell to the floor, and I stripped out of my pants. "They were using their blood to enhance their natural abilities—"

She gasped. "Blood magic?"

I frowned. "Maybe. Do you know much about it?"

She shook her head. "Not a lot. Thankfully, it's rare. But the people who use it are pretty nasty."

I ran my hand across the scar on my chest. If I squinted, it sort of looked like a tree with branches reaching up toward my shoulders, a long jagged trunk down the center, and a root system that ended at my waist. I suppressed a chuckle at the absurdity of the thought, stepped into the shower, and stayed there until the water started to run cold. Afterward, I stumbled over to the bed, and fell fast asleep.

32

March 19th

It was a clear, hot, and exceptionally humid day...which was pretty typical for New Orleans this time of year. The best thing I could say about the day so far was that I'd signed the paperwork finalizing the sale of my condo this morning. Which meant I owed Alisia a bonus.

But having that place off my hands was about the only good news I'd received over the last several weeks. Mind you, most of them had been spent in Scotland with Hayden's alter ego, Ignatius. One of my major disappointments concerned Timur. He'd committed suicide before we'd finished tidying things up in Grants. So, the Black Circle would get to keep their secrets. For now. We knew about them, and we were actively searching for them. It was only a matter of time before we turned up something.

I wish the same could be said about Ruth Miller. It seemed she'd dropped off the face of the earth. Alexander and his people were digging into her past, but they hadn't had much luck yet. Maybe we'd have a breakthrough with our investigation in Canada. I hoped that by locating the place where the Grants had first registered, we might be able to find out what name Ruth was using at the time. That was a longshot, however, since the province they claimed to be from was having trouble locating their files.

On the local front, Captain Hotard was back on active duty, but he was riding a desk until an informal hearing could take place to remove him from the police force. I wasn't sure that was such a great idea. As the captain, his hands were tied, to a certain extent. Once he became a civilian, God knows what mayhem he might cause. But that wasn't my decision.

I fumbled with the keys in my pocket as I approached the gate to my uncle's place. He and Isidore were in Rome for another summit. Which was good, because I really wanted some privacy for what I was about to do next. I made my way through the front door and was about halfway through the bookstore when my phone chimed. After pulling it out of my pocket, I tapped the mail icon on the screen.

Gavin, I wanted to thank you again for freeing me from my prison. I've read the journal you gave me, and you're right, I did need to know what was inside, and as such I've adopted the name. I'm going to guess you read it as well.

Please keep my secret.

You should know that you didn't destroy all the undead. The BC has been planning something big for the last few decades. When Ke'lets, one of the nine lich lords, was killed, they stepped up preparations.

What I'm trying to say is this: there's a war coming, and not everyone inside the Archive is your friend. Over the last few weeks, I've learned a few things about you...all of them good, in my opinion. You don't deserve what's coming. You once offered to help me if things got bad, and now it's my turn.

If you need me, get in touch, and I'll be there.

Jade

I wish her news was a bit more unexpected, but all it did was confirm what I'd already suspected. Plus, it lined up with what Hayden had

Dust Walkers | 231

said. Ever since Viktor's near-fatal trip to Siberia, the necromancers had steadily been coming out of the woodwork.

From my understanding, Mir, the man Viktor had working on the laptops, was still trying to crack the encryption. Even so, Viktor was actively recruiting, and the Ulfr were expanding their ranks. As for me, I'd added several more clans to my growing force of centurions.

One of the few victories worth celebrating was that Alexander had successfully convinced the holdouts to agree to the new laws. I wasn't sure how he'd managed it, but his actions had helped stabilize a volatile situation, and allowed Viktor's people to get back to their day job.

I couldn't be sure what the future held for me, but I was doing my best to be as prepared as possible. But how does one plan for an all-out war when the enemy was so far ahead? I didn't know the answer to that question, but I had a feeling I was going to find out the hard way.

If you'd like more in this series you can continue with *Shades of Fire & Ash.*

ACKNOWLEDGMENTS

Special thanks to Rick G., Steve W., and James N. You've all been so
very helpful, and supportive, which means a lot to a newbie.
Thank you.

ABOUT THE AUTHOR

Ken Lange is a current resident of the "Big Easy," along with his partner and evil, yet loving, cats. Any delay, typo, or missed edit can and will be blamed on the latter's interference.

He arrived at this career a little later in life, and his work reflects it. Most of his characters won't be in their twenties, and they aren't always warm and fuzzy. He is of the opinion that middle-aged adults are woefully underrepresented in fiction, and has made it his mission to plug that gap.

Translation: he's middle aged and crotchety.

ALSO BY KEN LANGE

Warden Global

The Wanderer Awakens

Sleipnir's Heart

Rise of the Storm Bringer

Children of the Storm

Vigiles Urbani

Accession of the Stone Born

Dust Walkers

Shades of Fire & Ash

Plague Bearer

Dawning

Coming soon:

Shattered Peace, Vigiles Urbani, Book 4

Fall of Eleazer, Withering, Book 1

Made in United States
North Haven, CT
28 January 2024